praise for h

"A delightful read!"

—USA Today RITA Award-winning
Bestselling Author Susan May Warren

"*How Sweet It Is* plunges the depths of human emotions including grief, loss and the difficult path to healing and forgiveness. This Fox Family debut is a gift of rich sweetness.

—Kim, Goodreads

"If you want a clean read with a wholesome message and characters you can care about, you'll find all of it in the story."

—Lisa, Goodreads

"I highly recommend *How Sweet It Is* to fans of contemporary Christian romance. Or, anyone with a sweet tooth."

—Michelle, Goodreads

"Not to sound cliché, but this story was sweet as could be and had me reading well into the night. It was great to return to Deep Haven and see familiar characters, but meet new ones."

—Lily, Goodreads

how sweet it is

A Deep Haven Novel

Fox Family ❈ Book One

andrea christenson

Edited by
susan may warren

sunrise
PUBLISHING

To all the dreamers.
Trust in the Lord, He will make your paths straight.

one

· · ·

Today, all of her dreams would begin to come true. Robin Fox added a flourish of gold leaf to the turret on the cake in front of her at le Château du Gâteau. If she got this cake right and won a spot in the Pastry World Cup, Victor would have to give her that promotion he was always dangling just out of reach.

"Monique, can you hand me that palette knife?" She gestured to the long thin spatula lying on the counter a few feet away. Monique handed her the tool with a sigh.

"I should be the one decorating that cake," the bakery assistant grumbled in French.

Robin caught a drip of icing before it marred the surface of the cake below it. Then she stood, arched her back, and took a deep breath. Her many years of French, first in high school, then later through an app on her phone, had more than prepared her to speak it now. "Well, Victor gave the job to me." Even with the cake almost finished in front of her, Robin still had trouble believing Victor had given her this monumental task.

Monique crossed her arms. "Fine. Have it your way."

Around her, the other employees at le Château du Gâteau

focused on their own work. Outside, the morning's early-January gloom wrapped the streets of Paris, but inside, the kitchen warmed and filled with the scents of yeast and sugar.

Four years ago, when Robin had been languishing in obscurity in a bakery in Los Angeles, California, she'd only dreamed of being featured in a bakery competition in Paris. Victor LaVigne had changed all of that for her. A friend of the bakery owner in LA, he'd swept into the kitchen one day declaring that he wanted to hire a new pastry chef and demanding that the chefs prepare him something so he could offer one of them a new job. He'd promised fame and excitement and a chance to shine in the City of Light. Robin had leaped at the chance.

Being an ocean away from the memories of her parents was just the gold leaf on the turret.

And now she was ready to taste some of that fame. She'd labored hard over the cake design in front of her, a towering confection of golds and pinks. Four cakes stacked on one another, then carved to resemble a palace basking in the light of a sunset.

Victor had entered his bakery into a contest. For two weeks, a judge traveled throughout Paris evaluating cakes and pastries and awarding the best entries a place in a timed competition, the Pastry World Cup, later in the year. The cake contest had grown to almost mythic proportions—the Tour de France of the baking world.

For the past few weeks, she'd spent every spare moment working on the design, tweaking the sketch she'd be working from, and trying out new flavor combinations. She'd even worked over Christmas, tuning out the twinkle lights and merry cheer as she focused on her work. Last week, Victor had approved her design. Now she had less than one hour before the judge was scheduled to arrive. Just enough time to put on the finishing touches.

Robin checked her laminated 3x5 cards where she'd written a

detailed schedule. Everything was going according to the plan she'd laid out.

In the courtyard of the castle, she placed the final small fondant figure. Two princes and one princess stood together near the drawbridge. A nod to her brothers, Grayson and Oliver, wherever they were in the world. She pushed that thought away. No good would come of thinking about her brothers now.

She checked the clock again. Perfect timing. The fifteen minutes before the judge arrived would allow her to clean up and put on a fresh chef's jacket. The one she wore now bore signs of the various colors she'd used. The pinks and golds went well with her curly auburn hair but surely wouldn't impress the judges.

In a small room off the kitchen, a row of black lockers lined the far wall. She popped hers open and reached for the clean jacket she kept there. A small yellow Post-it stuck to the inside of the locker door caught her eye. *Call Grandma Fox!!* Written in her roommate's signature loopy cursive, it had been stuck there since Elise's recent visit to the bakery.

"Your Grandma Elaine called again," her roommate had said. Elise had worn her white-blonde hair loose that day. Her bright blue eyes had sparked. "Haven't you called her back yet?"

"I know, I should have. I've just been so focused on that cake design. That has to take top priority right now." Robin had pushed the lump of guilt deeper in her stomach. It had been several weeks since the last time she'd talked to her grandmother. Wait. This wasn't about her grandfather's health, was it? Grandpa Jim had only recently recovered from a heart attack. "She did say it wasn't urgent, right?"

Elise crossed her arms, leaned against the lockers. "She said not to worry but that she really needs you to call." Elise's French accent deepened. "I don't get it. Shouldn't a family who has gone through the things you went through stick closer together?"

Robin hadn't answered. Had no answer, really. Elise had sighed, then tapped the Post-it. "Call your grandma."

Robin pushed away that memory. No time for calling Grandma right now anyway.

She had a contest to win.

She gave her hair a quick check in the mirror hanging next to the lockers, smoothed a stray lock that had escaped her messy bun. She tugged the bottom of her chef's jacket into place and straightened her shoulders.

In the kitchen, the other bakery workers scurried around. The sugar-and-yeast-scented air rolled over her in a humid wave. Hopefully the warm air wouldn't affect the frosting on her cake. The rest of the crew were following Victor's orders to stock every shelf, fill every basket, displaying all their most popular pastries. He said it wasn't enough to simply present a beautiful cake to the contest judge. They wanted to be sure to present a successful bakery as well.

"It's go time, people," said the man himself, dressed in an impeccable chef's white uniform, the signature tall hat towering above, pushing through the swinging door. Victor LaVigne was a little shorter than Robin's five-foot-seven frame. He made up for it in charisma. His square jaw and piercing blue eyes, dark-blond hair worn closely cropped, not to mention a perpetual half smirk, half smile that he wore, combined with his affable nature, would have made him irresistible.

Except for his incurable ego.

"Napoleon complex," one of her coworkers muttered under his breath. She suppressed a chuckle. Probably shouldn't insult the man who had given her today's opportunity.

"Listen up." Victor clapped his hands twice. "Today is a day when fortunes are made. Let's be sharp." He named two of the junior employees and dismissed them for the day. "We don't need extraneous people in here." The two scuttled out, heads down.

Robin walked toward the cart holding her cake. Victor met her there.

"Not bad," he said. He strolled around the cake, hands clasped behind his back. "A little dramatic, perhaps, but otherwise a fine showing."

Damien, the bakery clerk, poked his head into the kitchen. "Monsieur Clement is here," he whisper-yelled. He gave Robin a pointed look and a thumbs-up before disappearing back through the door into the front room of the shop.

Robin ran her palms down the sides of her pants. The man who could make her dreams come true sat on the other side of that door.

Just as she reached for the handle of the wheeled cart, Victor tapped her arm. "Allow me," he said. He must want to present her to the judge too—a prize-winning cake made by his prized pastry chef.

One of her coworkers held open the door, and Victor pushed the cart through, head held high. Robin followed close behind.

In the tiny dining room, barely a hundred and fifty feet square, sat the judge. Damien was in the middle of telling him a story, his arms making wide gestures.

"Damien." Victor cut him off. "I think our guest has had enough."

Damien gave a quick dip of his head and retreated back behind the till.

"Monsieur Clement, I present Castle in the Clouds." Victor bowed and held his hand palm up to gesture to the cake. He took a step back as the judge rose from his seat and walked a full circuit around the confection.

"Very pretty," Mr. Clement said. He walked back to his seat. "Of course, the proof, as they say, is in the pudding. As you know, taste is also a factor in this competition."

Victor waved a hand at Robin, shooing her back into the kitchen. "You heard him. Get something to cut this cake."

Earlier that day Robin had set out a cake knife, a wedge-shaped server, and a real china plate and spoon. She grabbed the stack and hustled back out to where the men were chatting. She heard Victor answering some questions about the construction of the cake as well as the flavors.

She waited for him to call on her to answer the judge's questions, but he never did. His smooth voice gave a reply to everything asked of him, sometimes getting the information wrong. She tuned him out, concentrating on cutting the perfect slice from the edge of the castle, coming back to the conversation in time to hear him tell the judge that the filling for the cake featured vanilla custard.

"Excuse me, Victor." She hoped her French didn't fail her now. "I think you mean mascarpone cream."

The look Victor shot her, his back turned to the judge, was heated. She had a sudden urge to step in front of the cake to prevent the frosting from melting.

"Thank you, Robin." Victor's voice was a hiss. "Of course I meant mascarpone cream, sweetened with vanilla."

The judge looked between them. Then lifted one shoulder in a shrug. Robin handed him the piece of cake. Her hands shook, and she slid them into her pockets, then took them back out again. Too casual. She finally settled for knotting them behind her back.

Mr. Clement tasted a tiny bite of the cake, measuring out a small amount of the frosting and filling. He closed his eyes briefly, then took a second bite. "Who is responsible for this creation? We will need your photo."

Robin's heart was a runaway freight train. Now was the moment Victor would introduce her.

Victor took a step forward. "I am."

What? Her heart plummeted to somewhere near her knees. "But I—"

Victor cut her off with a harsh movement of his hand. A quick chop through the air that was unmistakable. She opened her mouth to speak again. To defend herself. Victor held up one finger. She crossed her arms. Fine, if that's how he wanted to play it. As long as he followed through on the promotion and the spot in the Cup, she'd happily stand aside now.

The judge snapped his fingers. She realized then that there was a photographer standing in the corner taking candid shots. The judge moved toward the cake, extended his hand to Victor. Victor nudged her out of the way as he posed in front of her cake, shaking hands with the contest judge and smiling widely.

The rest of the event passed in a blur as the judge interviewed Victor, and the photographer took shots from several angles. Eventually Robin found herself back in the bakery kitchen, serving slices of her cake to the staff who were still on duty.

When Victor went to his small office off the kitchen, she followed him. She popped her hands on her hips. "What was that in there?"

"What was what?" He sat in his swivel chair and began moving it left and right in tiny movements.

"Why didn't you tell him I was the pastry chef on that bake? I should have been in those photos, not you!"

"Eh." He raised one shoulder. "My bakery, my glory."

"Are you kidding me? After all the hours I put into winning this contest? You're going to cut me out?"

"Robin, I paid you fairly for your hours. No one promised you more than that." He crossed one slim leg over the other.

"What about your promises of making me a partner?"

The chair creaked as Victor continued to sway. Seriously? How could he be so casual about this?

He lifted one hand, palm up. "It is I who should be upset. You embarrassed me in there."

"What? How can you say that?" She was aware that her voice had risen, that the kitchen, normally full of chatter, had fallen silent.

"Correcting my answers, inserting yourself where you don't belong."

Robin's face felt hot, her back prickly. "I'm starting to think I never belonged here."

Story of her life.

Victor just shrugged.

She started unbuttoning her chef's jacket, le Château du Gâteau embroidered on the chest. "I quit. I will find a new place to work."

Victor smiled his signature smirk. "Good luck with finding another position. I know everyone in this town. I will blacklist you."

"Good luck finding someone to fill in on short notice for the Cup," she shot back.

"Eh, I'm sure Monique would love the position." He gave a shrug and turned away.

Robin wrestled her arms out of the sleeves and dropped the jacket on the ground. She placed her foot on the fabric, then spun on her heel and walked out.

On the metro back to the small flat she shared with Elise, Robin checked the time on her phone. Mid-afternoon in Paris meant mid-morning in Deep Haven, Minnesota, where her grandparents lived. Robin's heart rate had settled into an ache, and the devastation from the afternoon was only a dull roar. Maybe hearing Grandma's voice would bring some comfort.

She pictured her grandma in the kitchen of Fox Bakery in Deep Haven. Grandma Elaine and Grandpa Jim had started the business together over fifty years ago. She had learned how to bake her first loaf of bread in their kitchen.

Robin cleared her throat, put on a happy voice as Grandma answered. As much as she longed for comfort, she wasn't ready to tell Grandma everything. She pictured her grandma on the other end of the phone. She was likely in the bakery chatting with customers. She would have her silver hair tied with a brightly colored scarf, wearing a pair of pastel crepe pants to match.

"How is Paris?" her grandma asked.

Robin closed her eyes, focused on the warmth of the words. "I don't know. Turns out I might not belong here."

"What do you mean?"

"Oh, you know." Robin kneaded her eyes with her thumb and forefinger. She would not cry on the metro. "The French have a different way of doing things." She cleared her throat, then opened her eyes and concentrated on the upholstery pattern of the seat in front of her. Greens whirled with oranges in a cacophony of color. "Sorry I've missed so many of your calls. What's up?"

"Grandpa and I are going to Florida," Grandma said. "Do you know anyone who could come and run the bakery for us for six weeks?"

"You're going to Florida?" Somehow she couldn't picture her Northern Minnesota grandparents lying on the beach down south.

Grandma's voice echoed through the phone connection. "The doctor recommended your grandpa take some time off from the bakery, and my sister said we could use her beach home in Florida."

Robin almost shot off her seat on the train. "Is he feeling okay?" When he'd had his heart attack, her grandma had insisted she shouldn't come home. "You said his heart attack was no big deal."

"And it was no big deal. But the doctor wants to keep it that way, so he said we should take some time off." Grandma cleared her throat. "Anyway, I wondered if you had any contacts from school who would be available to help us out."

Hmm, was there more to the story? "Sure. I probably do, but I have a better idea. I'll come home."

"I can't ask you to do that."

"It's okay, I need a break anyway." She couldn't bring herself to tell her grandma the whole truth—that she'd just lost her job at the bakery in Paris, that she was on her last thousand euros, that she'd completely messed up. "I can arrange a few things here and be back in Deep Haven by mid-January."

"You're an answer to prayer." She heard her grandma swallow then clear her throat. "Grandpa and I will send you the money for the plane ticket."

"You don't need to do that."

"Oh, please. I insist." Grandma promised to send the flight details and said goodbye.

Robin wasn't eager to go back to Deep Haven, as she'd never felt like she fit in there. But, sure, she'd work at the bakery, give things a chance to cool down over here. Then she'd be back. Paris was her dream. And she wasn't giving that up.

It might be a nice break, being back home. After the fast pace and intense pressure of her job here, running a small bread bakery in a small town would be a piece of cake. Or, er, maybe brioche.

She would go home, ignore all memories of her once happy family, run the bakery for a few weeks, and then figure out a way to get back to Paris.

Where she truly belonged.

⸺ ⸺ ⸺

DEEP HAVEN, MID-JANUARY

NEW YEAR, NEW SAMMY. THREE YEARS AGO SAMMY JOHNSON wouldn't have pictured himself here, spending so much time at Deep Haven's youth center, especially in the middle of the day. He would have imagined himself at the wheel of his semitruck, hauling lumber from Turnquist Lumber to the paper mill in Weyerhauser, Wisconsin. Or picking up a short-haul down to the mill in Duluth. But the accident, the aftermath, and the resulting therapy had changed all of that.

Now he couldn't imagine getting back behind the wheel of a vehicle. Ever.

He didn't know what he was going to do with the rest of his life. A question that plagued him more and more lately.

He pushed the thought away.

Instead, he focused on spending time with at-risk teens in between his courier and handyman gigs.

And this kid was doing fine. He just needed a little encouragement. Sammy stood next to seventeen-year-old Ben Zimmerman as he completed another five-minute sprint on the exercise bike in the youth center.

"C'mon, Ben, push it a little harder this time. We'll have you up to speed and ready for baseball season in no time."

A few years ago, Ben had been in trouble with drugs and had gotten a severe burn on his legs. Once his family had finally admitted he had a problem, they'd become supporters of the youth center, and Ben had slowly found better ways to occupy his time. Sammy was happy to help him focus on baseball instead of goofing off in the town gravel pit and getting into trouble.

Ben seemed to know where he was going in life. If only Sammy could say the same thing.

On the bike, the teenager pedaled a little harder. His designer joggers and sneakers belied the ache Sammy often saw in the teen's eyes. His smartwatch beeped—five minutes down. Ben stopped pedaling and Sammy handed him a water and a towel.

Ben rubbed the back of his neck with the towel, his dark hair glistening with sweat. "I don't know, Mr. Johnson. It's not the speed or the endurance part of the tryouts I'm worried about." The teen looked down at his Nikes. "I have a big history test coming up, and if I fail it, I won't qualify for the team. I'll be on academic suspension."

Sammy shuddered away a quick flashback to his own high-school experience. He almost hadn't made the football team for nearly the same reason. His friend Colleen had helped him in science. She'd been a great lab partner until they'd made a double batch of elephant toothpaste and their chemistry teacher split them up. Good thing he'd quickly been paired with Robin Fox, who'd also gotten him through math class. He'd had to work really hard the rest of the time.

What this youth center really needed was tutors. But in the meantime... "Look, I'm not super great at math, but what I am good at is learning study tricks." He waited until Ben looked him in the eye. "I had trouble in high school too. Let's get together and I can show you what I did to get myself through."

A slow almost-smile spread across Ben's face. "That would be great. Thanks."

"Hit the showers. I have some deliveries to make, so I'll need to lock up in fifteen minutes."

While Ben showered in the tiny locker room nestled in a corner of the building, Sammy sat in the makeshift office of the youth center. A few years ago, the town, under the guidance of Vivien Buckam, had tried to set up a youth center in the old Westerman Hotel—a plan that had gone up in flames. Literally. The old, rundown place had burned to the ground.

Vivien hadn't given up, however, and she'd drafted him and a team of other volunteers to look for a new place. They'd settled on this old building, not much more than a glorified pole shed. Sure, they had locker rooms, an ancient pool table, some donated exercise equipment, and a whole thrift store selection of old couches, but the building needed constant attention. Volunteers from around town loosely staffed the center. They offered a place for kids to go after school and on weekends.

He checked the volunteer schedule for the rest of the week. It looked slim. He added his name to a few extra slots. Sometimes this place was all a kid had. They could use a full-time staff. And tutors. And, he added to himself, a working treadmill, a computer station, and, if he was really dreaming, a kitchenette where they could cook and serve large dinners for kids who lived on free lunches at school.

Sammy scrubbed a hand across his face. So many needs. So little time. Vivien had done a great job getting the youth center up and running, and the directing board was full of supporters, but everyone was always so busy. It seemed everyone else had other things in their lives besides this volunteer gig. He would hit up the guys tonight at the VFW, see if anyone could take another shift.

The kids needed them.

"I'm ready to head out, Mr. Johnson." Ben's voice cut through his thoughts.

"Great. I'll walk you out." He locked the door behind them before zipping up his jacket against the early-January cold. He wound the scarf his mother had knitted for him an extra time around his neck. The fibers of the scarf caught in the stubble on his cheek. No reason to stay clean shaven in the middle of winter. Fishing in his pocket, he pulled out a stocking cap and tugged it down over his blond hair.

"Need a ride?" Ben asked, pausing with a hand on the door handle of a beat-up Chevy pickup.

"Nah, I'm good. Thanks though."

"You sure? It's cold out here."

The kid had a way with the obvious. "I'll be fine. See you Friday for study practice."

Ben raised an eyebrow but didn't protest any further. "See ya."

Sammy waited to make sure Ben's truck started, then threw his leg over the seat of his fat tire bike. He'd found the machine more than adequate for getting around town. He'd bought it last year after his physical therapist declared him finished with his treatment. And since he was never driving again, thank you very much, he'd needed a way to stay gainfully employed. He'd gotten a few odd jobs and worked as a courier for several businesses in town.

Making his way along snow-cleared streets, he navigated to

the small, in-town office of Turnquist Lumber, where he had to drop a package off for Seth Turnquist.

The receptionist waved him back into Seth's office. He almost laughed aloud at the sight of Seth sitting behind a desk and sporting a dress shirt and tie. On the back of his chair hung an honest-to-goodness sport coat.

His friend looked positively...respectable. Not at all like the Seth Turnquist who used to get into trouble with Sammy, or the rough-and-tumble Seth who'd knocked down fires in the wilderness. This Seth was clean-shaven and straightlaced.

Marriage looked good on him.

Seth looked up from his paperwork. "What are you smiling at?"

"I'm remembering the dunking we used to give each other when we practiced logrolling. Too bad you're all domesticated now."

"I'll have you know I can still roll with the best of them." Seth came around the desk and flexed one arm before patting his stomach. "Just because Ree keeps feeding me doesn't mean I couldn't put you into the lake." Seth punched his shoulder.

He took it back. Domesticated Seth was power under control. He certainly wasn't pulling his punches. Like a trained stallion who used his incredible strength to pull with a team. A hero. Marriage had changed him—for the better. Sammy rubbed the spot on his shoulder Seth had slugged.

"Here's your package from the architect." Sammy had picked up the package before meeting Ben at the center. The courier service he'd started to help pay the bills was picking up. "Got anything for me?"

"Nothing today." Seth opened up the manila envelope and scanned the pages. "Thanks for getting this over there tonight."

"It's what I do." The warmth in the office suddenly felt overwhelming. Sammy swiped off his hat. Stuffed it into a pocket.

"As much as I appreciate your business, I wish it wasn't

'what you do.' I want more for you than this." Seth went back to his chair and motioned to another one for Sammy. They both sat. "Have you thought any more about joining Tucker Newman's smoke jumping team?"

Sammy shifted in the chair. "I don't think so. I'm not ready for something like that." Seth had come home a few years ago after several summers on a smoke jumping team fighting wildfires in America's western wilderness. He had to admit, the job held a little appeal. He had toyed with the idea of being a firefighter his whole life.

"Come on, you're in the best shape of your life. Even from here I can see you're more buff than when we were on the football team together." Seth leaned forward, placing his arms on his desk. "You can be more than a courier or whatever. Aren't you itching to get on with your life again?"

Seth...wasn't wrong. But whenever Sammy thought about the future, a yawning cavern of the unknown greeted him. "Sure, when I was younger, I dreamed of firefighting, but..." How could he explain to Seth that now that he was here, with an opportunity dangling in front of him...well, the weakness he sometimes still felt in his knees—and his spirit—was proof that sometimes the known was the better road. Definitely the safer one.

And for now, the known had him on a bike around town couriering packages for small businesses. And if that didn't exactly provide the satisfaction and heroism he'd always wanted for his life...at least it was safe.

"Fine. I'll think about it." Anything to get Seth off his back. Maybe he could shove the idea to the back of the brain along with the whisper that Seth might be right.

"Well, don't think too long. A new group is starting in March. I'd love to see you join them."

"Speaking of joining, will you be at the VFW tonight?"

"I'll be there. See you soon."

Seth's words weighed on Sammy as he ran a few more

errands before biking to the VFW. It was trivia night. Tonight he and Seth were on a team with some other guys from town. He was looking forward to getting one of Jack Stewart's signature fish burgers.

At the restaurant, the other guys had already assembled at a table for six. He slid onto a chair between Seth and Boone Buckam. Across from them sat Peter Dahlquist and his cousin Nick. Deep Haven regulars filled the wood-paneled restaurant. He nodded at Adrian Vassos and his wife, Ella, over near the far side of the room. Closer to where he sat, Pastor Dan Matthews was eating a burger with his wife and kids. The ringing of the pinball machine and an occasional clacking of pool balls filtered back to where they sat. Near the front of the room, the small stage stood empty, since the local band, the Blue Monkeys, had trivia night off.

Sammy put in his order. Lately Jack had been experimenting with a coleslaw topping on his fish burger. Today's slaw featured green apple, raisins, cabbage, and a vinegar dressing. Mouthwatering.

Just as the meals arrived, Nathan Decker, a local real estate salesman, stopped by the table. "Sammy! I hoped I would catch you here."

Sammy poured a little ketchup onto his plate. "What's up?"

"I'm wondering about selling your property. I know you're still in the thinking stage, but if you aren't going to do anything with it, now is a great time to sell." Nathan tucked his hands into his pockets, rocked back on his heels. "It's a buyer's market, and I've got several people looking to buy property they can build on."

"I don't know, Nathan. I still haven't made a decision."

Nathan nodded, a short jerk of his head. "Well, let me know. I can get you a great price."

"What was that all about?" Seth raised his chin at Nathan's retreating back.

"He's been after me to sell my property for a while. He said there are people looking to buy a property to build a home on."

"Isn't that what you always planned to do?" Seth kept his voice low.

Yep. He'd even put a trailer out there and saved up money for a down payment on the cabin he hoped to build. Before the accident stole all of that away. "He's probably right. I should sell. Move on with my life. I haven't even been up there since before the accident." He'd needed full-time care for a while, so moving in with his mom had made sense.

"Are you sure that's really what you want to do?" Seth took a swallow of his Coke. "I mean, you've had that land for a long time."

"I'd love to live out there." He could even picture the log cabin he'd build. Loads of bedrooms, a great room with a floor-to-cathedral-ceiling fireplace... "But it's too far from town. If we had a big snowstorm, I'd be stranded with just my bike. Plus, I don't know how I'd afford it."

"Don't you have a check from the insurance company for your truck?"

The insurance check from his totaled semitrailer lay heavy on his mind. The settlement had finally come in almost six months ago. He still had a hard time believing that the accident had ruined his brand-new lumber hauling truck. He'd bought the rig with some of the cash he'd saved from his Army bonus. Had planned on making his job as a driver-for-hire with Turnquist Lumber a career, maybe picking up other driving jobs along the way.

"I'm not cashing that. I'm not even opening the red envelope it came in. I don't want a new truck. It doesn't really belong to me." It belonged to an earlier version of himself. Someone who could have been a hero.

"Seems a shame to let all that money go to waste."

He knew that, he really did, but taking that money seemed wrong somehow. Besides, "I think I survived that accident for a reason. I wish I knew what that reason was. Now that I'm not in pain every time I get out of bed, I'm feeling…something. I don't know…" Under the table he stretched his legs, and an ache crept up his thighs. "There must be a reason, right?"

"I don't know if we know the reasons for everything this side of heaven, but I do know that we should all make the most of the life we've been given." Seth pushed his dinner plate aside and laced his fingers together. "God has gifted each of us with a purpose. Even small things become holy in His hands."

Sammy finished off his fries, giving himself a minute to respond. "I know you're right. I hope I don't mess it up. I thought going into the Army was God's purpose, but two years as a mortar maggot before my medical discharge? Not very purpose-filled. Then I thought logging was His purpose, but…" He gestured at his legs. Remembered his…other reasons for never driving. "Neither of those things worked out. How am I supposed to know what to do?" He ran a hand through his short hair.

"I'm sure you'll figure it out." Seth started to say more but was cut off by the start of the trivia game.

An hour and a half later, armed with promises from the guys to help out at the youth center, Sammy ordered another fish burger to go. He'd bring this one home for his mom. As he stood to go, Vivien threaded her way through the tables.

She walked over to Boone and kissed the top of his head. There were a few catcalls, which she smiled at. Vivien's dark hair hung limp, and Sammy saw circles under her eyes.

"Sammy, I'm glad I caught you. I was up at the youth center and saw that you're on the schedule for tomorrow. The furnace finally gave out." She sighed and then sat down in the empty chair next to Boone. "You won't need to come in for your shift tomorrow."

Oh no. "Want me to come take a look at the furnace? I know a thing or two about HVAC."

"No, that's all right. We had someone come out from the

hardware store." She swiped a few fries from Boone's plate and dipped them in some ranch dressing. "He said we need to replace the whole thing. That baby's been running since 1987, if you can believe it."

Sammy had been in the youth center. He could believe it.

"We can't get the new furnace for a while. Well, we can't get the funds for a new furnace, anyway. You may as well plan on being off duty up there for several weeks. We'll have to drum up some donations."

Great. So much for his hard work convincing the guys to take more shifts.

The youth center received a tiny budget from the town and had a few donations trickle in every month, but Sammy knew that would never stretch to a project like this. "A new furnace for a building that size will cost, what, like ten grand?"

"Possibly even more if they have to retrofit any of the venting or anything." Vivien waved a hand as though the problems were gnats flying in front of her face. "Anyway, I'm trying to figure out everything that needs to be dealt with while the center is closed. I know the school had been hoping to hold their Snowball Dance up there in a few weeks, but they're going to have to move it back to the high school."

Sammy agreed to make a few calls of his own. He'd need to let Ben know they had to meet somewhere else. Maybe the coffee shop or the bakery.

Seth nudged him. "Too bad we don't know anyone with a pile of cash."

He shot Seth a look. Enough already.

The waitress walked over with Sammy's extra food already boxed to go.

Sammy stood. "See you later, everyone."

"I'll walk you out," Seth said, grabbing his jacket. They walked in silence until they got outside. "Want a ride?" Seth asked.

"Nah, I'm fine on my bike." Sammy stuck the food box in the

insulated bag he kept in the delivery basket on the back of his bike.

"Listen, promise me you'll at least think about what I said." Seth clapped him on the shoulder.

"About what, the house? The job?"

"All of it. The check too."

Sammy pulled on his bike helmet. "Telling you about that check was a mistake. And I'm not opening it." He swung his leg over the bike and pedaled off before Seth could respond.

He put the bike on the front porch of his mom's house, where it wouldn't get snowed on if those clouds blotting out the evening stars decided to let loose.

"Ma!" he called as he unwound his scarf, stepping into the front hall. "I brought dinner."

"You're a lifesaver." Meredith Johnson came out of the kitchen, wiping her hands on a dish towel. "The state of our fridge is atrocious." She reached out and brushed Sammy's cheek. "You had a little blue fuzz there. I'll get out a plate. Meet me at the table."

He shrugged out of his jacket and hung it on the coat tree.

Walking into his mother's kitchen was a bit of a time warp. He'd offered again and again to tear up the 1970s linoleum and replace the Formica countertops, but she insisted on keeping them. The rest of the house was tastefully updated, but this small room at the back of the house she kept in the condition she'd received it—harvest golds and seafoam greens and all. She said the linoleum remained pristine and the Formica was fine, so why bother?

He knew the truth was likely more complicated, as truth often tended to be. He suspected the real reason was the memories his mom had made in this room. She had lost both parents very young, and they'd left her this house.

He set the take-out box on the table nested within the banquette. "I picked up a fish burger and fries. Hope that sounds okay."

"I hope they didn't get too cold, what with being in your basket as you biked back here." Her voice held a gentle tease. "If my fries are cold because you still refuse to drive, I won't be held responsible for the consequences."

"Ma, we've been over this. I'll get behind the wheel of a car when I feel ready. Not a minute sooner." And not a minute all too soon. He wasn't ready—wasn't sure he'd ever be ready.

"I know, honey. I'm just razzing you." She lifted a plate out of the cupboard, and he filled it with the fish burger and fries, still piping hot from the bag. He sat at the table. On it lay a few unopened, letter-sized envelopes. The return address of one read *Williams*. He knew they were from the mother and son who he'd nearly run over on the worst day of his life.

Another thing he was never going to open.

"How was your day?"

"I don't know, Ma."

He thought about the youth center and the furnace. About all the decisions piling up. And he still hadn't found even one answer.

two

. . .

Robin glanced at the clock. Noon.

She just needed to make it through another few hours and then she could go to bed. She'd been back in Deep Haven for two days but hadn't yet kicked the jet lag. A yeasty aroma of baking bread wafted through the bakery. The bread she'd started early that morning must be almost done.

Robin opened the oven door. Perfect. She pulled the pans out of the oven and left them on the counter to cool.

When she'd gotten home on Saturday, Grandma Elaine had insisted they spend a few hours together at the bakery to show Robin the ropes. She'd explained that the bakery was open five days a week—they closed on Sundays and Thursdays.

"Grandma, I think I know the bakery." Knowing her grandparents, it hadn't changed any in the ten or so years she'd been gone.

"Still, I want to make sure you are comfortable there before we go." Though she was pushing eighty, her grandma still displayed her artistic bent in her stylish and flamboyant clothes. Her purple, hand-dyed tunic topped a pair of camel-colored wool slacks. A bright watercolor scarf knotted around her neck. "I think we're all packed. We should be good to go in the morning. It's not easy trying to decide what to bring for a trip this long."

"What's to decide? A swimsuit, a cover-up, a floppy hat, and a pair of fuzzy pj's. What more do you need when living on the beach?" Robin teased.

"Silly girl. You know I can't live without my scarf collection," Grandma Elaine teased back.

"You aren't going to miss the snow?" Up here on the North Shore of Lake Superior, snow was a guarantee.

"Never." Grandma Elaine held out a jangling ring of keys. "The key to the house is on there as well as the keys to the front and back doors here. I've left the recipe book next to the spice rack near the door in case you've forgotten the measurements."

She leaned over and gave her grandma a hug, breathing in her cinnamony scent. "It hasn't been that long since I baked a loaf of bread."

Grandma Elaine squeezed back. "I know your focus in Paris was on cakes and pastries. I wasn't sure if you'd be a little rusty at brioche." She pulled back and seemed to search for something in Robin's eyes.

Robin let go. Held her palms up in surrender. "True, but I made your signature cinnamon rolls every Saturday for me and my roommate. I'm sure the rest will be like falling off a log."

"Don't worry, we trust you." Grandma Elaine patted her arm. "I know you can do it. Just don't change anything around here."

Why would she change anything? She loved this little bakery. Even if it did bring back some painful memories. Okay, and maybe it did need some updating—the oven was older than the bakery itself. And she *would* enjoy adding a cake or two to the menu, but that wasn't really changing anything, right? Just improving it a little. Oh well. Best to do what Grandma asked.

She crossed her arms. "I won't change anything."

"I know you, you know." Her grandma brushed at a strand of Robin's hair. "You can't resist adding a little flair. Just keep things the way they are—simple—and you'll do fine."

"You have nothing to worry about." Robin had given her a hug, then pulled away. "Go to Florida. Enjoy your umbrella drinks by the ocean."

"I'll call once in a while to check in, but you don't need to call us except for emergencies."

Robin bit back a laugh, or maybe it was a sigh. Same old story. She'd just have to show her grandma she could do this. All on her own.

She'd been right. The bakery was nearly unchanged since she'd left for college ten years ago. The kitchen was one long rectangle with the cooler to her left, along with a small alcove for a computer from the 1990s. Straight across from her were the racks holding the baking supplies, alongside the commercial dishwasher, a small sink, and an ancient oven, which had probably been manufactured somewhere around 1952. A long workbench made of smooth hickory filled the center of the room. And to her right, the main sink nested in wooden cabinets, which were older than she was.

She wandered out through the swinging doors to the retail area and dining room. Reds and cream colors decorated the small space. Two floor-to-ceiling picture windows flanked the door, which faced the parking lot. The twin panes let in the weak January sun, warming the wood tables. Outside, three patio tables waited for summer weather to return.

A long display case filled most of the space separating the dining room from the kitchen. And on the wall behind that, a painted stylized fox ran through a meadow with Fox Bakery stenciled underneath.

So many memories were packed into the square footage. Over there at the front table was where her grandma had shown her sine, cosine, and tangent in her trigonometry homework. She pictured Oliver with his head bent over his science book and Grayson munching on a sticky bun after school. The scent of vanilla and cinnamon and yeast permeated the air, but the bakery didn't seem quite as warm without her brothers in it.

This, then, would be her kingdom for the next two months. No Victor criticizing her every move. No demanding instructors pushing her a little harder each class. Just a space where her grandparents believed in her enough to keep things moving like clockwork, serving their customers and fulfilling orders.

A movement on the other side of the lot caught her eye. She saw…wait, was that Megan walking toward the bakery, pushing a baby stroller? She hadn't seen Megan Carter in years but kept up with her life on social media. She supposed it was Megan Barrett now.

She flipped the Open sign to Back in 15 Minutes and grabbed her jacket.

Robin went out to greet her. "Megan! So good to see you."

"Robin?" Megan wore a long puffy jacket and fuzzy mittens, her blonde hair peeking out from a matching knit hat. She held out her free arm to Robin for a side hug. "Hi! I heard you were coming back for a while but didn't realize it was so soon. How are you?"

A thin, black-and-white cat cut between them before crossing the parking lot and disappearing behind another building. Who did he belong to? Based on his scrawny look, he was probably a stray. She'd leave out a little food and water just in case.

"I'm doing okay." Robin tugged her gloves on. "It's weird to be back."

"I'll bet." Megan adjusted the blanket covering the stroller. "Baby Rae and I are getting some fresh air. Want to join us?"

"I'd love a quick walk." Robin glanced at her watch. "I can afford to be gone a few minutes." They'd had a big rush earlier, but now the bakery was quiet. She could take a break.

They headed toward downtown Deep Haven, passing Wild Harbor Trading Post next door. To the left, Lake Superior stretched to the distant horizon, and sunlight sparkled off the water.

"So, you're married now. And have a new little one." She'd gone to school with Megan but hadn't known her too well. Still, in a small school like Deep Haven, everyone kinda knew everyone. "That's wonderful. Congratulations."

Megan tugged off a mitten and flashed her ring finger, blushing a little. "Thanks. Cole and I used to know each other when we were kids, before you were living here with your grandparents. When he came back to town, I knew he was still the one for me." She looked at her ring for a moment. Robin's ribs tightened, but she breathed it away. So what if she was twenty-eight and hadn't had time for a relationship? She could still be happy that Megan had found her happy ending. Maybe Robin's was out there too. He just hadn't walked into her life yet.

"Marriage looks good on you."

"Thanks. Since having this one," Megan said, "it's taken a while to feel back to normal again. I'll take all the compliments I can get. Enough about me. Let's talk about you. You were in Paris, what, five years?"

"Six years in LA, then four in Paris. Man, that time flew past. I still have to pinch myself that it really happened to me."

Megan pushed the stroller over a curb and onto the sidewalk, the movement causing the blanket to slip into the stroller. Inside, Megan's seven-month-old slept, her rosebud mouth open in a miniature O. A lump rose in Robin's throat. Her friend seemed to have it all.

"Baby Rae is beautiful," she said.

Megan gazed down at the baby, a smile lighting her face. "She is, isn't she?" She adjusted the blanket again, tucking it around the baby instead of over the stroller opening. "Okay, so I know you went to that cooking school in Los Angeles after high school, then what?"

"Yes, I was offered a job right out of my two-year culinary arts college at the Paris Patisserie in LA." Robin remembered the thrill of landing her first job. The excitement of making it on her own. "It turned out I was mostly doing the grunt work, but I figured I was paying my dues. Eventually they let me decorate cakes, and then they even let me try out a few new recipes."

"Aren't you a bread family?"

She laughed. "Yeah, Grandma and Grandpa asked me about that too. I had planned to specialize in bread, maybe add some new twists to ours here at Fox, but when I took the pastry unit in college that all changed." She remembered the feeling of that first class. It was like a whole new world had opened to her. "The colors, the creativity, the ways you can make a cake look like anything. It called to me. It was like art."

Megan waved a hand to stop her. "Not 'like' art, it *is* art. I've seen what some of those people can do. Did you learn other pastries too?"

"I spent six months perfecting a croissant. I can make them in my sleep now. Which came in handy when I moved to Paris."

"Yeah, how did that happen?"

She looked at the park sprawling out next to the water. The waves lapped at the boulders lining the far side. Across the harbor, a boat motored past the lighthouse. "One day after I'd displayed a cake I'd made start to finish on my own, a French guy walked in. Victor LaVigne. He kind of swept me off my feet. In a bakery sense." She'd been so blind. On reflection, there had been other warning signs. Why had Victor needed a pastry chef from America, for instance?

Megan laughed. "How can someone sweep you off your feet 'in a bakery sense'?"

She laughed too. But how else could she describe it? "After seeing some work I had done, he asked me to work with him in Paris. He said he'd just opened a bakery and needed someone with my talents." And naivete, but she wouldn't admit that part to Megan.

"Oh, right. That would do it." Megan maneuvered the stroller around a frozen lump of snow.

Robin ran her hand over the back of a park bench as they walked past, its bumps and pits rough against her hand. "He told me it would be a tough go for a while, but eventually I could be his partner and we would take the baking world by storm."

"Swoon! Was he handsome?"

"Megan!"

"What? I run a wedding planning business. I need to know if you're a potential customer." Her friend grinned at her.

"Yes. He is definitely handsome. He reminded me of a French Channing Tatum. The hair, the smoldering eyes." Victor *was* handsome. He also had a magnetism that pulled people into his circle. She was sure he would go on to great things—if he could keep his ego to a minimum and refrain from taking credit for other people's work. Although, the French seemed to not care about that as much as she did.

"Sooooo." Megan drew out the word. "Spill. Any sparks there? Ha! You're blushing. There were sparks."

"Of course there were sparks. It was a bakery. In Paris. With a Channing Tatum look-alike. It was practically a Hallmark movie." Robin's face heated even more.

They walked a few steps. Megan seemed like she was waiting Robin out. Finally she broke. "And?"

"And what?"

"Don't play coy. Now you're here. In Deep Haven. Unless you're hiding a French hottie in the walk-in cooler, I'm guessing there's more to the story."

Megan had no idea how much more there was. No need to spill all her secrets though. Just enough to satisfy her friend's curiosity. "Turns out real life isn't like the movies. First of all, he made it clear he wasn't interested in me in that way. Not that I'd set my heart on it or anything, just that I'd felt a few sparks, you know?"

"I'm so sorry, Robin. That's awful." Megan's face grew sober, all hint of teasing gone.

She waved off her friend's concern. "It's fine. I didn't really have any feelings for him." It was true. After the first few months of working for Victor, she'd lost any sparks of attraction and focused on developing her pastry skills. Realizing that Victor was a glory-taking, egotistical fraud hadn't hurt her romantically, just in all the other ways that mattered.

"I know something about falling for the wrong man." Megan stopped walking. She stared out toward the water for a moment. Robin recalled hearing about Megan and how the father of her son Josh had abandoned them when he found out Josh was on the way. Megan gave herself a shake. "Enough of the serious stuff. Are you ready to turn back?"

Robin nodded. Megan had no idea how much she wanted that.

"Someday, I'd love to see some of your cakes."

Finally! This topic she could get behind. "I have some photos on my phone." Robin tugged off a glove and tapped open her camera roll app. They stopped in the middle of the sidewalk.

"Robin! These are amazing!" Megan swiped to the next photo. "Looks like I was right before. You are an artist. Do you have an online profile?"

"No. I was working on one in Paris, but Victor convinced me to only post to the bakery account instead. He felt it would be better for business if my work was featured there and not split off on a personal account."

"This Victor person sounds like a real piece of work."

"You're not wrong."

"Are you thinking of adding cakes to the menu here?"

"No. Grandma asked me not to change anything while she's gone. I think she's worried I'm in over my head anyway. She forgets that I got a business degree along with my culinary one."

"This one looks like a wedding cake. It should be on the cover of a magazine." Megan had stumbled on Robin's secret dream, as well as found the photo of a cake Robin was particularly proud of. Three layers stacked asymmetrically, topped with a rainbow of flowers tumbling down the side.

"I baked that one for a woman celebrating her eightieth birthday. She was a hoot. She said she'd never married because the love of her life had died tragically right before their wedding. She wanted a birthday cake fit for a bride, but she didn't want traditional colors. Check out the next photo."

Megan swiped left. "I love the sparklers!"

"Her family added those instead of birthday candles."

"What a fun idea. You know, a cake like this would bring in a lot of money. We can't get anything like this up here. Most of my brides order their cakes from Duluth."

"Maybe someday."

In the stroller, Baby Rae began to shift, stretching her tiny arms out in a boxer's pose. Megan leaned over and laid her hand on the baby's tummy. "I should get going before Little Miss starts fussing. Thanks for the walk."

"Thanks for the chat."

"I'm serious about the wedding cakes. If you change your mind, let me know. I could send a few brides your way." Megan pushed the stroller, working her way to the door.

"If I change my mind, you will be the first to know." But being sole baker while her grandparents were away would keep Robin busy. No way she would have the time for multiple custom cakes, even if it did sound like a dream come true. "Maybe once I get my feet under me. But you shouldn't count on me anyway. After Grandma and Grandpa get back, I'll be finding a new job in Paris."

"Too bad. Deep Haven could use someone like you." Megan stopped outside the bakery. Her breath came in puffs of white. "Maybe I should grab some bread for my guys. I know Cole and Josh both love fresh-baked goods."

"Come in. It's freezing out here." Robin pulled open the bakery door, and a waft of honey and yeast billowed over them on the warm air from inside. "Let me wrap up a loaf for you."

"I'll take that one." Megan pointed at a loaf studded with raisins.

"Good choice. It's one of my favorites. I used to dream about my grandmother's raisin-walnut bread while I was gone. I've tried to recreate it hundreds of times, but I could never get it right. Grandma swears she gave me the full recipe, but I think there must have been a secret ingredient she left out."

"Maybe the secret ingredient is the Deep Haven air." Megan grinned over the counter at her. She smiled back.

Robin moved to the cash register and rang up the order. She kept her eyes on the keys even though she could have punched them in in her sleep. Grandma's charge to not change anything must extend to the register. It was still the same one they'd used for years.

The bakery sold bread, muffins, and sticky buns, and sometimes the customers liked to stay to eat. After attending a baking conference, Grandma and Grandpa had reluctantly added an espresso machine and a drip coffee system. On paper, coffee was their best seller, because almost everyone grabbed a cup no matter what else they were buying.

That morning, Robin had already seen many familiar faces. Pastor Dan Matthews had stopped in for a rosemary-and-olive focaccia, then Casper Christiansen had dropped by for an oatmeal loaf as he headed to Wild Harbor.

"Thanks again," Megan said, stashing the bread in the storage area under Baby Rae's stroller. "Seriously, I'm happy you're back. Even for just a little while." She gave Robin a wave and made her way out the door.

Robin grabbed a spray bottle and washcloth to wipe down the tables. Out in the main room, she gave each table a thorough wash, then looked around the space, stifling a yawn. Things were still quiet. She'd start the final dough of the day—one that needed to proof in the fridge overnight—and then she would think about closing up early. Wendy Matthews, the daughter of Pastor Dan and one of her part-time helpers, wasn't coming in today, and jet lag was hitting hard.

She walked back to the kitchen to take care of the few dishes and to start the dough.

Strange. The floor looked a little damp near the sink. Uh-oh.

She opened the cabinet. A steady stream of water dripped off the pipe from near the top valve. The bottom of the cabinet was discolored and soggy. She took a deep breath, remembered all the lessons her grandpa had taught her. Better get the water turned off. Locating the knob near the pipe, she gave it a turn.

It didn't budge.

Lying on the floor of the cabinet was a wrench as long as her forearm. She hefted it and tried to fit it around the spigot. No go. Maybe if she tapped the mechanism it would loosen. She reached in to give the metal fitting a whack, but then her knee slipped and she fell forward, hitting the pipe itself full force.

She wasn't sure if the clanging pop noise had come from the pipe or her heart as a gush of water spewed out of the ancient plumbing.

Welcome home, Robin.

ANOTHER DAY, ANOTHER DELIVERY.

God hadn't whispered His secret plans to Sammy over the past hours, so Sammy had no choice but to continue coasting through life. He'd run—make that biked—around town, dropping deliveries here and there. He'd also checked in with Edith Draper and repaired her front door.

The life of a delivery boy and handyman was not super glamorous. But it was honest work, if not very fulfilling.

He could really use some more caffeine. He'd woken in the night from a nightmare, heart pounding, sheets soaked. Every time he closed his eyes he saw not what had actually happened in his accident, but what had almost happened: his truck plowing over the Prius, the passengers inside unable to make it out before the whole thing was engulfed in flames.

Sleep eluded him for the rest of the night.

Sammy checked his smartwatch. The bakery would be closing any minute, and he'd promised his mother a baguette to have with their lasagna that night. After dropping off another packet of legal documents at Turnquist Lumber, he biked over to the Fox.

The dining room was empty, and no one was manning the till. Strange. Usually Elaine or Jim greeted their customers as they came in the door.

A scream pealed out from the kitchen.

He scrambled through the swinging doors. At first he didn't see where the scream had come from, but then he noticed a pair of petite legs sticking out from under the sink, where the pipes were doing their best Niagara Falls impression.

"Whoa! You need to get that valve turned off."

"I know that!" the legs shouted. Okay, it probably wasn't the legs. "The dumb thing is stuck."

He crossed over to the sink double-time. "Here, let me."

A woman's voice growled. "Be my guest."

He reached under the sink, his shoulders barely finding clearance, water spraying everywhere. The woman inched out, giving him room. He didn't look her direction—too much water spraying everywhere. Finding the water shutoff valve, he gave it a twist. It resisted, so he strained harder. It gave way and screeched as he turned it to the right. Mercifully, the water stopped shooting him in the face.

With a sigh, he wiggled out from the opening and turned. He sat down against the cabinet, ignoring the water seeping into his jeans.

The woman in front of him was soaked, auburn curls dripping onto her Fox-themed shirt. Freckles dotted her upturned nose beneath a pair of pale green eyes.

"Robin? Robin Fox?" He recognized her with a start. She'd changed since high school. More sophisticated or something. Cute, and grown up.

She gave a weak wave. "That's me."

"I haven't seen you since graduation!" He and Robin had shared a few classes during high school, graduating the same year. They'd been lab partners in chemistry. He still had a photo of the two of them proudly displaying a volcano they'd constructed together. In the years since, every time Robin had been home, Sammy had been elsewhere. Their schedules had never synced. She was home so rarely, especially lately. "Weren't you in Paris or something?"

"I'm back. Hi, Sammy." She brushed a hair out of her face. "Thanks for rescuing me."

"You had the right idea. You just needed some brute strength." He gave a playful flex of his muscle. It had the desired effect, as her face bloomed into a smile.

"Yeah, you always were great at that."

"Where did the dent in this pipe come from?"

"I guess I have some brute strength too. I tried to hit the spigot to loosen it, but I slipped, or the wrench did, and hit the pipe instead. It's not too bad, is it?" She stood and took a few small towels off a stack on a shelf. Tossed him one.

He wiped his face, then ran the towel over his hair. His jacket was soaked. Couldn't do anything about that for now. "I hate to be the bearer of bad news, but I think you're going to need a plumber. You have quite a swing. We could've used you on the baseball team." He stood next to her, a pool of water at their feet. He shucked off his jacket and laid it on the center island.

"Those pipes are ancient. They must've had a weak spot." Her shoes squished as she moved to put the dirty towels in a basket. "I need to get this water cleaned up."

He checked the time. His mom wouldn't be expecting him for a while yet. "I'll help."

"You don't have to do that."

"I'd like to."

She squished into the dining area, and he watched as she flipped the Open/Closed sign over, locked the door, and turned out the main lights. She showed him where the janitor's closet was, and they worked in silence for a few minutes, him running the mop and her sopping up the mess under the cabinet.

A memory struck him and he began chuckling.

"What?" Robin stared at him. He probably deserved it—he was cackling now.

He caught his breath. "Remember that time in junior year when the whole class had the water balloon fight in the hallway at school?"

She propped her hands on her hips. "I thought Principal Chase was going to have a stroke."

"I can't believe we thought we could get away with it." He shook his head.

She turned back to the mess under the cabinet. "Well, we kinda did get away with it. None of us even had to serve detention."

"I suppose they thought that mopping the entire school and publishing an article in the school paper about the dangers of high-school pranks was punishment enough." He still had nightmares about writing that article. His teammates had made him do the essay, and he'd never lived it down.

She speared him with a look. "It didn't hurt that the whole incident was spurred on by the football team."

"Yeah, that too." He shot her a wry grin. "So, you're back in town."

"I'm filling in for my grandparents while they take a sabbatical of sorts in Florida." She tugged a rubber band off her wrist and looped her hair up in a complicated maneuver. Suddenly she looked more like the high-school Robin he'd known. A grown-up version of her, anyway, complete with some new curves.

"I heard about your grandpa's heart attack. That must have been scary." His mom had made him deliver a meal to the Foxes after Jim came home from the hospital.

"It was hard being halfway around the world, but Grandma said it wasn't serious enough for me to come home. I wish my brothers would have at least made an effort, but I guess they had good reasons not to come home, just like I did."

He pushed on the mop, then wrung it out in the bucket. "He looked pretty good last week at church."

She stood up, bunching the towels she held into a ball. "I think he's feeling much better, but the doctor said that he needed to take some time off from the bakery. Getting up at four a.m. and working in a hot kitchen wasn't doing him any favors."

"Maybe they'll like it so much down there they'll stay."

"I can't see that happening. They love it up here too much. The last thing my grandma said was not to change anything. After Grandpa's heart attack, she can't stand the idea of more change."

He moved over next to her at the sink. "That makes sense. But as much as I'd dislike going against your grandma's wishes, I think this entire cabinet will need to be replaced." He opened the door under the sink, and they both stared at the sagging floor for a moment. "The leak was probably slow for the last few days, then just got worse. When you tried your Louisville Slugger act, it gave out altogether."

Beside him, she gave an audible sigh. "I guess I can use the sink by the prep station for a few days, but I can't leave this here like this. Like it or not, I'll have to get that fixed."

He ran the mop over the last of the water. "How are Grayson and Oliver?" Robin's brothers had been gone from Deep Haven for longer than Robin.

A shadow passed over her face. "I don't know." She half turned away from him. "Other than a quick call at Christmas, I haven't talked to them in a while." Her abrupt tone told him more than her words.

Message received.

"Where do you want me to put this wet mop?" he asked. She showed him where they kept the mop and the dirty laundry for the laundry service to pick up.

She lifted a container of flour from a shelf and began to

measure it out into a huge stainless steel bowl. "So, what are you up to these days?"

That was the question, wasn't it? "I do odd jobs around town. Mostly deliveries, but I'm also handy with a hammer." He was grateful that she didn't slow her work in response to his lame answer for a job.

She spooned a grainy, brown substance in next, then gave everything a quick whisk. "What happened to working out at Turnquist Lumber?"

His chest grew tight. "There was an accident almost two years ago, and I had to go on some medications that weren't compatible with using heavy machinery." *Just breathe, Johnson.* He took a breath. Two.

She measured out some water, weighing it on a scale before adding it to the bowl. "I heard something about that. I think Grandma sent me a link to a newspaper article Ree wrote. You were a hero."

He wished people would stop saying that. He was no hero. "I just stopped my truck. Nothing heroic there."

"And you pulled two people out of a car before they could be crushed, and your truck prevented the rest of the traffic from crashing into them. Pretty heroic, I'd say."

He wiped his brow. She must have turned on the oven, because it was suddenly hot in here. "Anyone would have done that." Besides, she didn't know the whole story. And he certainly wasn't telling her that the whole thing was partly his fault to begin with.

"That might be true, but you were there and you did it." She stopped measuring ingredients and fixed him with a stare. "Is there more to the story?"

The rest of the story. Right.

She meant the moments after he'd pulled the mother and son out of the crushed Prius. The split second between one life and the next.

The mechanism holding the massive chains around the

lumber on the back of his truck had snapped. Something about the cold weather and the age of the steel. Three logs had tumbled off the pile. One had landed on him, crushing his legs beneath. The other end had landed right on top of the Prius where the two people had been sitting minutes before.

He swallowed. A short answer would have to be enough. "My legs were crushed, but Colleen—you remember Colleen Decker?" At her nod, he continued. "She's a flight nurse now for the local Crisis Response Team. Anyway, she did some procedure to help while we flew to Duluth. At the hospital, they pieced me back together. Then physical therapy did the rest."

A gross understatement, but she didn't need to know about the nights staring into the dark, wondering why he hadn't died on that road. Or the nightmares where he felt that chopper falling out of the sky. Or the pain that he sometimes still felt in his right leg when he turned wrong... The few moments right before the accident. The blackness that had descended...

She leaned against the counter, stuck her hands in her pockets. "That sounds awful."

He didn't know how she'd gotten him to open up that much. Usually he wasn't this chatty. But, come on, this was Robin. She'd always put him at ease in school, and she seemed...he didn't know...familiar or something now. "I'm past the worst of it."

Crossing to the working sink, she washed her hands again, then returned to the mixing bowl. With a mighty grunt, she moved the bowl to a Hobart mixer standing in the corner. Her petite frame made the motion seem almost impossible. "So, what's next? Are you going to stick with being a delivery man?"

An unscratchable itch roiled through his chest again. "Honestly? I'm not sure. I have a few options out there. Nothing feels quite right though."

The Hobart started mixing the dough, and the rhythmic sound of it thump-thumping soothed his nerves.

"I hear ya." She clapped her hands together. "Okay, enough

personal stuff. What're the updates around here? Anything interesting happening?"

"This is Deep Haven. There's always drama."

Her laughter sounded like a wind chime on a summer day. "Well, tell me some of it. The dough has to mix for eight more minutes, and then I'll need to call the plumber."

She led them to the dining room. "Mind if I cash out the till while we talk?" He shook his head. The register drawer opened with a ping, and she began shuffling through the cash inside.

He spotted a spray bottle and rag sitting on the counter. He picked them up and raised his eyebrows at her.

"Be my guest," she said. "The glass on the display case needs a good clean. We had some kids in earlier with sticky fingers. Sooo..." She drew the word out. "You were going to tell me some drama."

He sprayed the cleaner onto the case. "Right now there's some jockeying going on at the school." He rubbed at an extra-sticky spot. "The high school had planned to hold its Snowball Dance at the youth center—some sort of ploy to get kids interested in using the center more. But their HVAC system died, and now the dance is back at the school."

"That's too bad. How soon can it be replaced?"

"I'm not sure. There's never enough money during a good month, so I'm sure there's no extra for a new furnace." He took a long look at the case in front of him. The glass shone.

Robin stuck the bills she'd counted into a bank bag. "Sounds like the youth center needs an angel investor. Someone who can just fund the whole thing."

A spark lit inside him at her words, but she was still speaking. "Remember the Snowball Dance our senior year?"

Boy, did he. Blue and white streamers had crisscrossed the gym, balloons everywhere. Girls dressed in shades of white, and boys sporting their fathers' ties. Colleen had shown up on the arm of Tucker, her high-school boyfriend, and Sammy had tried not to feel too jealous. He'd always liked Colleen but had remained firmly in the friend zone. She was now with Jack Stewart, and he was happy for her. He really was. He just wasn't sure why he never got the girl.

Robin was still chuckling. "I thought I was such hot stuff. Had my life all planned out. I was going places. School in Los Angeles and then the sky was the limit."

"Didn't you go with Paul Johnson? He was a real catch." He smirked at her. His cousin Paul had been homecoming king one year with Colleen as queen, and Sammy had never quite forgiven him for it.

"We made quite the pair. He thought he was all that and a bag of chips. Turns out he was just a big, dumb potato." Robin smiled, the laughter clear in her eyes.

In the kitchen, something began beeping. Sammy sobered. "He sure liked to play the field, and I'm not talking about football. I should've warned you about him."

Robin motioned to the back. He followed her into the kitchen. "Don't worry about it. I figured it out myself. Besides, we weren't that kind of friends in high school."

"That's not how I remember it. I remember loads of long talks on the bus to away games." Long talks where he'd tried to distract himself from watching Colleen sitting with Tucker.

"True, but those were mostly superficial." Robin lugged the mixing bowl back to the workstation. "Who liked who, details about the team we'd play that night, did you run sprints that day in gym. That kind of stuff."

"I always thought of you as"—he bit his tongue on the words *a sister*—no girl wanted to hear that—"as a good friend. I'm sorry I fell out of touch."

She laid her hand on his bicep. "Hey, don't worry about it. I fell out of touch too. Following my grand plan for my life, remember?"

The heat of her hand burned through his shirt sleeve. "LA, right? Then Paris? Good for you, following your dreams."

"Something like that." She sighed.

He could have kicked himself. Of course her dream didn't include coming back here to take over a rinky-dink bakery. "Sorry, I shouldn't have brought up a sore subject."

She removed her hand and his arm felt its loss. "It's not that. I just keep thinking about the youth center. Having a place like that would have meant a lot to me when I was growing up." She dumped the dough out onto the workbench and began cutting it into huge pieces with some sort of cutting tool. "Would you grab me that stack of square bowls and their lids?" He handed her the supplies, and she filled each one with a section of dough. "Grandma said the church needs new carpeting, too, but can't replace it yet. And The Garden group home needs a new van. Too bad no one in Deep Haven just has a pile of money lying around." She turned to the sink and washed dough residue off her hands.

An image of an unopened red envelope hanging on his mother's fridge flashed into his mind. He knew of at least one person in Deep Haven who had a pile of money lying around.

Maybe God was telling him something.

If only he could bring himself to cash it. Except, he was not in the business of lumber truck driving anymore.

three

. . .

Why had she ever thought this job would be easy? In between customers, another rosemary loaf for Pastor Dan and a few baguettes for Ellie Brewster, and sliding a batch of bread into the oven, Robin prayed the pipes would be an easy fix. She couldn't keep dodging around the plumber. And was this considered an emergency? Should she let her grandma know? No. She could handle it.

Robin pushed a stray curl out of her eyes. The smell of freshly baked bread permeated the air, but even that homey scent didn't make her feel any better.

Not with Mack Hill, the plumber, making all kinds of grunts under her cupboards.

She checked her watch. Mack had arrived an hour ago, three hours later than he had promised. Thankfully, business had been quiet, so she'd been able to bounce back and forth between the kitchen and the retail space.

With one last disapproving grunt, Mack slid out from under the sink. "It seems the whole town is having water issues," he said. "Winter in Deep Haven, eh?"

She agreed with him, but really, it had been ten years since she'd spent a winter here. She'd forgotten some of the basics, like leaving a tiny stream of water running so pipes didn't freeze. "What's the damage?" she asked Mack.

"All of your pipes will need to be replaced," Mack said from his squat in the Fox Bakery's kitchen. "I can patch it up for now, but it won't last long." Mack stood up, groaned, stretched his back, and then wiped his hands on a towel hanging from his belt. "I'm getting too old to be crawling around on the floor." The gray-haired plumber must have been pushing seventy.

"How long will that take?" She leaned a hip against the counter. She'd been using the small sink for the past few days. She really needed the regular one working again.

"The patch job? An hour or two. If you want me to replace these pipes, that will take a couple of days. I'd suggest converting some of these pipes from copper to PVC or even PEX. You're also gonna have to find someone to come in and fix this cabinet before mold sets in. Frankly, I'm surprised your grandparents got away with having a wooden cabinet in here for so long."

Suddenly Robin was seeing dollar signs. "How much is all this going to cost me?"

"I won't charge you for today, but your sink drainpipes will cost a couple hundred, your P trap will be a couple hundred, and the labor is added on top of that." Mack began repacking his tools. "If you want it done soon, I'll have to charge a rush fee. Tomorrow is Saturday, but I can maybe squeeze you in. I'm swamped with work. We need another plumber in town, or at least someone younger than me. I don't work as quick as I used to."

She wasn't sure. "I don't have time for my whole bakery to be torn apart. Maybe we should just do the patch job."

He speared her with a look. "Okay, but I don't recommend cutting corners. It really won't take too long—a day or two, tops."

The shrill tone of the bakery phone ringing cut between

them. She answered on the second ring. "Fox Bakery, how can I help you?"

"Yes, this is Dave Stewart, the Cook County health inspector?" His voice held a question. "Can I speak to Jim or Elaine, please?"

Robin's heart beat loud in her ears. Health inspector? Surely they hadn't been reported for the flood situation. "I'm sorry, they are unavailable. This is Robin, their granddaughter. I'm filling in for them while they are away."

"Oh. I'll speak to you then." She heard a rustle of paper on the other end of the line. "I'm calling to schedule your annual health inspection. Is Monday a good time to come by?"

Robin took a look around the kitchen-cum-war zone. "Um. Not really. Let's do the end of the month."

The inspector cleared his throat. "You can't keep putting off this inspection. I gave your bakery some leniency after Mr. Fox had his heart attack, but now I must insist it get done. Otherwise I will be forced to shut you down. If you can't do this Monday, it'll have to be the first Monday in February."

By the sink, Mack had finished packing his tools. His feet squished a little on the still-sodden floor. She closed her eyes, gritted her teeth. "Sure. Fine."

"We'll just be checking to make sure everything is up-to-date, and of course I'll want to check your walk-in. I'll try to pop in sometime around lunch in…just about two weeks' time." The click on the other end sounded before she could say anything else.

She swallowed. Hung up the phone. Turned to Mack with a slight smile. "When can you start?"

After the plumber left, promising to return the next day, Robin stood in the kitchen, staring at the wall. Her grandparents had been gone for three days and things were already starting to fall apart. Where would she find someone to fix the cabinets on short notice? She'd have to figure it out somehow.

She made a mental note to check with the laundry service

about the damp cloths she and Sammy had used yesterday to clean up. They needed to be laundered.

Speaking of Sammy, where had he come from yesterday? Not that she hadn't appreciated his help, and right when she'd needed him, but she hadn't thought about Sammy in years. Check that—she thought about him every time she watched a football game. She may have dated a football player or two, but Sammy was the one she always looked for on the field. As a lineman, he'd seemed to have a knack for always being in the right place to protect the ball. She wondered idly if he still played. And yeah, she could admit to having had a crush on him in high school. He'd grown into himself in the years since. More masculine.

In fact, Sammy Johnson had become one fine-looking man.

Of course, she'd heard about his accident and the heroics accompanying the event. Saving someone's life was just what the Sammy Johnson she'd known would do. It didn't surprise her to know he was a hero.

She moved to the nook where the computer sat on a small desk. Underneath, file drawers held financial statements and other business-related items.

Booting up the aging computer took forever, so Robin flipped through the product catalog in front of her. Drooling over fancy and expensive ovens always calmed her. She dreamed of a day she could purchase something like this for her own bakery. But those dreams would have to wait, as she had far more pressing needs.

Like saving the bakery her grandparents had trusted her with.

New plumbing and new cabinetry would cost money. She logged into her grandparents' banking program. Checked the numbers again.

Apparently, Fox Bakery was broke.

Well, not technically. The Fox Bakery made enough to pay its bills and the wages for their part-time employees, but there wasn't much left over. It looked like her grandparents routinely donated their product to any charity that asked them to donate to their silent auction or any church function that required fresh bread. There was even a record of them providing unleavened bread for an annual community Passion Play and Lord's Supper event every Easter.

All admirable, of course, but it didn't leave anything in the bank for routine updates to the building, like repairing ancient plumbing, for example.

She shuddered at the thought of calling her grandparents to ask them to pay the plumber. This money issue had probably contributed to Grandpa's heart attack in the first place. There was no way she was interrupting their quiet trip to Florida with a plea for more cash.

She'd figure it out. And figure out how to replace the cabinet too.

The scent of bread grew stronger, alerting her that the current batch was nearly done. She went to the oven to pull the loaves out. She kept turning the problem over in her mind, kneading at it like a stubborn rye dough that refused to relax.

After transferring the long, thin baguettes to the cooling rack, she reached for her phone. Video chatting with Elise would be a helpful distraction. She checked the time again. With the time difference, she should catch her friend getting off work.

"Elise!"

"Robin!" The miles that separated them fell away. The two had been roommates and fast friends since Robin's first year in Paris. Victor had introduced them, and when Elise had found out Robin needed a place to stay, she'd jumped at the chance to find a new flat together. She'd been looking for a way out of a bad situation. The two of them had soon become more like sisters than roommates.

Now her friend's warm greeting comforted Robin like biting into a fresh baguette on a spring morning. In the tiny video screen, she could see that Elise was sitting at her miniscule kitchen table. Her white-blonde hair topped her head in a tight knot. Even through the screen, Elise's bright blue eyes shone.

"How is Deep Haven?"

"Pretty much the same as how I left it." Those words should have been depressing, but somehow, finding Deep Haven unchanged had been a balm. Coming back had felt…right. She related some of her woes to Elise.

"I'm sorry. That sounds rough. Can I help?"

Robin barked a laugh. "I don't see how, when you're across an ocean."

"Moral support then." Elise smiled.

"Any way you can make several thousand dollars magically appear in my bank account?"

"That's a little beyond me, I'm afraid. Let's think about this logically. How long do you have before the plumber needs to be paid?"

"He said I could split his bill into three payments, and I could pay over the next couple of months."

"Okay, well that's more doable then." Elise hummed out a thinking noise. "You just have to figure out how to increase your sales by several hundred a month."

"Oh, is that all?" Robin propped the phone up on the countertop and wound her hair into a messy bun. She secured it with the hair tie she always wore on her wrist. "I'm sorry for the sarcasm. I shouldn't take it out on you."

"Can you open an extra day of the week?"

"I could, but then I'd have to pay someone to work it, and I don't know how quickly the town would catch on that we added a day."

"Advertise?"

"Sure, but that takes money too."

"Some moral support I am."

Robin had to laugh at Elise's self-deprecating tone. "Don't beat yourself up about it. I'll come up with something."

"I'll be praying for you. I know you'll figure something out.

Although, I was hoping the slower pace over there in Deep Haven would be a good thing for you. You know, give you a chance to practice some of your rusty cake-decorating skills."

Except for the occasional special order and the recent Castle in the Sky project, there hadn't been much opportunity to hone those skills in Victor's bakery. He'd mostly kept her busy making other pastries. Sometimes she wondered what he'd seen in her back in California. When he'd recruited her, he'd talked about her talents but hadn't elaborated.

She'd thought he meant with cake, but maybe he'd just meant she had a talent for being duped.

"Yeah, I don't really see that happening. If I'm going to make more money, I'll have to work harder, not less."

"Speaking of Victor..." Her friend trailed off.

"Were we speaking of him?"

"Never mind."

Now she wasn't going to let it go. "No, what were you going to say?"

"It's just, I don't know if I should say anything, but you should check *La Patisserie*'s online edition."

The French baking magazine was a big kahuna in the baking world. Robin had once harbored a hope of being featured in its pages.

"Hold on. I'm taking you off video." She minimized the phone app and pulled up an internet browser. She already had the magazine open on one of her tabs, so she hit the button to refresh the feed. "What am I looking at here?"

Her friend made a small noise. "Robin, this is a bad idea. Forget I said anything."

"Not. A. Chance. What am I supposed to see? Or not see?"

"Scroll down to the up-and-coming section."

Robin scrolled down the page and stopped. Her breath caught in her throat. A photo of Victor filled the phone's screen. He was dressed in his chef's whites and holding a cake.

Asymmetrical stacked layers held flowers cascading down the sides.

And on top? Sparklers.

Her cake.

Well, her design, anyway. This was a near identical copy of the cake she'd made for the eightieth birthday party.

The snake.

He'd stolen her idea. But how? She'd baked and decorated that cake outside of working hours. Victor couldn't have known about it.

Oh no. She must have left her sketchbook of ideas behind when she fled the bakery. She scanned the article. It was a standard fluff piece about Victor and le Château du Gâteau. The interviewer's last line was the icing on the cake:

> Full disclosure, I learned of Chef LaVigne and his bakery when my sister, Monique, started working there before the end of last year. I'm glad she introduced me to le Château du Gâteau. With cake creations like these, Victor will be one to watch.

"Robin? Still there?" Elise's voice cut through her distraction.

Robin closed the internet browser and took the phone off speaker mode. "Sorry. Still here. I can't believe he stole my design." Her shoulders tightened.

"Really? You can't believe that the man who took credit for your hard work and then threatened to blacklist you wouldn't also steal from you?"

Okay, Elise had a point. "I thought...well, I don't know what I thought." But then she remembered a time she had labored for hours over a special order, and when the client came to pick up the pastries, Victor had received all their thanks and praise without mentioning her. He'd waved it off later by saying they hadn't given him a chance to point out her efforts. "I guess he does have a pattern for undermining my work."

"I'll say. I didn't mean to upset you. I just thought you should know."

"Thanks, Elise. I appreciate it."

They exchanged promises to talk again soon and signed off.

She opened her phone again and navigated to the photo of Victor looking smug, holding her cake. She had to show the world what she could do. No more letting anyone steal her ideas and make her feel like a failure and a screwup.

Scrolling farther down the page she spotted an advertisement for *La Patisserie*'s annual Distinctive Bakes America competition in New York City. Each year, hundreds of pastry chefs were nominated by magazines all over the world to enter their best works into the contest. Winning a contest like that would be a dream come true. She read the fine print. Each contestant would be invited to compete based on photos alone. They were nominated for entry by the magazine's photographers. She imagined what she could do if she had that prize on her baking résumé.

Except, she had a business to run and bills she didn't know how to pay. Her eyes landed on the accounting spreadsheet on the computer in front of her.

What if the two things didn't have to compete? Cakes had a much higher return on investment than bread did. She remembered what Megan said about people needing high-end cakes in Deep Haven. If she put a little of her meager savings into supplies, she could probably pay off the plumbing bill in a couple of weeks.

Maybe she wouldn't be able to enter the contest, but that didn't mean she couldn't bake cakes to help pay the bills around here.

Putting the phone away, she searched the bakery for ingredients that would work for cake. The flour would be tricky, since she preferred a finer flour, but she could work with the all-purpose stuff they had for their cinnamon rolls. She looked around at the kitchen. Hmm. The only mixer was the huge Hobart in the corner. Holding up to a hundred pounds of dough, the behemoth worked wonders for batches of bread dough, not so much for a single cake. Hand mixing would have to do. She made a mental note to buy a smaller stand mixer for the countertop, then tried not to sigh. More expense.

Finding cocoa powder and baking chocolate gave her the idea for a cake filled with chocolate ganache. Good thing she had three recipes memorized. Dumping ingredients into a bowl and whisking them together, she decided on a basic chocolate cake, which paired nicely with the ganache filling.

When the mix was ready, she slid the pan into the oven. While it baked, she drew out a plan for decorations.

A few hours, several customers, and zero mishaps later, she had a beautiful chocolate cake filled with chocolate ganache and decorated with a chessboard theme, ready for an eager customer. She snapped a few photos of it for her records, then put it on a cake stand in the display case in the front of the store. Maybe she'd bake up a few cupcakes and put those in next to the sticky buns. It couldn't hurt to add a pop of color to the display area.

The front door chimed as a couple walked in, a breath of cold air preceding them.

"Oh! It smells divine in here!" The woman pulled off her gloves and stuffed them in a pocket.

"Hello," Robin said. She checked the clock. Almost three. One of her employees, Wendy Matthews, would be here soon to finish out the day and close up. A wave of relief washed over her. She'd been up since four a.m. baking bread, then finishing the cake. "What can I wrap up for you?"

The couple, who looked to be in their early thirties, both wore navy, puffy jackets and gray scarves.

"We're here for a few loaves of French bread," the man said, approaching the till.

"And some chocolate chip muffins, if you have them," the woman added.

"Coming right up." Robin busied herself wrapping up their order.

The woman wandered over to the cake on display. "This is so pretty! I didn't know you did cakes here."

"Thank you! It's a new thing. We're thinking about adding them to the menu." Hopefully Grandma could forgive her.

"Jacob, come here. Look at this cake. What a clever idea to use chocolate wafer cookies as the pawns."

Jacob took two steps closer to the cake. "Very nice."

Not very chatty, this one.

"Oh! I just had a brilliant idea. Do you do wedding cakes?" The woman's eyes sparkled with excitement.

Um. "Depends on what you're looking for."

"Jacob and I are getting married on Valentine's Day. Isn't that romantic?" She clasped her hands together.

Robin smiled in agreement.

"Well, we just got engaged, and every place we call says that they need more time than five weeks." The woman looked at Jacob, and he nodded in confirmation. "But since you are just starting to make cakes, maybe you aren't already full. Would you make our cake?" The woman looped her arm around Jacob's and leaned toward Robin, the brightness in her eyes palpable in close quarters.

Robin did some quick calculations. Most bakeries would never accept a commission so close to the event. But the woman was right. She was just starting with the cake biz and didn't have other orders waiting in line. Plus, one wedding cake could practically pay for the plumbing all on its own. This would keep her skills sharp, and she wouldn't have to call Grandma and Grandpa for help. Less stress for them, more practice for her.

Win-win.

She reached out a hand. "You have yourself a cake baker."

The woman grasped her hand and gave it a firm shake. "I'm Emily, by the way. Emily Lindstrom. And this handsome guy is Jacob Pine."

"Nice to meet you both." Robin couldn't help the pang that tweaked her heart at the warmth with which Jacob looked at Emily. "Should we plan to look at cake options at the beginning of next week?" Emily and Jacob agreed and gathered their things to leave.

The couple exited as Wendy entered. "Oooh, pretty cake," she cooed as she spotted it in the display. Wendy was the daughter of Dan and Ellie Matthews. Tall, with long brown hair, she looked just like a younger version of her mom. Wendy had worked for Robin's grandparents through high school and now picked up longer shifts between her online college classes. "Are we doing cakes now?"

"Temporarily." Robin held up her hand to stave off a wave of questions. "I just want to keep my hand in it." No need to tell Wendy about the money problems.

"I can't believe how great this looks. You are talented."

Victor would have called the cake a mess. That man was more of a perfectionist than she was, but she was proud of how it'd turned out. And with Victor, it wasn't that he thought she was so untalented but that he couldn't stand competition.

"Thank you. If anyone asks, I'll be making at least one cake a day, with rare custom orders. That should be doable. I may need to have you pick up a few more shifts though."

Wendy tucked a strand of hair behind her ear. "No problem. I have some extra time before my classes start again in February. Seriously though, I knew you had skills, but, girl, this is awesome."

The compliment lit a spark inside her. One she would love to fan into a blaze. But practical matters came first. "Be careful in the kitchen. Mack was in and fixed the pipes, but I think some of the floorboards are rotten. I'm working on a plan to get them fixed and to replace the damaged cabinets."

Robin stepped back from the case and looked at the cake again. It did look great in the display case.

It would look even better on the cover of a magazine... No. Best not to go there.

Now she just wanted to be able to bake delicious things and hold down the fort here until her grandparents were back. Besides, she couldn't make big changes to the bakery. Grandma had made her promise not to, and she intended to stick with that promise.

🐺 🐺 🐺

EXERCISE ALWAYS CLEARED HIS MIND, EXCEPT FOR TODAY. TODAY HIS mind buzzed with questions he didn't want to face.

Sammy wiped the sweat off his brow with a fuzzy towel. The weightlifting bench beneath him grew warm from his workout. He sat in the exercise room at the headquarters building for the Deep Haven Crisis Response Team. A team he barely belonged to anymore. Sure, the guys kept him around to answer phones sometimes, but not being able to drive put a damper on including him in rescue missions.

Hopefully he could get through this workout without his legs giving out. True, they had been strong enough for the physical therapist to release him from care. But would that last?

"Hey, Sammy, don't you hold the record for the power snatch in weightlifting?" Seb Brewster called from the treadmill, his breath coming in short bursts. His tall, lean form seemed made for running.

"That was a long ten years ago." Sammy had been on the football team at the time. His coach had encouraged him to enter a few weightlifting competitions to improve his game. He'd developed a knack for the power-lifting move known as the snatch. An explosive move, the snatch had an athlete squat, grab a bar fitted with weights, then stand quickly, lifting that bar up and over the head, maintaining the position for a heartbeat, then lowering the weighted bar to the ground. Not only had the move improved Sammy's overall strength but he'd found it'd improved his mental quickness too. A quickness he could use about now.

A move like that needed legs he could count on.

Near the wall, Seth pounded at a heavy bag. He paused between reps. "I bet you could still do it."

The men had ended up in the workout space after a training meeting for the Crisis Response Team. Jack Stewart, the dark-blond flight nurse, and Boone Buckam, the blue-eyed head of the Crisis Response Team, also worked out nearby.

"I could definitely beat you, anyway," Sammy said. "You always were a lightweight."

Seth put his hand to his chest in mock pain. "Lightweight?" He gave the heavy bag a few jabs. "Why don't you come over here and say that?"

Sammy laughed, the itchy energy in his chest easing.

"You're doing great after your accident," Jack said.

Okay, maybe the relief only lasted a moment. "Thanks to you and Colleen."

"Nah, Colleen was the hero that day." Jack walked over to where Sammy sat and motioned to the bar. "I can spot for you. Are you still in physical therapy?"

Sammy lay back down on the bench and wrapped his hands around the bar. "No. I've graduated." The months of therapy after his surgery stretched long in his memory. He'd moved past the physical limitations. Now if only he could figure out how to move his mind forward.

"You've done well coming back from that. Back to new." Seb slowed the treadmill to a walk.

"I won't be doing three-hundred-pound dead-squats again. But, yeah, I guess I'm doing okay." *If you don't count the nightmares.* He pushed the bar up and away from his chest, the burn in his arms not leaving any room for anything else. "I guess non-lightweight Seth will have to show us how it's done." An inch at a time, he brought the bar back down into place on the rack. A slight plink sounded as the bar seated into place.

"We could've used you last week on the snowplow," Seth said. "Any idea when you'll be coming back?"

And there it was.

A pain filled his gut momentarily. He really did enjoy being in the plow truck, clearing snow, contributing to the town he loved.

"I'm just not up to it yet." Sweat unrelated to the weight lifting popped out on his forehead, and he wiped at it again.

"Maybe you can ride along with us sometimes. Get back into the swing of things," Jack offered.

"Yeah, maybe." Get an up-close view of everything the accident had stolen from him? No thanks.

Sammy took Seb's place on the treadmill. For a moment the room echoed with the noises of the men shifting into their new positions. Their sweat filled the air with a sharp musky scent. Outside the window, the January sky hung overcast and gray.

"Did you hear that Robin Fox is back?" Seth called from the weight-lifting bench, his voice coming out in a grunt as he tried to press Sammy's weights.

"Who is Robin Fox?" Boone asked.

Sammy felt heat rise up his neck. "Just a girl we went to school with a long time ago."

"Just a girl with the last name Fox?" Boone teased.

"I think we need to hear more about this Robin," Jack put in.

Sammy increased the speed of the treadmill. "Guys, she's just a friend."

"Okay, sure," Jack said. "But is she single? Is she cute?"

Sammy ignored the ribbing and bumped his machine up until he was jogging.

"I seem to remember you two being pretty chummy." Seb caught his eye in the mirror hung on the wall, his face a picture of innocence. "I ran into you more than once having a study session."

"Oh." Boone leaned into the teasing now. "I think maybe you just need another study session. See if you remember any chemistry?"

Sammy missed a step, recovered, and held up his hands in surrender. "Okay. I give. She's cute. She's back in town, and I saw her the other day. She's all grown up."

Seth gave a loud, theatrical sigh. "Growing up happens to the best of us. Wasn't she in Paris or something?"

"Yep. She's back here now, though, running her grandparents' bakery." Her dripping hair and the ruined cabinet flashed through his mind. "She's got her work cut out for her. The oven is ancient, and she'll need to update some other things as well. The pipes under the main sink burst and leaked all over the floor."

"Sounds like she needs a handyman," Seth said, waggling his eyebrows so no one could miss his meaning. "Know anybody like that?"

"Ha ha. Very funny." His breath came in shorter bursts. "I'm not sure how much time I'll have between my other odd jobs and the youth center."

"Speaking of the youth center," Jack said, "what's up with the furnace? Colleen mentioned they need a new one."

"Uh-huh," Sammy said. His legs burned with the pace he'd set. "It's kaput. I checked it out to see if I could convince it to run a while longer, but it's a no go."

"Too bad. A lot of kids depend on that place." As mayor, Seb kept tabs on things like that. "I think it's great you're tutoring Ben and some of the other kids."

"Someone has to make sure he stays on the baseball team. We need a win at state this year," Sammy said. "I know I wouldn't have stayed on the football team if someone hadn't helped me."

"Was this someone named Robin?" Boone's voice singsonged in a tease. The group laughed.

"Remember our junior year when we went to state?" Seth said. "You took us all the way that night."

Sammy remembered the game in living color.

"We were down by two points, ten seconds left in the second half." Seth warmed to his subject. "The quarterback ran long for a deep pass into the end zone, Sammy making a way for him, clearing green-and-yellow uniforms the whole way." Using the heavy bag, Seth mimed Sammy pushing the opposing players out of the way. "Just as the quarterback stretched high for the catch in the end zone, our boy Sammy here spotted a linebacker out of the corner of his eye. He pivoted and leaped—he practically flew— taking down our opponent a breath before the player could tackle the quarterback." Seth raised his gloved hands in the air in a Rocky pose. "The crowd went wild." He danced around the heavy bag. Around them, the other men chuckled.

Sammy's chest swelled as he recalled the fans chanting his name.

"Too bad we couldn't stay in high school forever," Seth said. He sighed dramatically and put a hand to his chest.

"C'mon, Seth. Don't pretend. We both know married life is a lot better than high school," Boone said.

"You got me there. You're absolutely right," Seth said. He began clearing up the weights. "Speaking of married life, it's time for me to get home to my wife, gents."

A prick, and the balloon in Sammy's chest deflated. Most of the guys here had someone to go home to. Meanwhile, he was still living with his mom. And yet, moving back out to his lot and trailer all alone didn't hold any appeal either. He pictured cold, lonely nights without the benefit of being able to bike into town. "Don't bother with those weights, Seth. I'll clean up."

"I'm heading out too," Seb said. Boone followed them out.

Jack handed Sammy a bottle of disinfectant and a rag, and the two men wiped down the equipment. "How are you really doing?" Jack asked. "And I don't mean physically."

"I'm making it." Sammy swiped at the sweat drops he'd left on the treadmill, washing away the evidence he'd been there. In his pocket, his phone buzzed. He pulled it out and saw a reminder to take his meds. He slid the phone back in and his pill case out. Just as he flipped the cap, the case slipped out of his hand.

Great. Pills everywhere.

Across from him, Jack stilled. "Dude. Those looked like Vicodin. Are you still taking opioids?"

Sammy bent to pick up the pills. Two, three...where was that last one? "What? No. I'm not on any pain meds."

Jack took a step closer. "There's one under the treadmill. Listen, if you're using as a way to cope, you can tell me."

Wait... "I'm not using."

"I know what I can see." Jack thrust out a hand toward the pills in his hand.

"These are a prescription. Drop it, Jack."

Jack propped his arm on the weight machine. "I'm just saying—"

"They're seizure meds, okay?" Sweat popped out on his brow. "I have to take Neurontin for seizures."

"Oh." Jack lowered his shoulders. "I'm sorry, man. I should've known better."

"Don't worry about it." Sammy retrieved the final capsule from under the treadmill and stood up. "I just don't like to talk about it."

"You know having to take medicine for seizures isn't a sign of weakness, right?" Jack resumed wiping down the machines.

"Yeah. Sometimes I know that." But sometimes, the lie won. The feeling that he wasn't good enough, the hunger for something more out of life told him that even his strength wasn't enough.

"Well, it's true. Having a medical condition and having to take meds for it is its own kind of strength. I bet you had to overcome a lot to own that truck of yours."

"You got that right. I had my first seizure after an accident in the Army. Did you know it takes eight years seizure-free before you can get a commercial driver's license?"

Jack tossed the dirty rag he'd been using into a laundry bin. "I knew it was difficult. I didn't know it was that long."

Sammy sat on the weight bench with a thump. "I threw all that hard work away." Might as well come clean with the whole thing. "In the distraction of getting my truck, starting my new job at Turnquist, and managing the paperwork...I wasn't taking my meds regularly." A gnawing began in his stomach. "The doctor can't say one way or another, but I likely had a seizure coming down the hill that day. I've never told anyone this, but I briefly blacked out, right before I saw the Williams's Prius."

Jack began racking the weights. "That's some heavy burden to carry. Probably doesn't help that you nearly died a second time that day."

"I don't remember much of the rest of the accident. Comes to me in dreams sometimes."

"I get that," Jack said. "There are some things you just can't shake. I lost a buddy back when I was a paratrooper. Still have bad dreams sometimes."

Sammy hefted the barbells Seth had left behind, their weight cradled against his chest making him stagger a step. "At least you can still get into a helicopter. I'm having a hard time getting back into the driver's seat. I'm cleared for regular driving, but I just can't bring myself to do it."

"You wouldn't be human if it didn't still bother you sometimes."

Sammy absorbed the words as he put the barbells into their place. "Maybe you're right."

"Only maybe?" Jack smiled. "I know I'm right, man. Trust me on this." Jack grabbed the rest of the rags, now soaked with the smell of hospital disinfectant, and threw them into the laundry basket to get washed by the night shift. "It took me a long time to get back into that helicopter. Even now I have moments sometimes."

"Okay, wise guy. Tell me how I'm supposed to buy a new truck when I can't even get myself to sit behind the steering wheel without breaking into a cold sweat?"

Jack walked in front of him toward the door. "What do you mean, buy a new truck?"

"I have the check from the insurance company for my totaled lumber rig still hanging on my refrigerator door. Can't bring myself to cash it." He stuffed his ice-cold hands into his pockets.

Ahead, Jack stopped and turned around. His gaze searched Sammy's face. "You've been through a lot. You can give yourself a break."

"I guess." Sammy shrugged.

Jack met his eye. "But who says you have to spend that money on a new truck? Just a thought." Jack clapped Sammy on the shoulder. "I'm sure you'll figure it out. Give yourself some grace."

The little nudges to cash that check drummed on his brain.

What if he didn't spend the money on a new truck but on something else entirely?

Sammy walked to his bike in the lot. He threw his leg over and kicked the kickstand up into place, eager to get moving. As he pedaled out of the lot, the sun broke through the clouds, its rays warming his face.

He might not ever get back into a semitruck, but that insurance money could do a lot of good around town.

four

. . .

Maybe this would work after all. Robin tucked a leg under her on the couch in her grandparents' living room. A gas fire crackled in the faux fireplace set in the wall.

As long as she didn't look too closely at the photos of her parents and brothers lining the mantelpiece, she could pretend it didn't ache in her gut every time she thought about them.

Instead, she sat looking over her new idea notebook. She'd sketched out some loose ideas for cakes that would be easy for the bakery to carry—things that were simple to make and decorate. She could even train Bella and Wendy to do some of them. She'd included a few more difficult designs as well. Those she would have to handle, but she could charge more. She especially liked a red-and-purple-themed three-tiered cake she'd drawn near the end.

It seemed her plan to bring cakes to Deep Haven was off to a good start. Beside her, the phone rang. Grandma Elaine's number popped up on caller ID.

"How is the Florida life?" She pictured her grandparents strolling down the beach, arm in arm. She knew for a fact that her grandma had packed more than one Hawaiian-style shirt to wear, plus matching shorts for Grandpa. She bet they turned heads everywhere they went.

"To be honest, we're loving the sunshine, but your grandpa can't keep himself out of the kitchen." Her grandma laughed. Robin pictured the little head shake she always did when describing her husband's antics. "There's a lemon tree in the backyard, and he's developing new ideas for lemon-infused breads."

"Sounds fancy."

"We're having fun. How are things there?"

Gulp. She hadn't exactly told her grandparents about the mess she'd made of the kitchen. She rubbed at the back of her neck, contemplating.

Nope.

No need to bother her grandma about it when there was nothing she could do.

"I saw Sammy Johnson the other day."

"Oh, he must have stopped by for a baguette. He stops by every week now that he's living with his mom again."

"It was fun to reconnect with him." Robin looked over at the kitchen table, remembering study nights with Sammy in that spot. "Do you remember how we worked on that science project together?"

"A volcano, right?"

Robin had been the artist on the project, and Sammy had been the tech. He'd figured out how to feed extra baking soda into the "lava" every few minutes to make the volcano flow continuously. Robin had added colored dye to the inner workings to make the lava multicolored. By the time they'd finished, the whole thing had stood three feet tall and four feet wide.

"You made a mess of my kitchen for a week getting that thing to work right," her grandma said. "I didn't think Grandpa Jim was going to fit it into the van."

She laughed. "Hey, at least we won the science fair."

"You always knew how to make a project shine."

Yeah, she should definitely tell Grandma about the kitchen. "Grandma, I—"

On the other end of the line an alarm screamed.

"Robin, I gotta go!" A fumbling noise and then the phone cut out.

Robin tried her grandma's number again, but it went straight to voice mail. She got up from the couch to find the number for their landline in Florida.

Her phone pinged a text message.

GRANDMA

> Grandpa set off the fire alarm trying to bake lemon challah. All is well.

Robin smiled. Grandpa Jim kept things lively.

ROBIN

> Glad you are okay.

> Thanks for the chat today.

GRANDMA

> Love you, Chickie-poo. Talk again soon.

A weight lifted off her shoulders even as her stomach knotted. Sure, she hadn't told Grandma about the kitchen disaster or the cakes, but she couldn't put it off forever. *Don't change anything.* Her grandma's words tiptoed through her mind again.

Don't worry, Grandma. I haven't changed much. Just the pipes, and soon the cabinets, the flooring, and maybe the menu...

The front doorbell rang.

Through the frosted window glass, she saw a wavy outline of a strawberry-blonde in a blue puffy jacket. She opened the door.

"Colleen!" Her friend from high school stood on the front porch, cheeks rosy, green eyes bright in the cold air. "Come in."

Colleen held up a bag emblazoned with World's Best Donuts. "I hope you don't mind me dropping by. I wasn't sure what your work schedule was. I know sometimes you have to get up before the birds, and I hoped you weren't sleeping. I brought donuts as a peace offering just in case."

Robin gave Colleen a swift hug, then took her jacket. "You're always welcome, even when you don't come with gifts."

"I suppose it's funny to bring donuts to a pastry chef."

"There isn't a donut in all of Paris that rivals World's Best. Come sit in the living room. I'll make us a pot of coffee to go with the donuts."

Colleen sat on the couch, and Robin moved to the kitchen. The low wall separating the kitchen and living room allowed for chatter.

"I'm sorry about your grandpa," Colleen said. "How is he feeling?"

"He's doing much better." Robin dumped water into the drip coffee machine. "He and Grandma are in Florida right now, staying at my great-aunt's place on the Gold Coast."

"I heard they were headed down there and that's why you're back. I'm glad you're home. It'll be fun to hang out again."

"Oh, I'm not staying. I'm only here long enough to cover for Grandma and Grandpa and then I'm leaving." She leaned against the half wall.

"What? I was hoping you were back for good." Colleen's expression stopped just short of being a full pout. "Deep Haven needs you."

"Ha. That's a laugh. This town never really understood me. Remember that prom dress I reworked back when we were juniors?"

"The one you found at the thrift store? I remember those wings."

"The dress certainly didn't match the vision I had in my head, but I thought the wings were amazing. I worked hard on that dress." The coffee machine gurgled its last drips into the pot. Robin found and filled two cups. "Okay, so I won't win any fashion awards, but even then, I wanted to stand out. Northern Minnesota isn't a good place for original ideas. I still hear the echo of the other girls laughing at me." She carried the cups to the living room and then handed one to Colleen.

Colleen speared her with a look. "C'mon, it was high school. I bet we're more accepting than you think."

"You're probably right." But even time and maturity hadn't quite erased the sting of that night. Robin sipped her hot coffee. She'd never felt comfortable here in Deep Haven—didn't fit the Northern Minnesota mold. "It was hard to tell when everyone spent all their time giving me pitying looks. They never really knew me. They only saw my tragic story, and my weirdness."

"Pitying looks?" Colleen stared at her. "I think you're mistaken. They were being sympathetic. Everyone knew you'd lost your parents."

And that'd been part of the problem. She'd always been the girl who was an orphan. Never fitting in...but that wasn't Colleen's fault. "Sorry. I'm just out of sorts, I guess. It has been nice reconnecting with some of the regulars at the bakery."

"Have you seen Sammy yet? I know he stops there a lot."

Sammy's teasing from the other day flashed through her mind. "You could say that. He rescued me from a flood. You know, I always thought the two of you would get together." Robin aimed for a casual tone.

"No, we were always friends."

Too bad Robin hadn't known that back in high school when she'd had a pretty huge crush on the guy. But also, "I'm pretty sure Sammy wanted more than that."

Colleen waved off the suggestion. "It would never have worked. You would be a much better match for him."

Huh. "I mean, he's definitely attractive." Robin spoke quickly to cut off the interest Colleen showed in the statement. "But I'm *leaving*, so nothing can happen between us."

"Maybe you should keep an open mind," Colleen said. "I

never thought I'd move back home, but look at me now! Besides, life is always messy. There is never a perfect time to fall in love."

"Food for thought, I guess. All this talk about love—do you have a boyfriend now?"

"Actually, I am dating a guy named Jack." Colleen's face softened. "We're on the Crisis Response Team together."

Robin took a bite of her donut. Its sugar coating melted on her tongue, and she breathed in the slight hint of nutmeg. "Oh, yeah. I heard about him in a newspaper article Grandma sent me. You two were the ones who took care of Sammy, right?"

"Yep." Colleen bit into her donut too. "I thought we were all going to die. Scariest day of my life."

"I'll bet. I never really heard the whole story."

Colleen paused, took a long sip of her coffee. "We got an emergency call about an accident. There had been a big storm, and everyone was on high alert. I didn't know it was Sammy until I got there. I drove up and it was…chaos. Sammy's truck had jackknifed around a Prius. Cars and people were everywhere."

Robin imagined the scene, the cold and chaos.

"At first I didn't understand what I was seeing, then I realized that some of the huge pine logs on Sammy's truck had fallen. One of them lay on top of the car, and trapped on the other end was Sammy." Colleen closed her eyes for the space of a heartbeat. "Another team was working on the passengers of the car, so I ran to where Sammy was lying. Jensen Atwood and my boyfriend, Jack Stewart, and some of the other guys lifted the log off of Sammy's legs." Colleen shuddered. "His legs looked like meatloaf before it goes into the oven. We all knew we had to move fast or he would lose them."

Robin's heart sped up. She knew everything had turned out okay, but hearing about the accident from Colleen made the situation even more real. "So you called for the chopper?"

Colleen nodded, one jerk of her head. "He needed to get to Duluth, stat." Colleen adjusted her ponytail. "When Bill, the pilot, got there, the storm started kicking up again. We thought the storm ceiling was high enough to allow us to fly, but we were hit with an updraft, and the pilot couldn't recover. We went down in a field."

"Oh my goodness. So scary."

"You have no idea. Jack ran for help and I stayed behind." Colleen's wry smile took the bite out of her words. "Anyway, I had to perform a field surgery to alleviate the compartment syndrome developing in Sammy's muscles. It saved his legs."

"That's amazing."

Colleen raised her coffee cup in a mock toast. "It was shortly after that we hired Jae Washington as helicopter pilot."

Robin stared at her friend in wonder. "You're a bona fide hero."

"Sammy is the real hero." Colleen finished her coffee and set her cup on the low table near the couch. "What he's gone through with physical therapy is amazing. No one thought he would keep his legs, let alone walk again."

Seemed like her high-school science-fair partner held hidden depths.

"And you've moved back to Deep Haven for good?" Robin had a hard time imagining Colleen being back at home, as all she'd talked about in high school had been moving away.

"Yep. The volleyball queen is back." Colleen gave a flip of her ponytail. "Seriously though. I'm glad to be home. My time in Minneapolis was fun, and I learned a lot, but there's nothing better than living in a town that just gets you, you know?"

No, Robin didn't know. She thought again of that prom dress, the pity, the misunderstandings. "I guess I don't see Deep Haven the same way. Maybe it's because I didn't grow up here." She hadn't moved here until she was ten. After that awful year... She pushed the thought away, focused again on her friend.

"You were here for a long time. I think that counts. I guarantee that people here love you. People were always asking your grandma how you were doing in Paris. She was so proud to talk you up."

Huh. She'd always thought everyone had forgotten about her once she moved away for school.

Colleen dug in the donut bag and came up with a napkin. She wiped at her fingers. "Listen, Deep Haven has always been a great place to find a second chance, but this time I wonder if it's you who needs to give Deep Haven the second chance. People here could surprise you."

Robin nestled her own cup next to Colleen's on the table. "I'll think about it." She leaned over and gave her friend a quick hug. "Thanks for coming and for the donuts."

"Anytime." Colleen squeezed her back.

After walking Colleen to the door, Robin climbed the stairs and went down the hall into her bedroom. Grandma hadn't changed much in here either. Before Robin had left for culinary school, she'd taken down her posters and some of her school memorabilia and helped Grandma paint the room a neutral beige. She'd left her own books on the shelves, her hand-painted duvet, and a few stuffed animals. The room now felt partly like her own and partly like a guest room.

Which was fine, because she was a guest here.

She opened up the closet and pushed back the clothing until she reached the back few items. Her hand brushed something silky and she pulled at it. Soon, her prom dress slipped into the light.

She held it out in front of her. Made from a deep-blue satin, the dress looked just like she remembered. Turning it around, she found the iridescent butterfly wings she'd sewn to the back. Shades of purple and blue glimmered as she moved the wings. They still sparkled after all these years.

She could still hear the whispers from that night. The popular girls had teased her about her wings for weeks after the dance.

In fact, only one person other than her grandparents had told her that she looked anything other than "weird."

Sammy.

His words to her that night echoed through her heart. *Wow, Robin. You look amazing. Ready to fly.* His voice had been soft. Kind. Almost like he was in awe of her.

She'd certainly been in awe of him, dressed to the nines in his tuxedo… Robin shook herself and shoved the dress away. She shouldn't be thinking about Sammy that way again.

Because as nice as a relationship with him sounded, it would mean staying in Deep Haven indefinitely. Yeah. No, thanks.

HE'D PRAYED, WRESTLED HIS PRIDE TO THE GROUND, AND FINALLY made a deal with God over the weekend. He'd cash the check and find ways to use it. If God wanted him to have that money, then for Pete's sake, he was going to spend it.

When Sammy entered the bank on Monday in the early afternoon, well-worn check in hand, the cashier gave him a skeptical look.

"I'm sorry, sir. This check is almost expired, and for such a large amount, you're going to have to talk to a banker." She hurried over to the open door to one of the offices facing the street. A nameplate reading Fran Turner was mounted on the wall. He heard snippets of their conversation, things like "old check," "a hundred thousand," and "scam."

The last two days had been torture. He'd tossed and turned in bed, Robin's words ringing through his mind. *The youth center needs an angel investor… Too bad no one in Deep Haven just has a pile of money lying around…*

"Sammy Johnson?" Ms. Turner's voice cut through his reverie. "Come on in and we'll have a chat." The banker, a slim blonde in a frilly top, gestured to a chair in front of her desk. "I'm Fran Turner. Please, have a seat."

He sat down. Shifted once in his chair, then sat forward again.

"Would you like to take off your jacket? This could take a few minutes."

Was this going to be an interrogation?

"Sure." He laid his jacket over the armrest of the seat next to him and shifted in his chair again.

"Sorry for the hassle, Mr. Johnson," Ms. Turner said. "I assure you this is simply routine."

"No problem." And if it was, there was no way she would hear that from him. "I guess I shouldn't have expected to waltz in and open a new account to deposit a hundred thousand dollars without consequences."

She chuckled. "Good. I'm glad you understand. Really, there are two issues at play here. The first is that the check is almost expired. Did you know that checks expire after six months?"

Just under the wire. "I always thought that was a myth."

"Nope. It's very real. Now, if the person who gave you the check verifies—say your grandma gave you a check at Christmas and you just found it in your stocking months later, she can call the bank and tell us she still wants to give her favorite grandson that money." Sammy shifted in his chair a third time. Was she going to take the check or not? Ms. Turner went on. "So there are definitely exceptions to the six-month rule. The other caution we have here is the dollar amount on the check. It's somewhat unusual for our bank here in Deep Haven to have such a large deposit."

Sammy crossed his legs. His shoulders relaxed. "I can understand that."

The banker typed a few more notes into the computer, then turned back to him. "I've put through a request to deposit the money. We'll hear back in a few days." She slid a paper with his account information printed on it over to him. "You will want to speak to an accountant, however, to invest it wisely. The growth potential here is huge."

She didn't need to worry about that. Sammy planned to invest it wisely. He bet the growth wouldn't be monetary, however.

He would use the money to help Robin and to benefit the town he loved.

"Is there anything else I can do for you?" Fran folded her hands on the desk between them.

"I have a few checks to deposit in my regular account." He'd been paid a few times for his courier job, and Edith Draper had tucked a twenty into his pocket after he helped her with her door.

"We can certainly take care of that for you." She tapped a few keys on her computer as he handed her the slim stack. Soon, she printed out a new statement for his account. He looked at the small figure. It reflected the balance of his newly deposited checks as well as the tiny amount of money left from his short-term disability. Sammy had received those slips of paper reminding him of his uselessness every month since the accident.

He rubbed at the spot on his chest where the restless itch seemed to reside.

As the banker finished the transactions, Sammy glanced at his watch. He'd promised to meet Ben at the Fox Bakery this afternoon. He should have enough time to bike there and arrive on time.

Maybe a certain auburn-haired Fox would have time for a quick chat before he and Ben got to work.

He gathered up his paperwork, shook Ms. Turner's hand in thanks, and made his way out to his bike.

Outside, the crisp air caused him to zip his jacket higher. He fished his knit cap out of his pocket and thrust it on, then pulled on lightweight gloves. On days like today, the warm cab of a truck held a lot of appeal.

A few minutes later he arrived at the bakery.

Baked goods made good motivation.

A warm, chocolatey scent greeted him as he pushed through

the door. The bakery was deserted except for Robin, who stood behind the counter. A heat filled him that had little to do with the temperature of the room.

"Hi," Robin said from her place at the cash register.

"Hi yourself." Sammy took off his jacket and set it on a table. "Oh! Cupcakes! I'm going to need a half dozen of those. I don't care what kind they are."

"You look serious. Good thing I have some serious cupcakes."

He laughed. "I need them for a tutoring session in a few minutes."

Robin bent to retrieve his order from the display case. "Six delicious, cream-filled chocolate cupcakes coming right up."

Sammy set the cupcakes on his table as Ben walked through the open door. Ben sat down, and Sammy explained that they would be playing a game for cupcakes. They'd both make a rhyme out of history facts and then memorize them. Then they'd challenge themselves to write the facts down correctly, either in verse or just the fact.

Winner take all.

A half hour later they landed on the last fact. "Okay, one more right answer for the win." Sammy held up a notecard. "When was the Battle of Waterloo?" He and Ben wrote their answers down, then compared them. Sammy had written 1815, but Ben's card read June 18, 1815. Sammy flipped over the flashcard. "Looks like you win the cupcakes, my friend."

"Yes!" Ben did a fist pump and hooted. "I knew I could take you, old man."

"Hey, who you calling old man? I still got lots of fight in me." Sammy's mock horror made the smile on Ben's face stretch wider.

"I knew I'd win. You didn't stand a chance."

"All right, you won fair and square." Sammy stood and so did Ben. They gave each other a fist bump. "I can't wait to see the grade on your history test." Ben pulled on his jacket and grabbed the box of cupcakes.

"See ya later, Sammy."

Robin stood at the display case, wiping the glass. "Pretty smart idea, studying history facts like that."

Sammy shrugged. "You taught me that game. Don't you remember setting a pile of Oreos in front of me in study hall? Because of you, I passed chemistry."

"Oh yeah. I remember now. I had to switch to bringing Grandpa Jim's oatmeal cookies because you kept winning all my Oreos." She scrubbed at a spot. "It was fun to see you working with Ben when you could be doing something else."

Sammy stretched, then approached the case where Robin was working. "I suppose, but it doesn't cost me anything to spend some time with the kid. He's got a good mind. It just needs to be steered in the right direction."

"Well, today it cost you a half dozen cupcakes."

"True. I'm gonna need to buy some more. I actually wanted to win those. I promised my mom I'd bring something home for dessert tonight." Sammy leaned on the counter, being careful not to smudge her hard work. "When did cupcakes get added to the menu, anyway?"

Robin groaned. "I met with the plumber on Friday. He came in and did a rush job on Saturday. The amount it's going to cost for me to pay for those pipes is astronomical. I had to add in a few new items to make ends meet. Besides, cake baking is therapeutic for me."

He studied the cake in the display. "This looks amazing. That shiny stuff on it almost looks edible."

"Gee. Thanks."

"I mean… Sorry. That did come out wrong, didn't it?"

"A little bit." Her toothy smile belied her pretended offense. "That 'shiny stuff' is gold leaf. It's totally edible. I thought it worked with the school colors."

"It definitely does. People will be beating your door down for these cakes."

"That's the hope. Well, maybe not literally beating down my door. I have enough to fix up around here without having to replace that too."

"Yeah, your cabinet did look pretty sad the other day."

"Oh, now you're insulting my kitchen too? You're in trouble, Johnson." Robin put her hands on her hips.

He held his hands up in surrender. "I keep sticking my foot in my mouth. I think I need to fill it with a cupcake instead."

"Good plan, mister. I'll box up these chocolate ones for you. Lucky for your mom, I have a dozen left."

"While you do that, I'll take a look at your cabinet. It could be an easy fix." She waved him on back, and he lifted the opening in the counter, letting himself behind the bar. As he passed Robin, he caught a breath of her perfume or maybe her shampoo. Something floral and summery. He pushed through the swinging doors into the kitchen.

The cabinet didn't look any better than the other day. In fact, now that the plumber had poked around, it looked worse. Both doors had been taken off their hinges, and he could see the gaping holes the screws had made coming out. There was no way they'd ever go back in properly. The floor of the cabinet was in worse shape. It looked like Mack had put a knee through the board because Sammy could see the flooring underneath.

Robin came in through the swinging door. "What's the verdict, Doc?"

"Not good news, I'm afraid. This whole cabinet will have to be replaced. A few of these wooden floorboards too. The water seeped into them, and I'm concerned about mold. Not good for a commercial kitchen."

Robin wrapped her arms around herself. "I'll have to get someone in here to take a look at that, I guess. I've been out of town for so long, I don't even know who to call. Any ideas for me?"

"I'll ask around for you." Huh. Not two hours after taking his check to the bank, and God was already presenting him with an opportunity to use it for good. Though, if he chose to pay for Robin's repairs, he could never let her know it was him.

"I'd appreciate that. There may even be a cupcake in it for you." She shot him a wink.

His heart flipped. What was happening? This was Robin. He shifted his feet, suddenly aware of his large size in this small space.

"Uh, thanks for boxing those up." He reached for the box of cupcakes in her hand. Their fingers brushed as he took it from her. A spark buzzed up his arm, and it must have landed somewhere in his brain, because he heard himself say, "I'm sure they'll taste as good as you smell."

She stared at him. "What?"

"Never mind. I'd better get going." He hurried past her and out into the dining room. Setting the box on the table where he'd been sitting, he picked up his coat. Why were these sleeves all tangled? He forced his arms through, then threaded his scarf around his neck before tugging on his gloves and hat.

"You look like that kid from *A Christmas Story*, the one who can't put his arms down because he's wearing so many winter clothes." Robin had come out of the kitchen without his noticing. A heat crept into his face that had nothing to do with the winter gear.

"It's just above freezing out there. If I don't bundle up, it'll be a long, cold ride home."

"Wait, is that your bicycle in the lot?"

"Yep, that's my baby."

"How do you pedal it through the snow? And more importantly, *why* do you pedal it through the snow?"

He hesitated. But, yeah, he could talk about the bike. Something safe. "It's got specially designed fat tires for riding in the winter. Most of the roads around here are either cleared or the snow is packed almost as hard as concrete. It's easier than you might think."

"But why?" When he hesitated a second time she spoke again. "Never mind. None of my business. Forget I asked." She started to turn away.

Shoot.

"I started bike riding in therapy," he blurted. She turned back to him. He lightly banged his fist against his leg. "One of the low impact ways my physical therapist had me exercise was to ride the stationary bike." He tugged his gloves off. No need for them in a room this hot. "I got pretty good at it after a while, and when I felt better, I started riding around town. I guess I just got in the habit." No need to mention the nightmares he'd wake up from, blankets twisted in a vise around his legs. Nightmares where he would get behind the wheel of a truck and leave several people dead in his wake.

Yeah, he wasn't eager to get back to driving with those images in his brain. Even if they were only dreams, they felt real to him.

"So you ride even when it's snowing?" Her skeptical look mirrored the one his mother had worn when he'd told her he was outfitting his bike for snowy conditions.

"Hey, don't knock it until you try it."

"I guess I'll have to trust you on that one."

"No, really, you should try it. Sure, you get some crazy looks around town, but on a bike, you really get a feel for a place. Deep Haven is special, and it's easy to miss that unless you're out in it." He came to an abrupt stop. "Anyway…"

Her face softened. "Someday I may test out your theory."

"I bet we can rent you a bike from Casper Christiansen over at Wild Harbor. Anyhow, I gotta go. I'll be back tomorrow with a report on your kitchen issue."

Sammy pushed into the cold January afternoon. The darkening sky above showed the first stars. He breathed in a deep breath, willed his heart to settle down.

After strapping his mother's box of cupcakes into his basket, he pedaled off into the night. He hoped Seth was still in his office. The owner of Turnquist Lumber was just the person he needed to help him with a lumber problem. A few minutes later he was rewarded with the sight of Seth's office lights blazing.

"Are you here to take me up on my smoke jumping offer?" Seth said by way of greeting.

"Not today."

"I talked to Tucker again today. He said they definitely have a spot for you right now, but you have to give an answer by March first. The new recruits are starting their training on April first, and he can't hold a spot for you past that. He is concerned about your legs, though."

"I appreciate what you're doing." He really did. He just wished he felt a calling to the smoke jumpers. When he thought about the position, he felt…nothing. No tug at his heart. A tug at his ego, maybe. Who wouldn't want to be a hero, fighting fires in the wilderness with some of the strongest men he knew? "I'm sure I'm ready for it."

But Sammy had always loved Deep Haven, had dreamed of building his life here, not in some wilderness.

He shook off the thought. "But I'm here for something else. I was over at Fox Bakery. Robin needs a new sink cabinet and some flooring. Any chance you can hook me up with that?"

"I have some things I can show you. Most of the stuff we stock is for homes, but I have a few things that can be used in commercial applications as well. I'm almost done for the day. Want to walk out to the showroom?"

"Lead the way."

Seth showed Sammy several shades of wood flooring, and Sammy picked one that closely matched the bakery's existing floor. "I don't want her to have to replace the whole thing."

"I think we have a few floor-model cabinets that could work, but you may be better off with a custom build, especially if you're trying to meet code. Custom builds can be pricey, though. Are you sure she wants to pay for that?"

"Don't worry about the money." Sammy felt good about making that promise.

After all, he knew someone who had money to spare.

five

· · ·

If this cake idea was going to pay the bills, she needed more clients.

A few days later, Robin sat at a table in the dining room of the bakery and jotted down some ideas. In the days since the plumber had delivered the bad news, she'd been working through the accounts and calculating how long before she could afford to pay for the new pipes. She had made two dozen signature cupcakes and topped them with a stylized fox made from auburn icing. She planned to give one away with every order. Maybe if people got a taste of the product, they would be interested in making larger orders.

If she could fill three large orders, she could probably pay off the plumbing bill early.

Bella Hudson, her high-school assistant, came around the counter. "You should head home. I can lock up tonight."

"Thank you." Robin shuffled her papers back into order. "I think I'll take you up on that." She stood and gathered her belongings, intent on tucking them into the tiny cubby in the kitchen that masqueraded as an office.

"These cupcakes with the basketball on them are really cute," Bella commented as she passed by. "You should sell them at the game on Friday. I know the boosters will have a concessions booth again. We have a home game against one of our rivals. Should be a good fan turnout."

Robin tucked her notebook into the crook of her arm. "Thanks for the idea. Is Principal Chase still over there?"

"Yes." The teen smirked. "I think she will die at her desk."

"Just my luck, I've always been a favorite of hers." Robin paused by the bakery phone mounted on the wall behind the cash register. She looked up the school's phone number and dialed. "It's ringing," she mouthed to Bella, who shot her a thumbs-up.

"Hello, Deep Haven High," the disembodied voice on the other end said.

"Hi, can I speak to Principal Chase?"

"Sure, let me transfer you."

Robin heard a click and then harp music. She twined her finger in the spiral of the phone cord. Before Mrs. Chase answered, the bakery's front door opened, and Sammy Johnson walked in with an armload of lumber. What in the world?

Robin realized that Principal Chase had been speaking to her for a few moments. "Oh! Sorry, Principal Chase. This is Robin Fox. Maybe you remember me?"

The principal's sharp tone softened. "Robin! Of course I remember. I think you're old enough now to call me by my first name." Robin heard the smile in her old principal's voice. "So good to hear from you. I heard you were back in town. Holding down the fort for your grandparents, right?"

"Something like that."

Sammy walked through the room and behind the counter. She flattened herself against the wall as he brushed past with his overflowing armload. "What was that? Sorry." Sheesh. If she didn't pay attention, Mrs. Chase—Sheila—would notice.

"I said, how are your grandparents doing?"

"They're doing well." Her grandma had called the night before, full of a glowing report on the house they were staying in near Cocoa Beach. She'd said she and Grandpa Jim took a sunrise stroll on the beach and planned to do that every morning it wasn't raining. "It seems Florida is growing on them. It's been weird to be in the bakery without them, though. Even when I was working here in high school, they rarely took time off, not even to go home early."

Sammy walked past her again and out the front door. He had taken off his jacket and was rolling up the sleeves of his red-blue-and-green plaid flannel. The green stripe picked up the color of his eyes. He shot her a wink through the window.

"What can I do for you? Robin? Did I drop your call?"

"Sorry again! I must sound like a flake." She shut her eyes and turned away from the door. Whatever Sammy was doing would have to wait until this conversation was over. She couldn't afford to lose this potential job. "I'm calling because I was wondering about the possibility of selling some cupcakes at the basketball game on Friday. Bella Hudson mentioned the booster booth." She held her breath.

On the other end there was a pause. She imagined Sheila gathering her thoughts. "I'm sorry, Robin, but that just won't be possible. I promised the boosters they would have exclusive rights to concessions that night. There will be a big crowd, and they need the money for new uniforms."

Robin tried not to let her disappointment leak into her voice. "I understand. Are there any other game nights available?"

"Let's see. We have the Deep Haven Community Church youth group, then The Garden group home, then the youth center is doing a fundraiser for a new furnace." A rustle of paper over the phone line. "I could pencil you in for the game on March sixteenth?"

Her brilliant idea flamed over like a brûlée left too long under the broiler. "I guess I'll take that."

"You know, I bet the booster club would love it if you could donate some cupcakes, though. Should I give you the number for the parent coordinator, Megan Barrett? They're always looking for more treats. Your cupcakes would be a hit."

She heard herself agreeing to call Megan. Opening her eyes to jot down the phone number, she saw Sammy carrying a long toolbox into the kitchen. What was going on?

She thanked Sheila and hung up the phone. A crash sounded from the kitchen. She gave Bella a raised eyebrow and cocked her head at the kitchen door gently swinging on its hinge. Bella shrugged. Well, only one way to find out.

"Sammy, what is going on in here?"

Sammy knelt on the floor, a pry bar in his hands. With a screech, one of the floorboards came loose and popped out of place. "You needed a few boards replaced. I'm replacing them."

"You can't do that."

He popped the next floorboard. "It looks like I can."

"No, I mean, I can't let you do that. I thought you were going to help me find somebody to fix this."

"I did. I looked in the mirror and there I found him." He shot her a grin. Oh, those green eyes were going to be trouble.

She propped her hands on her hips. "How am I supposed to bake while you're in here?" How was she supposed to concentrate if he kept coming in?

"That's why I came in close to closing time. I know you usually have the bread dough in the proofing box or in the cooler by now, and then you come in mornings before the sun is up to bake. Late afternoon is a perfect time. No one is really using this area."

He had her there. Also, he knew her baking schedule? Something about that struck her as...sweet. Really, really sweet. She wove the pen in her hand in and out of her fingers to give her hands something to do.

"Okay, but you must have other jobs to do. I can't keep you from those."

"Not for the next several days at least." He spread his hands wide. "After three, I'm all yours."

Did he mean… No, she was reading too much into his words.

He cut into her muddled thoughts. "Listen, I talked to Seth about the cabinet situation. He had several ideas, but then he said that most modern kitchens don't bother with a cabinet under the sink. He suggested I build a frame for the sink and leave the piping exposed. That way you can see immediately if there is a problem. He also said you should consider tiling at least this area." He gestured to an area around the sink.

The wood floor of the kitchen glowed with the warm patina of many years of love. Every ten years, Grandma Elaine paid someone to refinish it in order to preserve the heritage floor. Putting in tile instead?

Grandma Elaine was not going to like that.

"I don't know. Grandma said not to change anything."

"Hey, no pressure. Seth just mentioned that the places he's consulted with do it out of concern for regulations. Some places get a failing score on their health inspections because they aren't up to code."

Yeah, no pressure.

Robin was caught between her desire to keep her promise to her grandmother and her concern that they pass the health inspection the following week. "Guess we'd better go for it. Let me know what it will cost."

"I was hoping you'd say that." Sammy stood up and brushed off his knees. "Be right back."

Robin set the pen down and pushed at a loose board with her toe. Why couldn't the pipe have sprung its leak when she'd been safely in Paris? She heard the front door open and close. Then open and close again. Then a "Whoa!" from Bella, and the kitchen door swung open.

"You should get a doorstop for that thing." Sammy walked in carrying a large box. "It would make my job so much easier if I didn't have to keep running into it." He nudged her shoulder with his own, a playful look in his eyes.

Heat shot down that arm.

"What in the world is in that box? Or better yet, how did you fit all this stuff on your bike? Are you Superman? Please tell me you're Superman."

He tipped his head back and laughed. "Practice. I fit it on my bike with practice. That and lots of straps."

She joined his laughter. "And in the box?"

He set the box on the floor and lifted out a 12x12-inch tile. "Seth had some tile left over from a job. I thought they would be perfect in here."

Her mouth dropped open. Red and cream swirls marbled the tile—a perfect match to the existing colors already in the Fox Bakery. Sammy wasn't wrong. The understated tile would enhance the look of the kitchen.

He moved a slip of cardboard aside in the box. "And the pièce de résistance…"

"Look at you, speaking French."

"Oui, oui, mademoiselle." He hesitated before pulling the tile out of the box. "Close your eyes."

Normally, she would never take the risk of closing her eyes— too many chances for failure—but she trusted Sammy, so Robin obeyed. She felt something smooth and heavy in her hands. She opened her eyes and looked down.

A tile, cream and red with a stylized fox scampering through a crimson forest, rested in her hands. She raised her eyes to Sammy's. His face was inches away.

"There's no way Grandma Elaine can argue with that tile," he said in a whisper. "It deserves a place in her bakery kitchen."

"It's perfect." She hugged the tile to her chest. "I never knew a person could fall in love with a tile."

"Seth had a whole set of woodland creatures." He leaned away from her, his normal voice returning. "He said he gets all kinds of orders for them up here for people's cabins and whatever. Anyway, I think if we do a grid about five tiles wide and three tiles deep, it should cover the area under the sink. That tile you are clutching will have a prominent place in the middle."

She found her throat was clogged and just settled on a nod.

"Of course, I am going to have to insist on payment."

Her heart thumped. Crashed.

Great. More bills she couldn't pay. Add it to the growing list. "Of course. I'd never ask you to do it for free. And these tiles must have cost a fortune." Out in the dining room, the cash register dinged a sale. Or maybe that was just a ringing in her ears. "What is your hourly wage?" She saw dollar signs, and her chest tightened.

"A cupcake an hour."

Wait. "What? No. I want to pay you money. Real money." She crossed her arms. "I insist."

He crossed his arms, mirroring her. "I can get money anywhere. What I can't get out in that cold, cruel world is a dozen of your caramel mocha creme cupcakes." He threw his arm wide. "I insist. It's cupcakes or nothing."

She laughed and put her hand on his bicep. Cupcakes were something she could do. "Fine. It's a deal. One cupcake for every hour worked. Keep track of your time, and I'll pay you at the end of the job."

"I may have to work extra slow." Then the man had the nerve to wink at her.

Something warm and inviting curled through her like the first bite of a caramel-covered sticky bun. Heat rose in her cheeks. "I'll have to keep my eye on you, Johnson."

His slow smile turned the warm thing into an inferno.

Her cell phone cut through the charged silence, and she dug it out of her pocket. Megan Barrett's name flashed up on the screen. "Hi, Megan," she said, moving a step away from Sammy and back toward sanity.

On the other end, a rustling sound preceded her friend's voice. "Hi, Robin. Sorry, I'm just getting Baby Rae settled. Okay. I'm back."

Robin smiled, grateful for a moment for her heart rate to slow. "No problem. What's up?"

"I just talked to Principal Chase. Since when are you making cupcakes? I thought you weren't going to go against your grandma's wishes."

"Well, that was before I needed some quick cash." She filled Megan in on the kitchen disaster and how the cakes would help supplement the bakery income.

Megan laughed. "Only you would consider baking works of art to be 'quick cash.'"

Robin couldn't help but laugh along. "Hey, baking is all I know."

"Well, after I found out about the cakes, I had a brilliant idea. Why don't I hire you to bake cupcakes for the Snowball Dance?"

"What? That would be great! But how are you involved in the dance? I didn't think Josh would be old enough to go."

Megan sighed. "Don't ask. I was at a PTA meeting for the middle school, and someone mentioned they needed some things organized for the dance. One thing led to another, and I found myself on the committee."

"Oh, Megan."

"I know, okay? I have issues with the word *no*. But about those cupcakes. We'd need around two hundred. Will that be okay?"

More than okay. She'd have to put in some overtime to get them ready the week of the dance, but her time didn't cost anything. "That's doable. What's the theme for the dance?"

"They're going with a general winter theme. Think white and snowy."

Robin began jotting down some notes. "Ah, the brilliance of high school. I think my high-school motto was *Carpe Diem*, and I thought I was the height of sophistication."

Megan laughed. "Tell me about it. But to these kids, this will be a magical night. Provided we can pull it off. I still need two more chaperones. I'll probably end up doing it myself." Megan stopped speaking. Then, "Wait a minute. Why am I chaperoning this thing? I have a seven-month-old, and I can barely stay awake past nine anymore. You should chaperone."

"Um, no, thank you." She sketched out a snowflake shape.

"You were the one who just told me I had a problem saying no. Help me say no by saying yes!"

"I'm confused."

"No, you're not, funny girl. Help me off the hook on this one."

Robin heard herself agreeing. "Fine. I'll have to be there anyway to deliver and set up the cupcakes."

"Great! I knew I could count on you." A baby started crying. "Oops, there's my signal that I've spent too long on the phone. Seriously, thank you, Robin. I owe you one."

Robin ended the call and stuck the phone back into her pocket. Sammy had stopped pulling up boards while she was on the phone, but now he popped another one.

"I think I'll take up these last two boards, then finish cutting out this area when you're closed for the night." Still kneeling on the floor, he showed her where a fine blue chalk line outlined a rectangle near the sink. "I'll also take out the ruined cabinet and prep the floor for the tile. That will probably take me a couple of hours. Unless, of course, if you'd rather I don't stay here on my own and lock up, I could just wait until tomorrow, but that would extend the project another day or two."

"No, I don't mind you locking up. I trust you. I'll be sure to put the padlock on the display case, though—I can't have you sneaking the cupcakes." Robin shot him an arched eyebrow, then laughed at his fake innocent face.

"Don't worry, ma'am, your cupcakes are safe with me." Sammy's terrible Western accent and doff of his imaginary cowboy hat caused a hooting laugh to erupt from Robin.

She caught her breath. "Honestly, though, I said it before and I'll say it again. You're a lifesaver." She wiped a hand across her forehead. "That was Megan on the phone. She wants me to chaperone the Snowball Dance. I haven't thought about that dance in years, and now it comes up every time I turn around."

"Was it our senior year when someone got sick and threw up all over the gym?" Sammy sat back on his heels and rested his forearms on his knees. His legs must not have been bothering him today. He'd rolled up the sleeves of his flannel shirt, and his blond hairs caught in the light, turning his arms bronze like a Greek statue.

"Yep. Senior year. I don't remember who it was that got sick, though. Ah, good times." Resorting to sarcasm might keep her mind off the healthy, not-at-all-sick male specimen in front of her. Escape would be a good idea. "I, uh, need to check something in the front." She needed to catch her breath.

Because somewhere in the past few days, Sammy Johnson, with his kindness and his care, had run an endgame past her defenses and back into her heart.

FIXING THE FOX BAKERY'S FLOOR HAD BONUS BENEFITS SAMMY hadn't counted on. Benefits like hearing Robin hum the theme song for *Gilligan's Island* and listening to her laugh with Ben Zimmerman.

Sammy was currently pulling up the floorboards in the bakery kitchen while Robin kneaded something on the worktop in the center of the room. Bella was out front manning the register.

Once he'd decided to help Robin and met with Seth, he'd laid out a plan. Tearing up the wood floor and laying down the tile should only take the two days he'd promised Robin. Right now, though, he was trying to decide if he could stall a little. The warm bakery with its sweet, yeasty scent wrapped him in a safe feeling, like a child's blanket after a scary dream.

He was glad Robin had agreed to his plan for the changes in the kitchen. They would streamline a few things for her as well as bring the kitchen up to code. Robin had said the bakery kitchen's layout and cabinetry had been grandfathered in because of the age of the building, but he didn't want her getting into any trouble with the health inspector.

Late the week before, at the lumberyard, he had picked out the right pieces to build the sink structure. Sammy took the lumber home. In his mother's garage he had a small wood shop complete with a heater for the winter months.

He had used his lathe to turn the 4x4 square lengths of wood into spindles for the new cabinet structure. After turning all four legs, he'd sanded them smooth and stained the wood with a deep red stain matching the Fox's existing color scheme. Now those pieces were waiting for him to finish the tiling so he could frame up the sink.

He sat back on his heels in the Fox Bakery kitchen. Robin brushed past him as she headed for the cooler, then again as she went out into the dining room. Her perfume mingled with the sweet, vanilla smell of the bakery. Smiling at the interruption, he inspected his work. One more board ought to be enough. He pried up the last of the floorboards and set it on the pile, making sure it was out of the way of the traffic into and out of the kitchen.

Underneath the floorboards, a layer of dust covered the sub-floor. Sammy got up and went to the janitor's closet tucked between the wall and the walk-in cooler. Out in the dining room, Robin was talking to someone, then she called goodbye. A moment later, she came into the kitchen.

"That was Ronnie Dahlquist." She gestured with a thumb over her shoulder. "It was fun to meet the woman Peter ended up with. They seem to be crazy for each other. There was a time when I thought he'd never be married. Isn't he related to everyone in town?"

Sammy laughed. "Yeah, poor guy. Good thing Ronnie rescued him from a lifetime of singleness."

Robin pushed a stray hair out of her eyes. "Speaking of rescue, did you know that the youth center had someone donate a new furnace?"

A Carrier Infinity 98 gas furnace with Greenspeed Intelligence? Yeah, he knew about that. "Really? That's great." He bit back a smile. When the bank had let him know his money was available, he'd gone straight to spending it.

"I guess they paid for the installation too. The crew will finish up by the end of the week. You'll be able to move your tutoring sessions back over there by the end of the month." She moved closer to where he was working.

Shoot. That was one cost he hadn't factored in. "I don't know. Your cupcakes are so inspiring, I don't think we can move."

Robin smiled at him. "You know you're welcome anytime."

"I'll hold you to that." He swept the dust into a dustbin, then reached for a washcloth and cleaning bucket. The tile grout wouldn't stick to a dirty floor.

"If you're really hard up for baked goods, I have an idea. Maybe you should help me chaperone the dance. I hear that pays in cupcakes too." She gave him a saucy wink.

"I'll have to think about it. I'd hate to face the demons of the dance floor. I remember being terrible at it in school." A sticky spot on the floor claimed his attention for a moment.

"Come on, Fred Astaire. What's to think about? It won't be that bad. You don't even have to dance." Robin knelt beside him and took the washcloth and attacked the stain. The spot disappeared. "Megan said she needed two people. Plus, you're so wonderful with kids, you'll do great." She took the bucket from him and refilled it at the sink. "Come along with me so I have at least one friend there. I don't know many people anymore, so you can smooth things over for me. Help me avoid any traps because I don't recognize one of the other chaperones as a former classmate now that they've gained twenty pounds or lost all their hair. Please, I need you."

So, it was going to be emotional persuasion. "Fine, you win." He was rewarded by a bright smile before she handed him the bucket of clean water.

The door chimed again, and Robin headed out to the dining room.

He finished cleaning the area to be tiled. As he put away the cleaning supplies, he saw a tattered catalog sitting on the office desk. He picked it up and flipped through the pages. Kitchen equipment.

Several pages had been dog-eared with notes running along the sides. The catalog fell open to a page more worn than the others. Next to the MIWE Cube oven someone—Robin perhaps?—had made a note "too expensive" with a tiny sad face drawn next to the photo. He flipped to the back. Robin's name and a Paris address were stamped on the address label.

Interesting. He hadn't known Robin was a doodler.

Now he wanted to tell Robin to let the floor dry, and he would come the next day to finish the tiling. When she didn't return after a few minutes, he decided to investigate. At a table in the corner, Ben Zimmerman sat, looking intrigued. Robin sat next to him, head bent over a book.

"You just need to imagine this circle like a real pie," he heard her say. What was happening here?

"Wait a minute." She got up from the table and plucked two round focaccia loaves from the display case. "Okay, these two are the same size. We could divide them into two pieces each or six pieces or ten or whatever, but it wouldn't change the fact that they are the same size. For example." She tore one of the loaves in half, then pulled one of those halves into three pieces. Leaving the first half-loaf in a stack, she picked up the other loaf, tore it in half and one of those halves into two pieces, setting the chunks on top of each other. "Which one of these stacks is one half of a loaf?"

Ben's face cleared. "They all are! I get it now. Thanks, Ms. Fox." He jotted something on the paper. "Like this?"

"You've got it! Well done, Ben." She patted him on the back and slid some of the bread toward him. Ben crammed a bite into his mouth.

"Math is a lot easier when there's food," he said around the bite.

Hey! Sammy didn't want to be left out of getting the snacks. "You got that right," Sammy said, clearing his throat. At the table, the math wizards looked up at him.

"Hi, Mr. Johnson," Ben said. "Ms. Fox is showing me equivalent fractions. She really helped."

"I'm glad to hear it." Sammy couldn't take his eyes off Robin. Had she changed her hair in the last five minutes? Something was different, but he couldn't put his finger on it. "She's good at that. She used to help me in math class all the time."

"You did just fine all on your own in math," Robin replied. "I just gave you a nudge once in a while. I hope you don't mind me helping Ben. He came in looking for you, but I didn't want you charging me a cupcake for time spent tutoring." She waggled her eyebrows at him.

Oh, her teasing went straight to the cracked parts of his heart. He could see himself falling for her.

"I don't mind at all. Just don't be spilling my secrets. A man has to have some dignity."

Ben looked from one of them to the other. A wide grin split his face, so different from the sullen looks Sammy was used to getting from him.

"Oh, secrets. You mean secrets like the time you gave a speech on cheerleading and almost broke your ankle demonstrating a high kick?" Robin propped her chin in her hand, her eyes innocent and wide. "Or that time you and Colleen nearly set the chemistry lab on fire? Are those the things I'm not supposed to tell Ben about?"

Speaking of lighting a fire, her spark was doing something combustible in him.

Ben laughed. "I like this lady, Mr. Johnson. You should keep her." The kid was always full of great ideas. Just then Sammy caught Robin's eyes. Green and deep. Yeah, he just might have to keep her.

Robin blinked, and her gaze shifted to his hand. "What do you have there?"

Oh. He was still holding the catalog. "I was flipping through this catalog. I hope you don't mind."

"Now who's telling secrets?" She winked at Ben. "Now Ben knows that I spend my downtime drooling over kitchen appliances that I certainly can't afford."

The kid had the nerve to spread his hands wide and spar right back. "Don't worry about it, Ms. F. We all got our little quirks. We won't tell anyone about your crazy love for kitchen gear, will we, Mr. Johnson?"

"I think I can keep that one under wraps." He watched Robin as she leafed through the catalog.

"You couldn't have found this very stimulating," she said, looking up at him. She looked back down and turned a few more pages. She must have landed on her dog-eared page, because the corner of her mouth quirked up.

Well, it wasn't the catalog he found stimulating.

Yep, fixing up the floor at Fox Bakery was turning into the best decision he'd ever made.

six

• • •

A few days later, Robin stood in the lobby of Lena Larson's veterinary clinic. The late-afternoon sun struggled to reach into the room, but Robin was grateful for its effort. The morning had been cloudy and gloomy, but after lunch the clouds had parted and a hint of blue sky had broken through.

She was looking forward to an hour away from the bakery and all thoughts of Sammy. She was grateful for his help and his friendship, but lately her feelings for him had become...jumbled. She needed space to get them back under control.

"Thanks for coming over," Lena said. "I wanted to say welcome home, but I didn't think I'd get down to the bakery anytime soon."

"No problem. I'm glad I get to see your space." Robin took off her jacket and hung it on a hook beneath a black-and-white framed photo of a kitten. Lena was dressed in scrubs, and with her straight brown hair pulled into a ponytail, she looked ready to face a pet health crisis at any moment. They'd been apart for the past ten years, aside from some phone calls and visits during the infrequent times when Robin was home. Though Lena was Robin's brother Grayson's age, she and Robin had always hit it off in school. And today, they were picking right up from where they'd left off.

"Let me show you around." Lena led Robin into the back area, and Robin's heels clicked on the tiled floor. "I have two exam rooms and a kennel area."

"Pretty impressive. I like the green and gray color scheme."

"It's clean and simple. Which is perfect for me." Lena opened the door to a kennel. "Do you mind if I check on Mischa while we chat?"

"Fine by me."

Lena led a husky out of the kennel and then lifted it onto the exam table. "This is Mischa. She belongs to Nick Dahlquist. Do you remember the Dahlquists?"

"Lena, I've only been out of the area ten years. I didn't forget everything about back home."

Lena grabbed a pair of bright blue exam gloves from a box on the counter. "Well, Nick runs dogsleds now. Hey, you should talk to him about making dog treats at the bakery."

"Dog treats? I don't think so. Grandma would have a heart attack."

"Just a thought. He makes his own dog food and sells it online. He makes a killing."

Robin reached out a hand to Mischa, then drew it back. "Can I pet her?"

"Sure, go ahead. It'll help distract her while I look at these stitches." Lena began doing something that looked complicated on the dog's flank. A sharp scent of antiseptic filled the air. Robin admired the quiet and matter-of-fact way her friend worked.

"How are you holding up?"

For a moment Robin wondered if she was talking to the dog, but then Lena looked at her expectantly. "I'm doing okay, I guess. We had a minor mishap at the bakery, but I'm handling it."

Lena bent toward Mischa, her face nearly engulfed in the

dog's fur. "Oh?" The dog's presence between them muffled Lena's questioning tone.

"Sammy Johnson is helping me replace a cabinet and some flooring."

"Oh?" Lena's voice rose an octave in a tease.

"Is that all you can say?" Robin grinned at her friend.

"Sammy Johnson, eh? Is he still basically Paul Bunyan's younger brother?"

Robin regretted the fact that she might have mentioned that comparison to Lena back in high school. Broad shouldered, great-looking in a flannel shirt, that day-old stubble on his chin? Yeah, he still reminded her of the famous lumberjack. Except better looking. She buried her face in the dog's fur for a moment to hide a blush.

"He's still broad and blond, if that's what you mean," she said.

"Interesting." Lena snapped off her exam gloves and tossed them in the trash.

"What do you mean, interesting?"

"I can't believe Sammy Johnson is coming and spending so much time fixing up your grandparents' place," Lena said, deadpan. "There must be something attracting him to the bakery." She gave Robin a look that almost passed for innocent.

Lena simply didn't know what she was talking about. No way was Sammy interested in her. Why were all her friends trying to set her up with him? That ship had sailed in high school. Besides, after she finished helping out her grandparents, she was on the first flight back to Paris. She'd even started surfing the job boards for possible openings over there.

Robin couldn't let that impression stand. "He's only doing it for the cupcakes."

"Oh, sure. The cupcakes. Everyone knows he's finished his short-term disability. All his other jobs are paying gigs. He needs the money." Lena stopped just short of rolling her eyes. She moved to the sink along the wall.

Wait, what? Sammy didn't have any money? Why hadn't he told her that? She'd offered to pay him. She'd honestly believed him when he said he didn't need any reimbursement. "All I know is that he is in it for the caramel mocha cupcakes. I paid him off yesterday."

Sammy had spent the better part of three days finishing up in the kitchen. The space looked completely changed. Okay, not completely. He'd freshened up the look of the place with the tiling he'd installed, and the open-air sink stand he'd built added to the sleek new look. The rest of the space was unchanged. Well, except for the shelving. Robin had asked Sammy to move it after he'd finished with the other work. It really was handier to have it next to the prep station. Hopefully it would be good enough to pass inspection on Monday.

"So he's all finished up?" Lena scrubbed at her hands.

"Yep. You should see it in there. The whole place used to be so cluttered. Sammy helped me streamline it." She pictured how the cooler flowed into the prep area seamlessly. And now she could reach the oven without tripping on the shelves. "We left the prep table in the middle though."

"Is that the one that's like a family heirloom or something?"

"That's the one." The butcher-block-topped table-slash-island was over one hundred years old. Grandpa Jim's grandmother had had it made for her own kitchen when she was a wealthy lumber baron's wife. Grandma claimed it was the secret ingredient in many of their recipes. They used the table for shaping the breads and making pastries. Even though it was meticulously cleaned, Grandma claimed that the tradition it contained seeped into every loaf.

She bit back a sigh. She could only pray that Grandma would see the changes as improvements and forgive her for making them without consulting her.

Across from her, Lena was still talking about Sammy. She pulled a few sheets of paper towels from the dispenser. "I think you've got to grab that guy with both hands and not let go." She demonstrated by strangling her paper towels.

Robin laughed. Her usually stoic friend was surprising her with her antics today. "Um, I don't think so. Besides, there's nothing to grab. He's not interested in me." Sure, there'd been a spark of…something…that afternoon when she'd worked with Ben on equivalent fractions, but that had only been the heat of the moment. "More importantly, I'm not interested in him." Liar. Maybe. "Or at least, not in a relationship. I have too much going on right now."

"Oh, come on. Look, I know running a business is hard—trust me, I know. But if I had an opportunity to date someone, I'd take it."

"It's not just that. I don't want to get into a relationship at all. I'm leaving when Grandma and Grandpa get back. It's not fair to get serious about someone."

"You wouldn't have to be serious."

"Lena!"

Her friend held up her hands. "Kidding. I'm kidding." Lena moved Mischa back into the kennel. "Have you heard much from Grayson and Oliver lately?"

Robin didn't miss the too-casual tone of her friend. Lena knew the family's troubles, and she cared about all of them. "Nothing more than a quick call at Christmas. I thought with Grandpa Jim's heart attack they'd—" She shook her head, and a stone sat in her stomach. The truth? Her brothers had left town much the same way she had—quickly and with finality. The three of them had never experienced the tight bond other siblings had. She mourned their loss but knew that their relationships wouldn't mend without effort. An effort none of them were putting forward right now.

Something had broken between them the day their parents died, and it had never healed. Another relationship she'd never fit into.

"Anyway, I'm not sure what it will take to lure them home

again. I sometimes wonder if all three of us will ever be in the same town again."

The two stood in silence for a heartbeat.

Lena crossed her arms. "I still think you should break something else in your kitchen so your lumberjack will come running back. You and Sammy would make such a cute couple."

Robin chuckled. Lena knew just what she needed to break the tension. "Never gonna happen. But...we are chaperoning the Snowball Dance together."

"What? You've been holding out on me. I need details so we can plan. Will he pick you up? What time will you need to be ready? What are you going to wear?"

Leave it to practical Lena to think of the logistics. What was she going to wear? In all the hustle at the shop, she hadn't stopped to think about it. "I honestly don't know."

"There aren't too many places in town that sell formal wear. You might have to get creative."

"Ugh. I was talking to Colleen about that the other day. Remember the dress I made for my prom junior year?"

"The awesome one with the beautiful wings? Of course I remember." Lena crossed to the door of the exam room. Robin followed her out into the waiting area.

"Awesome? People gave me such grief for that dress. If Grayson and Oliver hadn't already graduated by then, I think they would have disowned me out of embarrassment."

"Nonsense." Lena's brisk tone brought Robin up short. "It was a beautiful dress, and you looked amazing. You should thrift something again."

"I actually still have the dress." Robin leaned back against the check-in counter, bracing herself with her hands. "I found it in my old closet at Grandma's."

"And? Is it as bad as you remember?"

"No." Tears prickled Robin's eyes. "It's just as amazing as I remember. Why are you smiling like that?"

"I'm smiling because here is your chance to redeem that dress."

"What do you mean?" Robin tugged her hairband off her wrist and wound her hair into a messy bun on top of her head.

"Maybe you should give the dress a little glow-up and wear it to the dance."

The laughter from her prom whispered through Robin's mind. But she wasn't that young girl anymore, was she? She'd matured. She'd lived in Paris for several years, for Pete's sake. She knew something about fashion. "You know, maybe you're right. I'll need to keep my hair simple, and my dress can't be too over the top—I *am* working after all. But yeah, I can still shine."

Lena nodded once. "Good. Now, I hate to kick you out, but I have patients coming in any time now." She glanced at her smartwatch. "Let's do this again soon."

"Definitely."

As Lena walked Robin over to the rack to retrieve her jacket she asked, "Hey, did you hear that someone donated enough money for The Garden to buy that new van they needed?"

"No. I hadn't heard that. How wonderful." Robin slid her arms into her coat.

"I know. First the youth center, and now this."

"It's like there's a secret superhero in town, except instead of catching bad guys they're creating hope."

Lena leaned over and embraced Robin. "It's good to have you back in town. I hope it's for forever."

"Lena, I already told you, I'm heading back to Paris as soon as my grandparents get their feet under them again. Plus, after Grandma Elaine gets a look at her kitchen, I may be excommunicated!" She headed toward the door.

"Not if Sammy has anything to say about it."

"There's nothing happening between us."

"Okay, but there will be. You heard it here first!" Her friend laughed and waved. Robin waved back and turned down the sidewalk.

Really. Nothing was going to happen with her and Sammy.

When she got back home, Robin pulled the infamous dress out of the closet again. Hmm, maybe Lena was right. The A-line dress boasted classic lines and a long skirt. With just a little adjusting, including removing those wings, taking off some other glittery bits, and shortening it to tea length, this dress could be perfect for the dance in two days. Easy enough for her to do quickly.

A good thing, too, because she really didn't have time to go shopping. Her life was complicated enough. She jotted down a plan to alter the dress in her idea sketch book.

If only everything in her life could be that easy.

THIS WAS DEFINITELY NOT HOW HE REMEMBERED HIGH SCHOOL. OF course, back then he'd been the odd man out. Always on the fringes, never getting the girl. Even Colleen, who he'd idolized from afar, had never seen him as more than a lab partner.

When Sammy walked into the gym for the Snowball Dance Saturday night, he couldn't keep his eyes off Robin. Her navy dress hung in simple lines around her, hugging at all the right places. And, yeah, maybe it was the twinkle lights and the cupcake-scented air, but it seemed to him that this would be a night to remember.

At the other end of the gym, the band, made up of six students from the school orchestra, tuned their instruments. Sammy had heard through the grapevine that the band would play for the first half of the evening—something about needing the practice before a solo and ensemble competition. Then a senior student who worked part-time at the radio station would DJ the last half.

"Hey, stranger." Robin put her hand on his arm. "You're right on time."

He cleared his throat. "I didn't think this old gym could look so good." Balloons and silver streamers were tied around the room, and in a display just shy of garish, snowflakes papered the walls, bleachers, and anything else with a vertical surface.

"Right? The decorating committee did such a great job." She let go of his arm and twirled. Her blue dress shimmered under the lights. "Megan said they are expecting around a hundred students. Mr. and Mrs. Dahlquist and Principal Chase and her husband—and of course us—are the chaperones, but they don't expect much excitement. The guys on the basketball team have to behave."

"Yeah, I heard they are on thin ice, metaphorically speaking, after a series of pranks against some of the hockey guys."

"I seem to remember another group of high-school guys getting into trouble." And then she shot him a wink.

Around them, the gym full of students dimmed. In that moment, he only saw Robin. How had he not noticed her before? In all the time they'd worked on projects for science and she'd tutored him in math, how could he have missed how beautiful and smart and funny she was? She'd walked back into his life and changed everything.

They'd lost so much time, but maybe tonight could be the start of something new.

He chuckled. "Yeah, we thought we were such hot stuff."

"And for a tiny high school in the middle of nowhere, you weren't wrong." She shrugged, a one-shoulder lift that spoke volumes.

He laughed at that. "Big fish in a very small pond."

"Something like that."

He sobered. "This may sound a little weird, but I wanted to thank you for doing this." He gestured to the room already filling with young people, boys stiff in their dad's ties and girls dressed in all the colors of the rainbow. "The kids in this town are special. It means a lot to me that you would help out tonight."

"It's no biggie." She waved off his compliment. "All I did was bake some cupcakes."

"Not to mention giving up your Saturday night to hang out at a high-school dance."

"I'm not sure I'm giving anything up. After all, I'm out with Deep Haven High's starting linebacker." Robin put her hands on her hips.

"True, most girls would kill for a date with me," he deadpanned.

Wait. Was this a date? Because if he was going to date Robin, he was pretty sure he could come up with something more romantic than a room full of teenagers, even if the room was covered with enough twinkle lights to cover twenty-four Christmas trees.

Robin hooked her arm through his. "C'mon, football star, let's go pour some punch."

They stood next to the display of cupcakes Robin had provided. "These look amazing." Sammy reached for one. "There must be, like, two hundred here."

"Two hundred and six to be exact. Bella and I finished them up this afternoon." Robin looked at the cupcakes, a slight smile on her face. White frosting and a sparkling sugar snowflake topped each confection. Just now, under the twinkle lights, the cascades of cupcakes looked like a beautiful blizzard.

Out on the dance floor, couples slow danced to a song Sammy couldn't put a name to. Something about an enchanted evening. The other chaperones had spread around the room.

A few kids lined up for a treat, and he and Robin worked together to pass them out. Robin loaded each cupcake onto a tiny plate, and he passed the plates to the waiting crowd.

"We're turning into a well-oiled machine," he said. Robin flashed him a smile. He could get used to working by her side. "This reminds me of my time in the military. Load, aim, shoot."

Robin arched her back in a stretch. "Based on what you've told me, you couldn't have been in very long."

He'd never even had a chance to prove himself. "Nope. Less than two years." He rubbed his jaw just below his right ear. "I was medically discharged."

"What happened?"

"I was an infantryman." He'd scored so low on the exam that the Army had just shoved him in a grunt job. "We called ourselves mortar maggots." No real action, no real brains—at least, not in the positions he'd held. Just point the gun where the officer told him and shoot. He'd never even made it overseas. "One day while training, we had a short round—a shell didn't fly like it was supposed to. It landed a few feet in front of the mortar." He picked up a cupcake and demonstrated the shell landing on a plate a few inches away. "It exploded and I was knocked back. I hit my head. Earned me an early release." But no commendations.

Robin's eyes widened. "Wow! That's terrible." She put her hand on his bicep. "Do you still have issues from it?"

Issues. Ha. Yeah, he had issues.

But no need to dredge all that up. "Headaches sometimes."

"I'm sorry. That sounds rough."

"I know one guy who lost his sense of taste after an injury." He picked up the exploded ordinance cupcake and took a bite. "Now that would be a tragedy."

The rest of the evening passed quickly. Pouring out punch and chatting with the kids kept his mind and hands occupied. Hands that itched to take Robin's and hold tight.

On the stage, the saxophone player leaned into a mic. "All right, everyone. This will be our last song, and then there will be a short break while DJ John James gets set up. Please enjoy the first movement from *Winter* by Vivaldi." The violinist took her place and the music started. The orchestral band had been playing easy-to-dance-to arrangements of popular modern songs, so at this driving and haunting melody everyone stopped.

Sammy leaned over and whispered in Robin's ear. "How are you supposed to dance to this?"

"I have an idea—come on." She grabbed his hand and pulled him out on to the floor.

"Wait—" But she didn't let him finish.

"Don't worry, it'll be fun. We did this in my Zumba class once. Follow me."

She kept a tight grip on his hand and stepped forward and back in time to the music. Sammy followed her lead. Then she added a step-behind vine move. Alongside her, Sammy counted out the steps, swaying when she swayed and stepping left and right in time. She began calling out the movements as she made them, and soon everyone on the dance floor was moving together in a line dance of sorts.

When the song slowed in the middle, Robin swung into Sammy's arms and led him in a kind of waltz. Around them, the kids paired up as well, swaying in time to the music. When the song came to its upbeat staccato crescendo, she called out, "Everybody shimmy!"

He felt the loss of her as she broke contact with him and shook her shoulders in a shimmy. The whole dance floor joined in. Sammy tried to alternate his shoulders but failed to keep the rhythm, so he broke out the one move he did know—the sprinkler. Robin threw her head back and laughed.

As the last note reverberated around the room, the group broke into applause and laughter. Then the gym filled with chatter.

Sammy grabbed Robin's hand and spun her to himself. "That was something else."

"I didn't think you'd be able to keep up," she teased.

He smiled down at her. "Don't worry about me. I can always keep up with a pretty lady."

"It's hot in here," she said, fanning herself. "We should take a spin around the school halls. Make sure everyone is behaving themselves."

He let go of her hand, but tucked it into the crook of his arm. "Lead on, m'lady."

They wandered into the common area just outside the gymnasium. Students milled around talking and eating cupcakes.

"Looks like your treats are a hit."

"What it looks like is they are keeping the students occupied. No shenanigans here." Robin dabbed a hand at her forehead. "Let's head toward the math wing." They walked a few minutes, Robin's blue heels clicking on the tile flooring. "It's so strange to be back here after all these years."

"I know what you mean. Everything seems smaller." The hallway was quiet and cool after the press of the gym.

"I suppose you've come back many times since graduation day."

"I've been back once or twice. Mostly in the past few years. Some of the kids I've tutored have been in the school plays and stuff."

"Was it weird to come back?" Robin paused and looked fully at him, waiting for his answer. Like she actually cared what it would be.

"Kind of nice, actually." Sammy hesitated. "I always felt a little lost in the Army. A little fish in a big pond. Coming home was good for me. I wasn't the big fish I used to be, more of a just-right size."

"Ah, the Goldilocks of fish."

"You got it."

They walked in silence a moment more.

"I have to know, where did you get those moves?" Sammy pulled Robin to a stop at a pillar near the ninth-grade math room.

She leaned against the brick. "I told you—Zumba. I also took some swing dance lessons when I was in California at culinary school."

Looking at her with that half smile on her face, he knew he was a goner.

"A better question is, what exactly did you think you were doing at the end?" She laughed and mimicked his improvised sprinkler.

He caught her hand. "No, it's more like this." He twirled her around and pressed her back against him, then showed her how to do the dance move, rhythmically shooting their arms out shoulder high, then bopping them in the air.

She laughed and spun back to him.

His breath stilled.

She tipped her head up, and he brushed a strand of her hair behind her ear. Her eyes held his, a question in them. He leaned closer and she nodded slightly. He closed the final gap and pressed his lips lightly on hers. Heat radiated in the inches between their bodies. She deepened the kiss, tucking her arms around his neck, one hand tangling in the short hair at his neck.

This was nothing like high school.

seven

. . .

Some enchanted evening. The music filled Robin's senses.

Sammy filled her senses.

When he'd walked into the gym earlier that night, her breath had caught as he'd stood there dressed in a light blue shirt topped with a gray jacket, a blue-and-gray tie around his neck, his broad shoulders straining at his sport coat. She'd crossed over to him and, oh, wow. He smelled divine. Woodsy and warm, with a hint of cinnamon.

Then they'd danced that wild, off-the-hook dance, and he'd made her laugh. And the dance again in the hallway a moment ago and locking onto his forest green eyes... Swept up in the moment, she'd kissed him.

Was still kissing him.

Her arms wrapped around his neck, one hand buried in his hair. He had one arm around her and the other propped above them.

This was not good.

She couldn't be kissing Sammy. She was leaving. She needed to stop. Like, right now. He needed to know she planned to go back to Paris.

Stop. *Now*.

She pulled her head back, breathing heavily. His slow smile quieted her words for a moment.

"That was—"

"Incredible," she said. Then she sighed and stepped away. "But it can't happen again."

His face clouded. "Why not?"

She took a few more steps away. She needed space. "Sammy, I'm leaving."

"What, the dance?"

"No. I'm going back to Paris as soon as I can. I don't want to live in Deep Haven. I don't want to lead you on. I shouldn't have kissed you."

"Mr. Johnson?"

At the voice, Robin sprang farther away from Sammy, bumping the wall behind her. Her face heated.

Sammy spun around.

Ben stood there with Bella, both of them grinning wildly. "I thought that was you!" Ben shot them two thumbs up. "Way to go, Mr. Johnson." And before Robin or Sammy could respond, the pair sauntered off down the hall.

Sammy turned back to Robin, his eyes wide.

She met his gaze, hoping he read the apology in her eyes.

He shoved his hands into his pockets. "That was awkward. Ben and Bella will have quite the story to tell."

She broke off their look and reached up and patted her hair. "We should get back." She wouldn't meet his gaze again. "We're the ones who are supposed to be breaking up this sort of thing." She ducked around him and started back down the hall.

"Wait, Robin. Stay a minute." He reached for her, but she dodged his hand. Too much temptation to keep holding on to him, but that would just lead him on more.

She wrapped her arms around her elbows and led the way back to the gym. The DJ was playing Barry White.

And yeah, "Can't Get Enough of Your Love, Babe" wasn't exactly the song she would have chosen right now.

The kid spinning records was actually pretty good. He interspersed his song choices with a little patter, mentioning his classmates, calling out inside jokes, and generally keeping the mood light and fun.

Robin sensed Sammy trying to interact with her all night, but she avoided him as much as she could in the crowded gym. Sure, she would have to fully explain herself to him, but right now she was working.

"That's a wrap, everybody," the DJ said. "Like the oldie song says, you don't have to go home, but you can't stay here."

"Actually—" Principal Chase grabbed the mic. "You do have to go home. Curfew is in forty-five minutes." The gym filled with laughs and groans.

Robin began disassembling the plastic structure displaying the cupcakes. All that remained now were some dark crumbs dotting the once pristine white tablecloth.

"There you are," Sammy said from behind her. "I thought maybe we'd have gotten another dance."

The fluorescent lights in the gym came on, bright in their artificialness, a stark change from the soft twinkly lights of the evening. She blinked a little. "Sorry. I got caught up in other things." She avoided looking directly at him and continued stacking trays.

"Let me help you." He unscrewed the plastic tiered tray he held and added it to her stack.

"Thank you."

He put a hand on her shoulder, and her arm heated in response. "Robin." Picking up the courage to meet his eyes, she waited for his next words. "I feel like you've been avoiding me. Can we talk this through?"

He speared her with a look. She wilted, sighed, because he was right.

"Fine. I have been avoiding you." She set the last tray on the stack. "I have to get this stuff back to the bakery. Maybe we can talk next week?" Coward.

His lips tightened. "I'd love it if we could talk now. I just want to understand what is going on." He held a hand out to her. "Can I help you bring these to the bakery and we can hash things out?"

Running from Sammy wasn't an option, and putting off a conversation wasn't fair or mature. She nodded, and he lifted the stack of trays. She packed the rest of the supplies into a lidded tote. They walked together out of the gym, stopping by a rack in the hallway for their jackets.

Outside, the twinkle lights seemed to be replicated by the light snow falling in the moonlight. The air was so cold Robin's chest ached a little when she breathed in. She zipped up her puffy coat, grateful for its fleece lining.

They passed Sammy's bicycle, leaning to the side in the bike rack near the entrance.

A laugh bubbled up in her, the sound echoing into the cold of the night air. "Did you really bike up here?" she asked, looking at him fully for the first time since their kiss. Suddenly it wasn't the cold air stealing her breath.

He tugged at the blue stocking cap on his head and nodded.

"You're crazy." Her mouth quirked to the side.

"Just a little."

"Tell you what. Come back to the bakery with me in the van—there's plenty of room for your bike in the back—and then I'll take you home. The temp is supposed to drop even further tonight."

They loaded up the delivery van, a white Ford with a stylized fox running toward a stack of bread painted on the side.

She slid into the cold leather of the driver's seat. The engine didn't respond to the turn of the key. "Grandpa said it can be temperamental." She put both hands on the steering wheel and gripped it for a moment. Getting stuck in the school parking lot? Not an option. She tried the key again. The engine roared and they took off.

"Grandpa and Grandma decided to give up their other car

when they realized it sat idle most of the time. They use this van to get everywhere in town, and if they need something different, they just rent it." And yeah, she should tone down the chatter, but being this close to Sammy ignited something in her she couldn't succumb to.

A few minutes later, they pulled into a parking spot behind the bakery lot. Sammy went to the back of the van and wheeled out his bike, moving it out of the way. Then he grabbed out the tote of supplies while Robin fumbled with the lock to the back door.

Pushing the door open, they both sighed with relief at the warmth of the kitchen. A hint of chocolate cake lingered in the air.

"You can put that tote over by the dishwasher. I'll need to clean everything before putting it away," she said.

"Can do." He set down the tote. "I'll go grab the rest of the stuff from the van."

"Thanks. Want some coffee?"

"I'd love some. Be right back." A quick wash of cold filled the kitchen when he went out the door.

She busied herself with the coffee and planning out what she wanted to say to Sammy. He came back in, balancing the stack of supplies.

"Did you know you have a stray cat out here?"

"Was it black and white?"

"Yep."

"I've seen it around sometimes."

The kitchen filled with the welcoming scent of fresh coffee. Robin poured them each a cup and handed one to him.

"Too bad the kids ate all of those cupcakes," he said.

She smiled. "That's the benefit of being friends with the baker." She headed to the walk-in cooler, emerging a moment later with a cupcake in each hand. "Extras."

"Are you an angel? Did I die and go to heaven?"

"Always the tease."

He reached for the pastry and brushed her fingers. They locked eyes. He took a bite of the cake.

Robin blinked, looked at the floor. "Look, Sammy, kissing tonight was a mistake. Okay, not a mistake exactly, but I shouldn't have done it." She wrapped her hands around her coffee mug, willing the warmth to work its way through her.

"I don't understand. What did you mean back at the school about Paris?"

There it was. The thing that sat between them.

"I'm only here to keep the bakery open for my grandparents. After they get back, I'm going back to Paris."

"I thought you lost that job."

"I'll be looking for a new position. Victor's bakery isn't the only place in Paris. Getting recognized in Paris for my talent has always been my dream. I want a place where standing out from the crowd isn't seen as being weird. A place I can call my own." Robin pleaded with her eyes for him to understand. "When I said I shouldn't have kissed you, I meant I shouldn't have let you believe we could have a relationship. I'm not sticking around. I don't want to bake bread in my grandparents' shop for the rest of my life."

He shoved the last bite of his cupcake into his mouth. Swallowed.

She could hear the condenser on the cooler ticking.

Sammy took a long drink of his coffee. Was he ever going to say something?

He swallowed again. Looked at the floor, then straight into her eyes. "Robin, I know we're just getting to know each other again. I think we have a connection. We can take it slow if you want. But don't say no to something good because it's not perfect timing."

Robin pushed away from the counter and began pacing. "You're a great guy, and I can't deny that I'm attracted to you." She avoided his gaze. "Sammy, I watched you tonight. It's obvious you love this town and the kids, and just everything."

She made a wide gesture. "I don't want to get in the way of that. I'm not sticking around and you are. Simple as that."

"You're right, I do love this town, and I've always dreamed of having a family here." Sammy set his cup in the sink, then rested both of his hands on the edge. She longed to touch his shoulder, make this easier for both of them. He turned. "But I also want to explore where this is going with you."

"I'm sorry. I really am. But I think it's best if we just stay friends. I'm leaving. I don't want a long-distance relationship. I don't even know if I want any kind of relationship."

"I guess that's it then." He straightened, grabbed his jacket off the center island. "Don't worry about taking me home. I can take my bike."

"Sammy..." But what could she say? "I'd like to stay friends."

"Sure," he said, opening the back door. A wave of cold air hit her. "Friends." And then he was gone.

She swigged the last of the coffee in her cup. A few pieces of the beans floated in the last swallow. Their gritty bitterness log-jammed in her throat.

🦊🦊🦊

EVEN THE NIGHT SKY MOCKED HIM.

The clouds had cleared, and Sammy rode his bike home under the cold starry sky. *I think it's best if we just stay friends.* Robin's words chased him. He blew out a frosty breath. Some enchanted evening this had turned into. He was never the guy the girls chose.

Around him, Deep Haven lay frigid and silent. He passed through a neighborhood, windows darkened at this late hour. Half standing on the bike's pedals, he strained up a hill near his home. One tire rotation at a time, carrying him farther away from the warmth of earlier that night.

Maybe he'd just gotten caught up in the moment, but kissing Robin had felt right. Like they belonged together or something.

Too bad she didn't feel the same way.

He turned into his driveway and then stowed his bike in the garage. He smelled the sweet pine scent of his latest woodworking project—two new sets of Ping-Pong paddles. He pictured Ben or another teen going head-to-head in the round-robin-style tournament coming up at the youth center. A few more coats of varnish and he'd be ready to take them over there.

The garage was almost as cold as the outdoors, so he quickly went through the door and into the kitchen.

His mom sat at the kitchen table in her pajamas, sorting a load of laundry. Her hair had gone silver over the past few years, and tonight there were tired circles under her eyes.

"Ma. You didn't have to wait up for me."

"I couldn't sleep." She shook out a towel, then folded it and placed it on a pile. "I thought I'd be productive until I felt sleepy."

He brushed past her, fully intending to head straight for bed.

"How was the dance?"

Her question stopped him in his tracks. "It was good. Interesting."

"Interesting? How?"

Shoot. He shouldn't have let that slip. Now she'd be on him for details like a dog on a bone. "We had fun." He tugged off his jacket and hat and laid them on the table, then sat down across from his mom. The kitchen held a faint chocolate aroma.

She threaded a dress shirt onto a hanger, then hung it on the back of a chair. "Tell me more."

He leaned back in his chair and told her about the dance that Robin had taught the kids, the one from her Zumba class. By the end of the story, they both were laughing.

"Robin's cupcakes were a hit. And the kids all behaved

themselves. They barely needed chaperones."

His mom quieted, smoothed the tablecloth in front of her. "Seems like I've been hearing a lot about Robin lately." She kept her eyes on the table as she spoke.

"Yeah, she's a good friend."

"Maybe more than a friend?"

"Naw, we just keep running into each other, that's all." The kiss from earlier that night lingered, but so did her *I'd like to stay friends* announcement.

"I know that look. It's exactly like the time Colleen broke your heart. You looked just like that when she turned you down." His mom gave him a sharp glance. "I know Robin has a place in your heart."

"Ma, I'm telling you, we're just friends." And after tonight, they'd stay that way.

"You might be telling yourself that, but in your heart, she's always had a bigger place." She snapped another towel. "I remember watching the two of you study together. You always were so in sync. She taught you a lot that year. You made a good team."

"That might be true, but it doesn't matter anyway. She's leaving town." He might be too, come to think of it, depending on the situation with Tucker and the smoke jumping gig. Robin was right to cool things off. Maybe.

"Already? She just got back. I thought she was home for a while."

"She says she's only here until her grandparents come back from Florida, and then she's moving on to bigger things." And wasn't that a kick in the teeth.

"That's too bad. I always liked that girl. She has style, like her grandma."

He smiled at that. "She sure does. And if anyone can make a name for themselves, it's Robin. She has big ideas and the chops to back them up." He thought about her helping Ben learn math. Yep. She was special all right.

He got up from the table.

"Wait," Mom said. "What have you decided about joining Tucker's crew?"

"I don't know. I like the idea of doing something heroic, but I've never wanted to leave Deep Haven." Sammy bent and rubbed at his knee. Sometimes a phantom ache would crawl over his legs, reminding him of what he had given up.

His mom began stacking the folded laundry back into the basket. "There are more ways to be a hero than fighting fires in a wilderness."

"I know that. I wish I knew what that looks like for me." He ran a hand over the back of his neck, sat back down.

"Sometimes I worry you've been searching so hard because you never had a father around to encourage you." Sammy could see the fraying edges of the bathrobe she wore over her pajamas around the house. "You missed out on the steady influence of a dad."

Sammy's parents had married young and had Sammy less than a year later. His dad had died shortly after that of an aortic aneurism. He had been in the military straight out of high school for a four-year term, and then he'd been a firefighter. It didn't take Sigmund Freud to see why Sammy might want to follow the same path. His mom had always said that his dad was a good protector.

He leaned forward, resting his forearms on the table. "I never knew Dad, so how could I feel the loss of him?"

"That's just what I mean. You never had a hero in your life to model yourself after. Not really. All the stories in the world about your dad couldn't replace him in your life. You've had to be your own hero."

"I had you." He reached out and took her hand. His mom was worth ten dads as far as he was concerned.

She smiled at him. "Not the same and you know it."

"I had my football coaches, Coach Presley and Coach Knight,

and the guys at church." He let go of her hand and leaned back again.

"True." She reached for another towel from the laundry basket.

"But all those people can't help me figure out what to do with the rest of my life."

"God has answers for you if you ask." Mom flicked out the wrinkles in the towel and then deftly folded it. "You'll figure it out. You always do."

"Good night, Ma."

"Love you, Sam. Oh—take those letters with you."

He took the two envelopes perched on the corner of the table. The same ones he'd been ignoring for the past few days. The ones with the name *Williams* marked in the upper left corner.

Upstairs, he dropped the envelopes on a stack of other envelopes which threatened to tumble over. He opened the drawer in his bedside table and swept them all inside. The lamp on top wobbled as he jammed the drawer shut with a satisfying *thunk*. One white corner of an envelope mocked him, its dogeared corner sticking out the top of the drawer, but he turned his back to it and searched for some pj's.

Moments later he'd changed clothes and climbed into bed. With his hands propped behind his head, he stared at the ceiling, then leaned over and flicked the lamp off. Darkness engulfed him, with only a small amount of light creeping in from the window and under the door. But even that didn't reach Sammy.

God has answers for you if you ask. His mom was right. Only, it seemed like, lately, all his prayers were doing was tumbling around in his mind before evaporating into the winter air.

He tossed off the covers and sat up in bed. Keeping his voice low, he tried again. "Jesus, I don't know what's going on. I don't know what to do." He stood and began pacing in the dark. "I don't know what You want out of me. I don't even know what I want out of myself." He rubbed at the ache in his leg again. The physical therapist had cleared him for all activities, and Sammy knew he was as strong as before, but the ache kept creeping back. His physical therapist called it a pain memory.

"I want to stay in Deep Haven, but there doesn't seem to be anything for me here. Being a courier and a handyman doesn't cut it anymore. I can't go back to driving a truck." A shudder ran through him at the image of him at the wheel of another lumber truck. "But I feel restless. Joining Tucker's crew doesn't feel right either. I know my mom said You have answers and would show me what to do, but I don't even know where I am. It seems like every choice is a bad one."

He took a fifth lap around the room, then a sixth. "Help me out here. Maybe this is unfair, but can You just show me what to do?"

He waited in silence for a few moments. No voice, not even a still, small one, answered him.

A verse drifted through his mind. *He will make your paths straight…* How did that verse begin? Something about trusting the Lord. Easy to say, difficult to do.

At least the ache in his leg had eased. He lay back in bed, again staring at the ceiling, now out of sight in the dark.

Time to face facts. His body was healed. And thanks to the insurance check, he wouldn't need much extra money for a long time. God probably wanted him to use the lumberjack build He'd given him to fight fires in some wilderness. He didn't know why he had ever thought he wanted to build a different life for himself.

He'd call Tucker tomorrow after church, see what it would take to join his crew. At least that was a proactive step he could take. He didn't have to make all the decisions at once.

In the living room, the clock chimed one o'clock.

Sammy's mind drifted. He saw himself on the highway north of town. Rain and snow pelted the windshield of his semitrailer. No big deal. He'd driven in worse. He hummed along with a country music song on the radio.

He wanted to rewind, to not see what came next.

His semi went around a bend in the road. He looked down to change the radio station.

Don't look down! he wanted to scream to himself.

A darkness descended and then a flash of blue ahead in the storm. Suddenly the rain and sleet lit up red with the brake lights of the compact car. A mama deer and her fawn leaped out onto the road.

He pumped his brakes, engine screaming.

He couldn't stop.

He couldn't breathe.

His truck hit an icy spot, and he knew he was about to plow over the small car in front of him. He pulled the wheel to the left, then right, steering around the Prius.

Too late.

He saw he'd overcorrected, and then the semi jackknifed. He wrestled with the wheel until the truck came to a stop, cradling the car in a vee between his cab and the load of lumber he carried. His trailer listed to the side, load top-heavy and groaning.

Heart pounding, he hopped out of the truck. *Please.* A whispered prayer for the people in the blue Prius.

That's when he heard it. Metal screaming, snapping, overlaid with the cries of a child.

"Help me!"

Sammy jolted upright in bed. His sheets tied him in place, twisted around his legs. Sweat bathed him from head to toe.

He groaned and fought off the sheets, then sat up on the edge of the bed, breathing hard.

This nightmare held him tight.

If only he hadn't messed with the radio.

If only he had double-checked his lumber load.

If only he'd taken his meds.

If only—

If only he could break free from the darkness he was living in.

eight

. . .

It would have been better if the night at the dance had never happened. Robin sat in church trying hard to pay attention—really, she was. A silver-haired woman shared about an orphanage in India that needed funds and then they sang a hymn. Robin couldn't remember which one.

Now Pastor Dan stood in the pulpit delivering a sermon she was sure spoke to her heart, straight from God's Word, if only she could concentrate on it.

The sight of Sammy and his mom sitting up two rows and over three seats kept snagging her gaze. She wondered if his thoughts drifted to the night before too.

Probably not. He'd probably written her off as a crazy tease.

Enough. She needed to focus. She'd already decided starting a relationship right now would be a mistake. She. Was. Leaving. Heading back to Paris or LA or wherever. Deep Haven wasn't home, and she didn't want it to be.

She needed to stay strong.

Sammy and his generous heart wouldn't turn her head.

She tuned back in to Pastor Dan.

"Listen to this verse from Romans five. 'But God demonstrates his own love for us in this: While we were still sinners, Christ died for us.' Friends, you don't have to clean yourselves up for God." At the pulpit, Pastor Dan held his Bible up. "God loved us before we were perfect. In fact, it is only through His love and Christ's sacrifice on the cross that we can be made holy. Some people believe they aren't good enough for God to love them, that they've somehow strayed too far. That's just not possible. Turn with me to Ephesians 3:18."

Pages rustled all around her. Pastor Dan read the verse out loud. "I'll start a little earlier, in the second half of verse seventeen. 'And I pray that you, being rooted and established in love, may have power, together with all the Lord's holy people, to grasp how wide and long and high and deep is the love of Christ.'"

Robin didn't hear Pastor Dan's closing prayer or the final hymn. As she sat in her seat, her brain still spun on those final words. God's love was colossal indeed. She brushed away a sudden wetness in the corner of her right eye, tucking the thought away for later. That kind of love was its own kind of home.

"Excuse me." A voice broke into her thoughts. "Are you Robin Fox, Elaine's granddaughter?"

She shifted in her seat, then rose and greeted the woman who had spoken. The older woman from earlier, with silver-gray hair, held the arm of a man of similar age. Robin guessed them to be in their seventies. They must be friends with her grandparents. "Yes, I'm Robin."

"I'm so pleased to meet you," the woman said. "I am Jean Adams, and this is my husband, Palmer. We know your grandparents. Megan Barrett said you make cakes?" Jean gestured to where Megan stood with her family, bouncing her baby on her hip. Megan gave a quick wave, then turned back to Cole.

Where was this going? "Yes, I run my grandparents' bakery here in town. I've added cakes to the menu."

"Oh, wonderful." Jean reached out and took Robin's arm,

leaning in close. "I knew any relation to Elaine would be someone who would help us. You might be exactly the person to solve our little problem."

"I'll do what I can." Robin glanced around. She hoped this wasn't a donation situation. She wanted to be as generous as possible, but right now, paying the plumbing bill was much more important.

"Just tell the girl what you want her to do," Palmer said.

Jean smiled at her husband. "Palmer and I will be celebrating our fifty-fifth wedding anniversary in February."

"Congratulations! That's the emerald anniversary, right?"

"Thank you. And yes, it is. It's not too often you find a young person who knows about those things," Jean said.

"Really, it's a miracle I've put up with her all these years." Palmer's long-suffering tone was undercut by the twinkle in his eye.

"Oh, you." Jean gave him a little swat. "Anyway, our son asked if he could do a photo spread for his magazine, *Lake Panache*. Maybe you've heard of it?"

Robin had heard of it. She saw it on the newsstand at the grocery store. An aspirational monthly with beautiful spreads of people living their best lake life. It was widely circulated in the United States, as it featured lake communities from almost every state.

Jean now had both hands clasped together in front of her. "He wants us to have a small gathering of friends at our cabin to celebrate our anniversary, and he will photograph the party."

"What an honor." Now Robin had no idea where this conversation was going.

"Jean," her husband said. "You still haven't told her anything. Give Robin here a chance to say yes or no."

"I'm getting to that. Well, if we're going to have a party, we really ought to have a cake. And if we're featuring the town of Deep Haven, it ought to be a Deep Haven cake."

Robin caught her breath. Did she mean— "And?"

"And we want you to bake it," Jean finished with a lilt, clapping her hands together.

"You want me to bake a cake that will be featured in *Lake Panache*?" Could a part of her dreams really be coming true? Ha! A print magazine. A photo spread in *Lake Panache* would also give her the exposure she needed. Maybe someone would even nominate her for the *La Patisserie* contest. This could be the biggest thing to happen to her.

Take that, Victor!

"Now, we can't promise anything about being featured." Palmer's quiet voice did little to squelch the squealing she was doing internally. "But we do want you to bake a cake, and we do have our son coming to take photographs and do interviews."

Apparently her mouth understood before her brain did, because Robin heard herself saying, "I'll do it."

"I'm so glad," Jean said. "The party will be on February twelfth. Now, we'll get the details together later, but Palmer and I never had a proper wedding." Jean looped her arm through Palmer's and looked at him with enough heat that Robin almost blushed. Jean looked back at Robin and smiled. "In the sixties it was all free love and getting married by the JP. I'd love to have a beautiful wedding-style cake for our anniversary party."

Um. Oh no. Was Robin dreaming or did she just commit to making a second wedding cake? Jacob and Emily's on February 14 and now the Adamses' only two days earlier. The bakery wasn't equipped for something like that. They'd barely put cakes on the menu at all. Her heart sped up, and she felt beads of sweat forming on the back of her neck.

No. She would not panic.

She would make this work.

She'd give Wendy and Bella more hours. She herself would map out a plan for baking and frosting the cakes that would fit the schedule. It would all work out.

It had to.

After making plans to meet the Adamses to work out the

details, she looked around for Sammy. He would love to hear about this. But it seemed he and his mom had already left, as she didn't see his broad shoulders anywhere.

She ignored the shot of loss that pinged through her.

Just as well. She was supposed to be forgetting about him. She needed to treat him as a casual friend, not as a partner.

Even if it meant not having someone to share her joy.

A BIT OF THE LYRICS FROM ONE OF THIS MORNING'S HYMNS ROLLED through Sammy's mind. "O the deep, deep love of Jesus! Vast, unmeasured, boundless, free..." Sammy appreciated the reminder from Pastor Dan's sermon that the love of Jesus would never fail. Even if he wasn't sure of his own path forward, that truth was something he could hold on to.

After grabbing a quick lunch with his mom at home, it was time to bite the bullet and follow through on his late-night decision. He went to the garage and turned on the small space heater he used while woodworking. A faint aroma of burning dust filled the garage, layering over the pine and lacquer usually present.

Sammy dug out the scrap of paper with Tucker Newman's phone number on it and dialed.

A man's voice answered. "Tucker here."

"Hello, Tucker, this is Sammy Johnson."

"Sammy! Seth mentioned you might be calling. Good to hear from you. It's been ages. What, like ten years since high school?"

"Yeah. Something like that." Sammy scooted onto a stool he parked next to his workbench. Pictures of him in uniform—first football, then Army—lined the back of the bench. A small clock made from the end cut of a log rested nearby. "Seth said you might be looking for a few more crew members."

"Yep. We'll have a new bunch starting their training in March. The season usually starts ramping up by May, and our training program lasts five weeks."

"How soon would you need an answer?" Sammy tightened his grip on the phone.

"The field is usually pretty competitive, but we seem to be in a lull year. I'd like to hear a yes or no by mid-February. I can't hold the job for you, not even as an old friend."

Sammy scrubbed a hand down his face. "No, I'm sure not. I wouldn't expect you to."

"Do you mind if I ask you a few questions? Kind of a preliminary interview?" Sammy could hear papers rustling on the other end of the line.

"Sure, that's fine by me."

"Seth did give me a sketchy outline on your story since the last time we saw each other. I know you played football in high school. Seth said you did a short stint in the Army. Lumberjack for a while. Am I on the right track?"

"Yes. That's the outline."

"Gotcha. Okay, would you say you are still physically fit?"

Hoo boy. That hit below the belt. "Did Seth tell you about the accident?"

"He mentioned that you no longer work for him because you heroically pulled some people out of a car at great cost to yourself."

There was that *hero* word again. People couldn't seem to let it go. He was no hero. "Yes. My lumber semitrailer jackknifed around a car. The car had braked suddenly to avoid hitting a deer, then I tried to stop behind it." He heard again the screech of tires, felt the pull of the wheel in his grip. He squeezed his eyes shut. "I was able to get out of my truck and helped a mom and her son get out of the car. And that's when the chains holding the lumber snapped." His breathing quickened. "I...I was trapped under one of the logs."

"Mm-hmm." A scratching sound came from the other end of

the line. Sammy imagined Tucker drawing a big *No, thank you* across his paper. "This was a few years ago, right?"

"Almost a year and a half."

"How are you feeling now?"

There was no way Sammy would admit to feeling fear or mention the nightmares he sometimes woke up from. And he would be able to get behind the wheel of a car by March, right? "Stronger, for sure. I'm back to my high-school weight." He hoped the wry humor translated through the phone lines.

"Physical therapy?"

It was phrased as a question, but Sammy was immediately transported back to the room that smelled of sweat and disinfectant, the voice of his physical therapist telling him "Just one more minute. You can do anything for a minute." He swallowed. Pushed back the memory of the pain.

"I completed my PT. The doc signed off several months ago."

"Okay. So you can carry gear of up to a hundred and fifteen pounds, learn how to jump out of a helicopter, and are confident in your ability to use your legs?"

That was the question, wasn't it? Could he trust himself?

Maybe it was time to try. "Yes."

"I'll tell you what. I'm still concerned about the strength in your legs and your ability to trust them. My team has to be able to rely on each other for their lives." Tucker paused, and Sammy could hear the second hand ticking on the clock. Then Tucker broke the silence. "But I'm going to give you the chance to prove yourself. I'll send you the forms you'll need to fill out. The application, a doctor's waiver, stuff like that. I trust Seth's judgment, and Seth trusts you. That goes a long way. Think it over. Talk to Seth. Then send in your application. Let's get you on the team."

Wait. Tucker still wanted him?

Even after his injuries, someone still trusted him? Maybe it really was time to trust himself.

"Thank you, Tucker."

"I'm not making any promises. That injury of yours could be a deal breaker. But if your doc says you're ready, I'll give you a shot."

Okay, so not the vote of confidence he'd hoped for, but it was something.

Sammy hung up the phone and immediately dialed Seth. "I just got off the phone with Tucker Newman."

"And?"

"And he said I fit the criteria, and as long as I have the doctor's go-ahead, he has a spot for me on the team."

Seth's hoot caused Sammy to pull the phone from his ear for a moment. "That's great! When are you sending in your paperwork?"

It was great news, and Sammy should feel better about it, but something still tugged at him. He didn't feel excited about the idea. Shouldn't he be thrilled with the chance to prove himself a hero?

Instead, all he felt was…nothing. Or maybe a tiny bit of fear.

Because, what if he really didn't want to fight fires and explore wildernesses? What if he didn't want to leave Deep Haven?

"I'm still thinking about it."

Sammy waited for Seth's rebuttal, but his friend went easy on him. "Hey, you missed trivia night at the VFW last night."

"Yeah, I was busy." The space heater must be working double time. He turned down the temp.

"Busy with what? A Saturday night fix-it job?"

"If you must know, I was out dancing." Shoot. After the razzing he'd gotten from the guys the other day, maybe he shouldn't have mentioned anything.

"Did your mom talk you into doing that square dancing down in Beaver Bay again?"

Sammy laughed. "Actually, square dancing with my mom was a lot of fun. But this time, it was more like work. Robin Fox and I chaperoned the Snowball Dance at the high school. She got roped in somehow, and then she thought she'd share the torture."

"Man, I haven't thought about the Snowball Dance in years. Remember when that kid got sick?"

"This is sounding eerily like a conversation I had with Robin," Sammy said.

"Sounds like you're having all kinds of conversations with Robin."

"It's kinda natural since I've been over there fixing the kitchen."

"Uh-huh. I'm sure it's only natural."

His friend's teasing hit close to the mark. He had been thinking about Robin. A lot. He loved hearing her laugh, seeing her easy way with others, but most especially he admired her determination to do the right thing. He'd have to keep his distance if he had any chance of keeping his promise to be just friends.

On the phone, Seth was wrapping up. "Okay. Keep me posted. Both about the smoke jumpers and this nothing-is-happening with Robin." Sammy could practically hear his friend winking through the phone line.

He ended the call and stuffed the phone into his pocket. The Ping-Pong paddles sat at the end of the bench, waiting for Sammy to deliver them to the youth center. No time like right now. He had nothing better to do this afternoon. Plus, he could check on the new furnace. He picked the paddles up and stuffed them into the courier pouch on his bike. After flipping the space heater all the way off, he opened the door to the kitchen.

"Ma, I'm going out," he called into the house.

"Be safe," she called back.

He grabbed a set of gloves from his workbench and headed out.

Straight into a snow shower.

The snow fell from heaven in giant flakes, eddied about on

the wind. The road didn't look slippery, so he pushed off in the direction of the youth center.

A fifteen-minute ride later, he pedaled the last few feet into the parking lot near the center. He put his bike in the rack and went inside.

A clicking noise coupled with the whir of a fan and the warmth of the building told him the new furnace worked fine. He went to the closet to check it out. At the back of the glorified pole shed that served as the youth center, the janitor's closet did triple duty as the electrical room, cleaning supply storage, and a catchall for sports equipment.

Sammy pulled the chain to turn on the bare lightbulb, and light illuminated the space. Once he located the bucket of Ping-Pong balls on a shelf, he put the paddles next to it.

At the back of the five-by-five-foot space hummed the new furnace. It was a beauty. The compact machine put out enough heat for the whole building while still being energy efficient. As an added bonus, it ran quietly. The kids who came to the youth center brought enough noise as it was. He checked the thermostat. Everything looked great.

His phone buzzed and he looked at the screen. Casper.

CASPER

Sammy, got time to help me with something at Wild Harbor?

Sure, he had time to help Casper Christiansen at the outfitters he ran in town.

Except for one snag.

Wild Harbor Trading Post practically shared a parking lot with the bakery. And he was definitely, absolutely, one hundred percent not thinking about Robin. Or casually riding past her place to see if she was in. Or imagining her in the kitchen kneading bread dough, a smudge of flour on her cheek.

This didn't count though, right? Helping Casper was about

as innocent as it got. So what if he cycled past Robin's place of business? Emphasis on *business*.

SAMMY

Be there in 20. Need me to bring any tools?

Helping Casper usually meant light construction work. If he had to stop at home, that would add to the travel time.

CASPER

Think I've got everything. See you in 20.

Sammy locked up the youth center and headed out on his bike. The fat tires were sluggish on the sloppy snow accumulating everywhere. He pedaled harder, enjoying the burn of his muscles against the sucking pressure of the snow. Fat flakes still fell. Each one swatting his face proved they were more water than snow crystal.

As he came down the hill into town, he spotted Owen Christiansen in a snowplow clearing the streets. The truck spread sand from its load in the back, a spinner connected to the rear bumper distributing it out evenly on the road. Owen responded to his quick wave with an equally short beep of the big truck's horn.

A few minutes later, Sammy pulled into the Wild Harbor lot. And yeah, despite his best efforts, he'd clocked Robin's van in the bakery lot, the lights of the bakery shining out the plate glass window, and a certain auburn-haired bakery chef ushering two customers inside. He pushed aside the questions in his mind about who Robin was meeting with and why she was open on a Sunday.

He hoped Casper's project took a lot of concentration.

Because that might be the only thing that kept his feet from carrying him straight over to breaking his promise to be "just friends" with Robin.

nine

. . .

Robin opened the front door of the bakery and let Emily and Jacob in, setting the bell on the door jingling. Behind them, a cold wind blew in a mini hurricane of snowflakes from the Deep Haven streets.

"It's good to see you again, Jacob and Emily." She shook their hands and led them to a table for their cake-tasting meeting. She'd come here straight from church, made a pot of coffee, set the table with a knife, forks, plates, and coffee mugs, and chosen two samples: a caramel mocha cupcake and a raspberry-filled vanilla cupcake, both flavors suitable for their non-traditional wedding.

"Thank you again for agreeing to do this for us." Emily tugged off her jacket and hung it over the back of her chair. Her eyes sparkled brightly. "We're doing everything in such a rush. I just bought my dress at a thrift store yesterday." She plucked her phone from her carpetbag-style purse and opened her camera app. "Want to see a photo?"

"Of course!" Robin reached for the phone. The photo showed Emily standing in front of a mirror in a satin A-line dress with fitted sleeves. A Chantilly lace overlay was threaded through with pops of green and blue thread. Robin felt her mouth drop open and eyes go wide. "You found this at a thrift store? It's gorgeous."

Emily beamed at her. "Pretty awesome isn't it?"

"Awesome doesn't even begin to cover it." Robin handed the phone back. "Are you going with those greens and blues for your wedding colors?"

Emily slid her phone back into her bag. "Yes. I know it would be more traditional to do reds or pinks for Valentine's Day, but I've never been known to do the normal thing. I'm having a wedding on a Tuesday, after all." Her laughter bathed Robin in joy.

"I suppose you aren't going to want a traditional cake then, either?" Hopefully they weren't looking for anything too complicated. She still had the normal bakery to run with a shoestring staff, after all.

"Jacob actually had an idea, didn't you, Jacob?" Emily turned to her fiancé, who up to that point had been so unobtrusive that Robin had almost forgotten he was sitting there.

Jacob pointed to the plate in the middle of the table. "Can we get those?"

"You want to try them? That's what they're here for." Robin picked up the knife and sliced the cupcakes into quarters. "I like to cut them up, but you can eat as much as you want."

"No. Well, yes." Jacob grabbed a piece of caramel mocha cupcake as his face reddened. "I mean, we want cupcakes at our wedding."

"Oh! That is a fun idea." Her mind started buzzing with the possibilities. Having their colors include green would work out great. Better than great, actually. With the emerald theme for the Adamses' anniversary cake, she could save a little on getting extra ingredients. "Tell me more about what you're thinking."

Jacob seemed to have used his quota of words, and Emily jumped in. "We don't really know what we want. We were hoping you might have some ideas."

Robin flipped open her sketchbook where she'd noted a few

pages last night in preparation for this meeting.

"What about something like this, except adapted for cupcakes? And maybe in green?" She showed them a sketch of a delicate lace pattern in black. The design wrapped around a cake and over the top, but she could pipe a portion of it onto each cupcake to make a cohesive look. "It could mirror your dress a little."

Emily shook her head. "I like that, but it doesn't quite feel right."

"Okay, no problem. How about this one?" The next page held a sketch of simple flowers, which could be piped in various colors. "I could make these in shades of green and blue, maybe a teal or purple, whichever way you would lean."

"I like these." Emily pointed at three of the tiny flowers.

With a few quick strokes, Robin drew out how the cupcakes could look. A smooth fondant top with a perfect flower perched on one corner of the frosting.

Emily clapped her hands. "I love it. It's perfect. I have another idea. I have a spare piece of lace from my dress. I don't know why, but it came in a bag on the same hanger. I'll drop that by and you can use it for arranging the cupcakes. If we do these flowers and the fondant in the same blue and green shades as the lace, that could tie things together."

The concept sounded…interesting…but Robin was willing to give it a go.

Jacob and Emily ate the rest of the cupcake samples with Emily chattering on about all the details. When they finished after an hour or so, Robin stood and thanked them for coming in. She walked them to the door and locked it behind the engaged couple.

Outside, clouds crowded out the afternoon sun dipping low in the sky. She stood for a minute admiring the glow of the sun along the bottom edges of the low-hanging clouds. A few snowflakes still floated down to the ground.

One cake figured out. Now she could dream about the

Adamses' cake. She needed something that would pop, something to wow the photographer.

If she could only get her cake into that magazine. Then she could enter the *La Patisserie* contest. And then she could work her way back to Paris. Maybe she'd go to San Francisco first, reacquaint herself with some of her old culinary school friends.

Suddenly she remembered the design she'd sketched a few days before. The perfect idea took shape in her mind. A marble effect in jewel tones. She'd substitute the reds and purples for emerald, aqua, and some sort of deep blue. Three tall layers for a round cake. The bottom could be a swirling design. The middle should be white so she could easily add in a stylized *Happy 55th Anniversary* message in gold along the side. The top layer would stand above the others on a pedestal with sparklers popping out to give it even more height.

Sparklers were quickly becoming her signature.

If she used a twelve-inch cake on the bottom, topped with a nine-inch and then a six, that should be perfect for their hundred expected guests. She imagined it in a potential table setting, using accents of gold and silver.

She hummed a hymn as she made her way into the kitchen to prepare poolishes, the starters which would add a depth of flavor to the next day's bread. She lifted a few mixing bowls off the shelf and moved them to the island, then measured out enough water for each poolish, using a digital scale for an accurate measurement.

Doing a dance twirl, Robin pirouetted to the supply shelf and reached for the yeast container. The box felt light. That was weird. She shook it. Then opened it, and the pit of her stomach dropped.

Empty.

That couldn't be right. An order had come in on Friday. She rummaged through the shelf. Everything was in its place as usual in her very tidy workspace. No yeast.

Forcing down the bile rising in her throat, she booted up the computer. Surely there was some error. She just needed to check her online order. A few minutes later the evidence was in front of her in black and white.

She'd forgotten to order yeast.

She dropped her head into her hands. How could a competent person forget to order the one thing most essential to running a bread bakery? Answer: she'd been too distracted with these stupid cakes and Sammy and just…everything.

She raised her head and looked at the clock. The single grocery store in town would still be open. Maybe she'd get lucky and they would have what she needed.

She tugged on her coat and gloves and then jogged the city block to the store, slip-sliding on the newly formed ice on the sidewalks.

In the baking aisle, she looked at the three minuscule sleeves of yeast they had on the shelf. These would last her, like, half a day.

She grabbed the packets. Better than nothing.

A quick check of her watch confirmed that she *might* be able to make it to Duluth before the Diner Depot, the store where they ordered all their yeast, closed. They didn't keep late hours on a Sunday.

As she slip-stumbled back to the bakery, a man got on a bike in front of Wild Harbor. Sammy, she realized, a pang of regret pinging her heart. She wanted to call to him, to apologize. Or at least get back to the friendship they had.

Too bad she was leaving.

🐕 🐕 🐕

HE DEFINITELY WASN'T LOOKING AT THE BAKERY.

Sammy gathered himself to head home. He planned to keep his eyes on the tire in front of him without a glance right or left.

But then, as he pedaled past the bakery's parking lot, he heard a metallic clang. Like it was operating on its own, his head turned toward the sound. Underneath a streetlight, Robin was wrestling with a tire iron near the delivery van. Even from across the lot he saw the tire was completely flat.

Aw. He couldn't ignore that.

He pedaled into the lot. "Need some help?"

She gave the wrench another push. "I think it's iced over."

"Let me give it a try." Sammy crouched down next to the flat tire. Robin moved aside and sat on the spare tire nearby.

"Grandpa Jim taught me how to change a tire before I moved to California, but I've never actually had to do it."

The cold of the ground seeped through Sammy's jeans as he kneeled to tug on the tire iron. No give. He stood. "Looks like I'm going to need some leverage." He checked to make sure the car jack was stable, then bent and put all his weight into cranking on the wrench.

It started to give and he nearly stumbled backward.

"Now we're cooking." He finished taking the lug nut off and then worked his way around the others.

Robin rolled the spare tire over to him and helped him attach it to the vehicle.

When they were finished, Robin stamped her feet and rubbed her hands together. "Thanks. I would've been out here in the cold for a long time if you hadn't ridden by."

"It was no problem. What are you doing out here, anyway?"

A shadow that had nothing to do with the passing clouds brushed over her face. "I need to drive the two hours down to Duluth today. And if I don't leave in, like, the next ten minutes, I'm not going to make it at all." Her voice choked out at the end.

"I don't know if that's a good idea. The storm has left everything super slippery."

"I don't have a choice. I…" She ducked into the van and turned the key and started the engine. There wasn't any indication she was ever going to finish that sentence.

"You what?" He held the doorframe.

She put both hands on top of the steering wheel and let out a long breath. "I messed up."

Whatever he'd expected to hear, it wasn't that. "Okay. Want to talk about it?"

She gave a little noise that could have been a laugh or a whimper—he wasn't sure which. When she spoke again, he had to lean in close to hear her words. "I forgot to order yeast."

"Yeast?" Now he was confused.

Her eyes blazed, and he was tempted to step back, but maybe she wasn't mad at him. "How ludicrous, right? I run a bread bakery, for crying out loud. How could I forget the one critical piece of running the place?"

Oh no.

"Can't you just get some at the grocery store?"

She barked a short laugh. "I tried that. They barely had enough in stock for half of what I need for one day. My next shipment doesn't come in for three days, and even ordering it online with rush shipping won't get it here fast enough." She pounded the steering wheel in time to her words. "This ridiculous tiny town in the middle of nowhere." Her hands stilled, and she looked him in the eye. "So yeah. I have to drive down to Duluth. The Fox can't afford to be closed more than one day."

Well, he had a few things to say about that, but it was clear she was in no mood to hear it. "Okay. But you're not going alone. I'm coming with you."

"You can't do that. What about your customers? You're not going to make any money if you keep bailing me out."

"I don't have anything on the schedule today. Everyone is pretty much closed on Sundays. I was just headed home." *Please say yes.*

She buckled her seat belt but didn't respond. The tight look on her face convinced him she shouldn't be alone.

"Fine. You win." She threw her hands in the air. But he

caught the slightest trace of a smile on her lips. "Do you want to put your bike in the bakery while we're gone?"

"Nah, it'll be fine under the overhang of the roof. Give me a sec." He moved the bike, then trotted around to the passenger side. He swung in as she adjusted the heating controls.

"Should be warm in here in no time."

"I saw the plow truck spreading sand while I was cycling down here. Hopefully it will have worked its magic by now."

They drove through town in silence. The ice from the storm shimmered everywhere. Out in the harbor, white caps chased each other across the waves.

"Do you need directions? I can navigate." Sammy wiggled his cell phone in the air.

Robin kept her eyes on the road. "No. I know how to get there. Thanks, though. Maybe I should have asked if you wanted to drive."

"Nah, I'm good."

"You're not one of those macho guys who always needs to be in control of the car?" She flipped on the windshield wipers. For a moment, their *swish-swish* was the only sound in the van.

He swallowed. Looked out the window. "The truth is, I haven't been behind the wheel of a car, or anything on four wheels, since the day of my accident." The words hung between them like fog over a frozen pond.

"Oh."

Was that all she was going to say? The silence stretched thin. Okay, he probably owed her more than that. "That's why I ride my bike all the time. I've tried to take my mom's car out sometimes or my truck, but I just freeze up. I can barely turn the car on, let alone put it into drive." And yeah, it wasn't the only reason, but it was the main reason.

"So, like, PTSD?"

"Pretty much. Except that my therapist said it's a little different since I developed it from one traumatic event instead of a long, sustained season of trauma. They call it ASD or Acute

Stress Disorder." An image of the Prius a moment before impact flashed before his eyes. If he'd been one second slower...but no. His therapist said not to dwell on what-ifs. The truth was, he had been just fast enough to keep from crashing his semitrailer into that tin can of a car.

"I guess that makes sense." She glanced at him, her expression unreadable, before looking back to the road.

"Most of the symptoms are better." Except the nightmares. "My therapist said that when my need for driving becomes greater than my subconscious desire to avoid it, I will give it a try again. For now, I'm content on my bike."

"I think you're brave."

"I'm not though." In fact, in the moment before he'd pulled that mother and son from the car, he'd panicked. He still broke into a cold sweat thinking about it. He'd panicked and wasted precious minutes before doing anything to save them. "You're the brave one. Moving halfway around the world. Pursuing your dream."

"Some dream that turned out to be."

"What happened over there?"

"My boss, Victor, asked me to make a cake for a contest." Robin reached over and turned the heat down. "I spent hours perfecting the design, then even more time building and decorating the cake. But when it was done, Victor basically stole it from me, telling the judges he'd made it."

"That's not right."

"The thing is, it was his bakery, so it was his right to claim the cake, but then he humiliated me in front of the whole staff, and he gave Monique, my coworker, the position he'd promised me."

"He sounds like a jerk." Sammy clenched his hands.

"Yeah, he kind of is. I can see that more clearly now. I'm mostly over the injustice of the situation, but I can't let go of the idea that I never got to show anyone what I can do. There I was, in Paris, and I missed my chance."

"Well, you're showing them now, right? Managing a bakery,

making amazing cakes."

"I guess. But sometimes it feels like it was more than a cake that was stolen from me. Like it was my whole life. Now I just feel stuck." She adjusted her hands on the wheel. "All I want is to get back to finding a place where I fit in. I'd started doing that in Paris, but maybe I'll never fit anywhere."

They drove awhile in silence. Robin leaned forward slightly in the driver's seat. Her words sank in. They had some things in common.

"I get that. Not the cake part, obviously, but I do feel stuck, you know? Like I never got out from under that log. I want more for my life, but I don't really know what that would be."

"Do you have any ideas?"

He tapped his hands on his knees. "Seth wants me to join his old smoke jumping unit." He snuck a glance at her, but her focus didn't leave the road. "Do you remember Tucker Newman? He runs an outfit in Montana now."

"And how do you feel about that idea?"

"I don't know. I like the idea of using my brawn for good. God made me strong for a reason. Plus, my dad was a firefighter."

"I don't really hear any passion in your voice when you talk about it."

"I'm not sure what else I would do. It's not like I have any other training."

"I think you should work with kids. You light up when you're around them, and you're really helping Ben."

"Uh, I don't think so. I'm just a volunteer. Any permanent job would likely require a college degree, and I'm not interested in going back to school."

They reached Duluth at last. Robin flipped the blinker on, and they drove into the lot for Diner Depot, a restaurant supply store. Its "Open" light shone from the front window, and Robin visibly relaxed. She shut the van off and turned to look at him. "Have you tried praying about it?"

He thought about the wrestling match he'd had with God a few nights ago. "Yeah. I never seem to get any answers though."

She gave him a half smile. "We all feel like that sometimes. I'm sure you'll figure it out."

"Thanks. In the meantime, I had an idea." They got out of the van and walked toward the store. "I'll help out at the bakery."

Robin stopped walking. Stared at him a moment. "But...you don't know anything about bread. Or cake."

"I'm a fast learner. Besides, I've watched you plenty of times. I'm also great at following directions."

Say yes. You know I can do it.

Although, he didn't know why this was so important to him.

He just couldn't stand by and watch the woman he lo— No. It wasn't that, not yet. But he admired her, and he wanted to see her succeed. "Pay me in cupcakes."

"Fine, you're on." Robin held out a mittened hand and shook his. "Welcome to the Fox Bakery team."

They went into the store, and Robin grabbed a basket from a stack near the door. She headed down an aisle marked Baking Supplies and stopped next to the section with yeast. He'd never seen so many choices. Robin chose several foil-wrapped packages and put them in the basket.

"As long as we're here," she said, "I need to grab some gel coloring for frosting. Did I tell you that I'm doing cakes for a wedding and an anniversary within two days of each other?" They walked to the food-coloring aisle, where a rainbow of tints greeted them. Robin put a tube of Grassy Knoll in the shopping basket.

"And you need green? Is it for St. Paddy's Day?"

"Ha! No, both of them have a green-and-blue color scheme, if you can believe it. The anniversary is fifty-five years, which is emerald. And the bride has unique taste. I've actually got the anniversary figured out, but now I need to work on some way to display the ten dozen cupcakes for the wedding."

"What, like a cake stand?" His mind started cataloging the wood he had available in his garage.

"I don't know, maybe? I was thinking about something not quite so traditional."

"I could probably make something."

"You would do that for me?" She turned startled eyes on him.

"Sure, what are friends for?"

Right.

Friends.

Robin tossed a few more items in the basket and then paid for her order. "I'm starving," she said. They walked side by side in the brisk air to the van. "Let's grab dinner before heading home."

Sammy did a quick check of the tires. "The spare still looks fine, but you'll need to replace it in Deep Haven after this long of a drive." He climbed into the passenger seat as Robin fired up the engine. "Want an adventure?"

She glanced sideways at him. "Sure?"

"Let's eat in that rotating restaurant. I've never been there. Have you?"

"I'm game. I've never been there either. Let's do it."

A dark night had fully encompassed them by the time they arrived at the restaurant.

"Whoa. I was not expecting to need sea legs tonight," Robin said as they stepped into the restaurant. Situated at the top of a hotel in the center of Duluth's steep hill of a downtown area, the room was ringed by glass windows. Beneath them, the floor spun slowly.

Sammy laughed. "This will take some getting used to. But the 360-degree view of the harbor will be worth it."

Lights twinkled in from outside. The waiter led them to a table and took their order. They both ordered that evening's special—almond-crusted walleye with a side of mashed potatoes and lingonberry jam.

After the food arrived, Sammy dipped his head and said a quick prayer for their meal.

"Thank you," Robin said. "My grandpa used to pray before every meal, but I've gotten out of the habit."

"I've always admired your grandparents." Sammy took a bite of his walleye. The buttery fish melted in his mouth.

"Yeah, they're pretty great." Robin pushed some potatoes around on her plate. "They're basically the only parents I've known."

Sammy remembered a little of the story. "Your parents died in a boating accident, right?" She nodded, kept her eyes on her plate. "I'm sorry. We don't have to talk about it if it's too much."

"No, that's fine." She put her fork down. "We were out boating on Lake Superior, just off the harbor in Deep Haven, when a storm came up. I don't really know much about boats, but Dad was trying to get us in to shore somehow when Mom was knocked overboard." She hugged her arms around herself. "Dad went in after her but it was too late. Hypothermia. Dad couldn't get back in the boat either. They'd both been pushed too far away by the waves." She unwrapped her arms and went back to playing with her fork.

Sammy reached across and took her hand in his. It was freezing. He held it between his hands, rubbing gently. "That must have been awful."

She looked up, a wetness in her eyes. "It was."

He reached for her other hand, and she placed it in his. "I'm so sorry." Her hands began to warm.

"Thank you. The weight of it isn't so heavy anymore. The grief still hits sometimes, but mostly I remember the good memories."

"So, is that when you moved in with your grandparents?"

Robin gave his hands a squeeze and let go. She picked up her fork and scooped a bite of fish. "No, first we lived with my mom's sister in Madison, Wisconsin."

"It must have been a comfort to live with her."

"You would think, but it didn't turn out that way. She used to get so upset with us for making any kind of a mess. She needed everything to be perfect."

"That would be difficult." He took a long drink of water, the liquid cooling him a little.

"One time I had decided to make an art project and drew a hundred beautiful flowers. Each one was different and colorful. I was so proud of myself."

"Seems like a good thing. You were expressing yourself."

"It was on the wall."

He barked out a laugh. "I'm sorry. I shouldn't laugh. Your aunt must have been livid."

"She was. She yelled about how I was ten years old and should know better than to draw on the walls." The color was high on Robin's cheeks. "She took us straight to my grandparents the next day and dropped us off. She barely said goodbye."

"What a terrible thing to do to a hurting kid."

"I know. I look back now and see that we were a big disruption in her life. She'd just lost a sister and was grieving too. Also, she was a really well-known real estate agent in her area, in high demand. We didn't really fit into her well-ordered life. I tell myself I can give a little grace because she was in a tough spot."

"Life is messy. No getting around that." He took another bite of his food.

"Thanks for listening. I don't talk about that time in my life very much." Robin took a huge bite of potatoes.

"That's what friends are for."

Right. Friends. Tell that to his traitorous heart. Because right now, all he wanted to do was walk around the table and take her in his arms. Whisper in her ear that he would always be a safe place for her to land.

So much for keeping his heart at a distance.

ten

. . .

Robin wished for a moment that she could throw a little tantrum this morning. She stood in the kitchen of the bakery looking at her dead oven—the one that just a few hours ago had been happily pumping out heat and baking bread to a crackling perfection. Now it was cold and dead, like her dreams for this stint in Deep Haven being easy.

After dropping Sammy off at his house last night following their shopping trip and supper in Duluth, she'd come back to the bakery and prepped dough for its overnight proof. She'd been forced to buy a new brand of yeast at the store as her favorite wasn't available, and she'd prayed it would be okay.

When she got to the bakery by four this morning, the bread dough had risen beautifully. The sight of the doming loaves was…perfection. The yeast she'd bought must have been as fresh as they'd advertised on the packaging.

Sweet relief.

Maybe she would recover from her lapse after all. Now she just needed to pass the health inspection scheduled for later that day. She rotated the breads through the baking process, carefully monitoring each bake. After the loaves finished baking, she put them on a rack to cool, listening to them sing and crackle in their signature music.

In celebration, she'd mixed a batch of her grandma's cinnamon coffee cake. Once she'd poured the batter into the pan, she'd swung open the oven.

Which was stone cold.

Now she held herself back from giving it a kick. Who could she call to fix the dumb thing? She knew next to nothing about oven mechanics.

She checked her watch. It was ten a.m. in Cocoa Beach. Even though she didn't want to admit she needed help, she'd have to call her grandparents. She flipped through the book of instructions they'd left for her and spotted a note about the oven. But just then the bell on the front door chimed. She closed the book and went to the front.

With any luck, it would be Sammy, showing up to help her bake as he'd promised. He might even know how to fix the oven.

Hope died a swift death.

A short man, who looked to be about forty, dressed in a suit and tie with an honest-to-goodness trench coat, stood in the dining room. He held a clipboard and was making notes. Must be the health inspector.

Great. Perfect timing.

He walked over to her. "Hi, I'm Dave Stewart." He stuck his hand out and she shook it, his chilly fingers giving her a shiver. Health inspector confirmed.

"Welcome to the Fox Bakery."

"I've actually been here before." His dour expression did not give her any confidence. At least the work Sammy had done in the kitchen was finished. Maybe he wouldn't ask if the oven was functioning. She resisted crossing her fingers behind her back.

"Of course you have." Maybe a dose of charm would help. "You must know my grandparents, Jim and Elaine."

"Yes."

Okay, maybe not.

"I've been in Paris for the past few years, so I'm not sure how an American health inspection works. What would you like me to show you?"

"Just stay out of my way, and I'll ask you questions as I have them."

Hoo boy. Alrighty, then.

She stood back and motioned broadly to the kitchen. "My space is your space."

He jerked a nod and jotted more notes on his clipboard.

She went into the kitchen, covered the coffee cake mix with plastic wrap, and tucked it into the cooler. It wouldn't hurt for it to rest a few hours. If she couldn't figure out how to fix her oven today, she would take the pan home and bake it there.

She flipped back to the oven page in her grandparents' book. Eureka! Grandpa had penciled in a note about needing to replace the wonky heating element. He'd even purchased one before leaving. She prayed Dave would take his time in the front half of the store as she rummaged through the supply closet until she found the electrical piece.

Her heart pounding in her ears, she switched out the heating elements, an uncomplicated process helped along by the illustrated instructions on the package.

Dave took his time examining the front of the store. Then he spent an equally long time looking at the new sink area, even getting on his knees to check the drainage lines. The scratching sound of his pen on the clipboard ran across Robin's nerves.

She busied herself with cleaning the equipment she'd been using for serving the few customers who came in.

When the front door jangled and Sammy came in, something let loose in her chest.

"I'm here for my shift." He smiled at her. "I heard you pay in cupcakes." His waffle-knit, green Henley fit close to his chest, and his jeans topped a pair of sturdy shoes perfect for working in a bakery.

When she walked back to the kitchen, Sammy in tow, Dave

was fiddling with the knobs on her oven. "This doesn't seem to be working."

"I know. It just went out. I finished my bakes for this morning, but just barely. I replaced the element, but haven't turned it on yet."

"I've been telling your grandparents for years that they need to buy a new oven, bring it up-to-date. Elaine kept insisting this one was fine."

She gave a weak laugh. "Sounds like Grandma."

Dave was warming to his topic. "They have so many great ones now. Steam, convection, brick-lined, the list goes on. This one barely passes inspection every year. Tell your grandparents I don't want to see this hunk of junk when I come again next year."

She had to resist looking at Sammy. "I'll tell them."

The inspector flipped the oven knob to Bake before scribbling some more in his notebook.

"I'm glad she finally had the sense to upgrade her sink area. It never sat right with me to write that off every year." The inspector tore a sheet off his notebook and handed it to her. Behind him, a curl of smoke puffed out of the oven. "Here's your copy of my report. You'll have to sign both copies. Keep yours on file."

Robin started to speak.

Then the oven just…exploded.

Behind the glass door, sparks shot from the electrical fitting of the heating element.

With a pop, the glass tube burst into a million bits.

Dave hit the floor like he'd been shot.

Inside the oven, a fire raged, more sparks flying from the element.

"Where's your fire extinguisher?" Sammy yelled.

Mutely, Robin pointed a finger at the cabinet. He dashed to it and yanked the extinguisher from its place.

There was a loud snap, and all the lights in the bakery blinked out.

"I think we blew a breaker." Sammy pushed past Robin and Dave. He tugged the oven door open and sprayed inside, dousing the electrical fire. "Give me a hand here."

Robin joined him, and they pulled the hot oven away from the wall and Sammy pulled the plug. "I think the fire was contained to inside the oven. Must have been a faulty element."

On the floor, Dave groaned. Robin dropped to her knees beside him. "Are you okay?"

He patted his arms and chest. "I guess so. I thought I was a goner for sure." He ran a hand across his face. "I've had some angry owners on the job before, but I've never been afraid for my life until today." He stood, knees visibly trembling. "Obviously, you'll have to get that oven fixed. Or better yet, replace it. I'm going to have to make your inspection provisional. Give me back your copy of the report."

Fleetingly, she thought about hiding the paper behind her back. Gave herself a little shake, then handed it over.

"Sign here, and here." Dave's hand shook as he pointed to the additional lines on the form. She did so quickly, and he grabbed his copy, then pushed out the door without looking back.

Robin finally looked at Sammy. She couldn't hold back the nervous laughter anymore. They both erupted. "That was... something else." She wiped a tear from the corner of her eye. Suddenly her knees gave out, and she braced herself against the counter. "I thought the inspector was bad enough. Then the oven...talk about going out with a bang. I sure made an impression."

"You did great," he said. "Want me to look at this oven? I can check it more closely if you want."

"That would be great. I'll figure out how to reset the electrical breaker for the building." She grabbed the binder again and flipped to the correct page. "I hope it was just the heating element. I really should think about buying a new oven, but the bakery can't afford to spend several thousand dollars right now. I'm just glad it broke after I finished baking for the morning. Well, almost finished. I have a pan of coffee cake I'd hoped to bake." She realized she was babbling, but the release of shock kept her mouth moving.

"We can't have a good coffee cake go to waste. Let me see what I can do."

Before she could protest—but really, was she going to?— Sammy slipped out of his jacket and tugged the huge oven a few more inches away from the wall. He poked around for a few moments. She found the instructions for resetting the breaker, and soon she got the lights on again.

"I'm going to need my tools." Sammy passed by her and out to his bike. A waft of his aftershave tightened her belly. Sammy sure had smelling good going for him.

She came back in and tried to stay occupied as he tinkered with the inner workings of the oven, but the bakery remained quiet, and there was only so much busywork she could do. The bakery was strangely devoid of customers, so she didn't even have sales to distract her. She found herself staring at Sammy's green Henley, slim jeans, and broad shoulders more often than she would like to admit.

What if he couldn't get the oven fixed? Did needing a new oven count as an emergency? Maybe she should be calling her grandparents. She drummed her fingers on the worktop.

Sammy pushed the oven back toward the wall. He dusted his hands together. "I think I got it now. I put the old heating element back in, and the oven is turning on. This happens sometimes when the element doesn't quite fit correctly. This will only be temporary, though. It looks like you will either need all new parts or an all-new oven."

"That's what everyone keeps telling me." A tight muscle in her back loosened. One problem postponed.

"Do you have a ShopVac somewhere? I'll clean out this glass and get it back in service."

Robin helped Sammy clean out the oven and the powder from the fire extinguisher. "Thank you, Sam," she said. "You have an uncanny knack for walking in right when I need you."

He looked into her eyes. "I have a Spidey sense for when you need my special skills."

Gulp. Was it hot in here? Must be the oven's preheat cycle. "Should we start on the next batch of bread?"

"Yep. It's baguette day, right?"

"You're in luck. I finished those before the oven conked out. You won't have to learn the trickiest bread to make until another day. Let me get this coffee cake in first." She slid the pan into the now-hot oven. "It should be ready just in time for a break. We'll share a slice." Wasn't she supposed to be cooling things off between them? Offering a man her fresh-baked goods was not cooling off. But what was she supposed to do when he kept rescuing her?

"Sounds like a plan."

"We make a good team—as friends, I mean." She couldn't look him in the eye.

"Right." His voice was flat.

Rats. But that's what she wanted, right?

SAMMY MADE HIS LAST DELIVERY AND TOOK A DEEP BREATH. THE heaviness in his chest stayed put. He checked his watch. Time for him to get to the youth center. He'd promised to be the judge for a Ping-Pong tournament after school today.

The trip to Duluth on Sunday with Robin hadn't felt like a drive between friends. And when they'd baked bread together yesterday, he'd kept being reminded of how he and Robin could work well together. They had an easy friendship that wouldn't take much fanning to blaze into love. And then at the bank, Fran Turner had said something about building a home with the rest of his money.

He'd tossed and turned all last night. Not with a nightmare this time, but fighting off dreams of a snug log cabin, his arm around Robin in front of a roaring fire. He still had the land outside of town even though Nathan Decker kept pestering him to sell.

A nice dream, but the conversation at the bakery threw cold water all over his passion. *As friends, I mean.* Robin's words stuck in his mind like a stubborn knot in a piece of wood marring the surface.

He swung a leg over his bike and pushed off, his gloves gripping the handles. The late, bright sun warmed his face. As he rode to the youth center, he dodged here and there, avoiding the snow that had melted into slush piles. The warm spell wouldn't last, but it was nice while it was here.

He coasted into the driveway of the youth center as a minivan pulled in. Ronnie Dahlquist, her husband Peter, with his distinctive dark hair and beard, and her brother Tiago piled out.

"Hi, Mr. Johnson," Tiago called and then raced for the front door.

"T! Manners!" Ronnie called after him. Ronnie wore her long hair pulled up in a high ponytail. The Latina woman was good for Peter Dahlquist. She kept him on his toes.

"It's no problem." Sammy wheeled his bike into place in the fish-shaped rack he'd built last fall after the old one had fallen apart. Scales formed the slats for the bike tires, and he'd given the whole thing several layers of sealant until it shone.

He walked with Ronnie to the door. "Are you here for the Ping-Pong tournament?"

Ronnie pushed the door to the building open and held it for him. "Yes, Tiago has been talking about it for a week. This place has been so good for him."

"He's a good kid." Ronnie's kid brother was quickly becoming a favorite at the youth center. Gangly and tall with a mop of dark hair, Tiago was working to fit in. He was always quick to help. And if he was sometimes also too quick with a joke during a serious moment, he could be forgiven for that. Sammy was often accused of the same thing. "I'm glad the center exists for kids like him. And for the many others who need a place to go."

Ronnie nodded. "Too bad the town can't get someone to manage it full-time. A real director and a consistent schedule would mean so much to so many kids."

Sammy agreed. But... "It's gotta be hard to find the right person. Wouldn't they need a degree and specialized training?"

"I don't see why they would. They'd maybe need some background checks and a love for teenagers, but they shouldn't need a degree. A willingness to work for peanuts and a deep enjoyment for working with teenagers would be harder to come by."

Plus, they'd have to want to live in Deep Haven, Sammy thought.

Though, who wouldn't be attracted to the small town together with its quirks and blessings? Sammy believed it was the best place to settle down and raise a family. When he'd been young and fatherless, the people of Deep Haven had been a family to him. He wanted that safety for his own kids.

He realized Ronnie was looking at him, waiting for a reply. "Teens aren't so bad. They just need a listening ear and someone who sees that their problems may not be huge to adults but they're the whole world to a kid."

"I don't know how you do it. I always have to count to ten and back when Tig answers me with a grunt instead of actual words."

Sammy laughed. "If that's the worst thing he does, I'd say you're doing pretty well."

Ronnie crossed her arms and nodded affectionately at Tiago,

who'd picked up a paddle and was hitting a Ping-Pong ball in the air. "Since we came to Deep Haven—well, after we settled in—he's been like a whole new kid, ya know? I was worried my marriage to Peter would upset his balance, but he seems to thrive in our new little family." Across from Tiago, Peter—still in his fireman's uniform—had picked up a paddle and was challenging the boy to a contest. The two laughed as they tried to outdo each other in bouncing the ball on their paddles.

"Seventeen!" Tiago crowed. "Beat you by a mile."

Peter slung an arm around the boy. "Nicely done. You're going to need all those skills in a few minutes."

Just then the door opened and more kids streamed in, laughing and jostling each other. The school bus must have let a bunch of them off at the corner. A blast of cold air came in with them. Sammy heard the new furnace cycle on to combat the cold.

Sammy clapped his hands together to grab everyone's attention. "All right, everyone! Let's get this show on the road."

The tournament proceeded round-robin style, with each kid having a chance to participate. Shortly after the games began, Vivien and Boone showed up and joined the adults in cheering, refereeing, and keeping score.

The mood of the group was generally good-natured, but Sammy intervened once when one kid accused another of cheating.

Once the tournament was over and most of the kids had gone home, Sammy walked Boone and Vivien to the door. "Thanks again for showing up." Sammy clapped Boone on the back.

"No problem. We believe in this place too." Boone tugged a knit cap over his blond hair, and Vivien looped her arm through his.

"You did a great job with these kids." Her deep-blue eyes flashed with humor. "You're almost dad-like in your ability to make bad jokes."

"Hey, don't knock my skills." Sammy tucked his hands into his pockets. Behind them, he heard Tiago challenging Ronnie to one last game. "See ya later." Sammy made sure the door was shut securely behind Boone and Vivien, then joined Peter on a couch.

And promptly sank almost to the floor.

"There's nothing left of the springs in this thing," Peter said. "I should have warned you."

Sammy adjusted himself in his seat. "Yeah, they're kind of all like this. We could use some better furniture, but I think people are reluctant to give the good stuff to a bunch of kids."

"I noticed you're not afraid of giving good stuff."

Had Peter found out his secret? "What do you mean?"

Peter watched Ronnie serve, and when Tiago couldn't return the Ping-Pong ball, she did a little dance and crowed. "Just that you're always willing to step up and help out. You don't hold anything back. I admire that in a person. You've always been that way."

"Thanks, I guess."

"Like on the football team. I know the linemen don't get a lot of credit, but you were always there to take a hit so the team could score. Anyway, not trying to get all sappy or whatever. Just thought you might appreciate knowing someone noticed."

Sammy cleared a sudden tightness in his throat. "Thanks." He stood. "Want a soda? I've got Cherry Coke in the mini-fridge."

"Sounds great."

Walking to the fridge gave Sammy a minute to think. New furniture for the youth center should be a priority. He wondered where he could find durable quality stuff that would hold up to the beating it would get from the teens.

He grabbed the Cokes and a folding chair, unwilling to brave that couch again. "Here ya go."

They popped their drinks, and for a few beats the only sound was the *thwack* of the Ping-Pong paddle against the ball.

"It's fun to see you as a family man," Sammy remarked.

Peter scrubbed a hand through his hair. "I never knew life

could be this great. I've always loved living in Deep Haven, but having a family too—man, it's amazing."

"I've always dreamed of building a life and family for myself here too. Even when I was in the Army, I pictured coming back here, starting a life. Maybe getting married, having a bunch of kids."

"That's the dream, man."

"And now you're living it."

They both swigged back a drink.

"Attaboy, Tig," Peter called out. "Take 'er down."

Ronnie put her hands on her hips. "Hey! Whose side are you on?" The smile spreading across her face told them she wasn't really offended.

When the players went back to their game, Peter spoke up again. "Last I heard you were looking to find some of that dream at a certain bakery." That last part said oh-so-casually.

Sammy slammed back the last of his beverage, the sweet fizz tickling his nose, irritating it. "Yeah, I'd hoped so too. But she's not interested."

"She's not interested, or you're not taking the leap?"

Sammy shot his friend a look. He'd hit close to the mark. "I'm not a coward." At least, not when it came to a certain auburn-haired baker.

Peter held up his hands. "I'm not saying you are. But one thing I've learned from Ronnie is that you can't just expect people to know what you're thinking. You gotta tell them. Be vulnerable once in a while."

Okay, maybe he was a coward. Because right now, telling Robin how he was feeling was the scariest idea in the world. "I don't know. She was pretty set on us being just friends. She's got the bakery to run. And she wants to move back to Paris ASAP."

"I don't have all the answers. I'm just saying if you want to have a sure thing, you gotta lay it all on the line." Peter finished his drink, crushed the can, and threw it to the garbage can in the corner. It fell in with a rattle. "Two points!" Then he laughed.

"But what do I know? I'm no expert. I haven't been married long enough."

Peter hefted himself out of the saggy couch and crossed over to Ronnie and Tiago. He gave them each a high five before swinging Ronnie into an exuberant hug.

Sammy's heart squeezed. He let out a long breath. Then waved goodbye to the family.

He wanted that someday.

Maybe even wanted it with Robin.

But he'd learned the hard way that he didn't get what he wanted.

Not, at least, without a fight.

eleven

. . .

Robin had spent the last few days praying her grandma's ancient oven would hold, and it had. Now it was Friday, and two workmen had shown up in an Anderson Equipment truck to deliver an oven.

"What oven?" Robin said.

The driver consulted his clipboard. "Looks like a MIWE Cube:stone and MIWE Cube:air combo."

The oven she could only dream about.

"But I didn't order an oven." She crossed her arms.

"It says here you did." The driver showed her the clipboard. Sure enough, under the line for Buyer it said Fox Bakery.

"There must be some mistake." She checked the phone number for the company and called them from the kitchen. The rep she talked to assured her that the oven was ordered and paid for.

"If that isn't the oven you want, we can make it right," the rep said. "We can exchange it for another one. It was a rush order, so if you've changed your mind…"

"No, I'll take it. I just don't know how it ended up here. Who does it say ordered it?"

"I can't tell you that, ma'am."

"I suppose those things are confidential, but it's my bakery. I'm the only one who could order it. Unless, did an Elaine or Jim Fox call?"

"No, it's not for confidentiality. I've never seen this before, but the order says 'Anonymous.' I guess you just have an enthusiastic fan."

A very enthusiastic fan. This model was top of the line. In fact, it was the very model she'd been drooling over ever since attending a baking trade show in Germany. Victor had taken her there but had been absent most of the time. She shook off that thought and concentrated on the part of the memory where she'd attended a baking demonstration with the oven model now being connected in her kitchen.

It was a modular rack system with a normal convection-style oven on top, and several rack layers of brick-lined oven on the bottom. She'd be able to bake cakes and bread at the same time and at different temps.

She leaned against the counter and watched as the workmen finished up, thinking of the recipe she wanted to try first. In Paris she had been working on perfecting a complicated baguette but hadn't returned to it. The oven here had been great for simple breads, but anything that required a specialized baking process had been a no go.

Even Grandma Elaine couldn't argue with a change like this one.

The men cleared away the packaging, and one of them handed her the owner's manual.

"The warranty information is in the back," he said. "You'll want to register the machine right away. You should be good to go, but if you have any troubles, there's a help line number in there too."

She thanked him and walked with them to the door. She'd flipped the Open sign off when the men arrived, and she turned it back on now. Wendy wouldn't be here today, and she hadn't thought she could handle customers while the kitchen was in disarray.

Out in the parking lot, a plow truck scraped away the inch of snow that had accumulated during the night. A light snow was still falling, and that stray black-and-white cat was out scampering in it.

She turned back to the kitchen. Opening the manual, she began the process of firing up the new oven. The front doorbell dinged. "Be right with you!"

A moment later the kitchen door swung open. "I hope you don't mind if I let myself back here. I'm here for my shift."

Sammy. He had little snowflakes clinging to his hair and scruffy cheeks, a dusting across his shoulders. They glinted in the light, giving him a sparkle.

"I don't mind at all." Robin gestured to the oven, which now put out a radiant heat. Or maybe that was her heart, which had begun beating a step or two faster. "Look at what was just delivered this morning."

"Hey! Look at that! A working oven." He walked toward it. "I hope you don't get in trouble with Grandma Elaine."

"I think she'll come around. Look! It's brick lined—perfect for those dark crusts you get on European breads. If that doesn't win her over, nothing will."

"What about this top part—is it a convection oven?"

How did he know about that?

She searched his face. As she stared at him, he began to blush and wouldn't meet her eyes. Then she remembered the strange conversation about her oven catalog. "Sammy Johnson, what do you know about this oven?"

He shrugged. "I'm no oven expert."

"That's not what I meant, and you know it. Do you know how this oven got here? My dream oven? The oven I've been drooling over for a year? The perfect oven for bread *and* cake?"

He widened his eyes. "Dream oven?"

"Don't lie to me." Robin propped her hands on her hips. "I

can see right through your innocent act. Did you call my grandparents or something?"

He held up his hands in surrender. "Okay. I don't want to lie to you. Ever. That day I saw the catalog on your desk, I noticed which one seemed to be your favorite. Then when your old oven went kaput, I bought this one for you."

Robin was aware that her mouth had dropped open. She stared at him, a roaring in her ears. "You bought me an oven?" Even after she had rejected him, the man had bought her an oven?

"You needed it." He spread his hands wide. "What you do here is art. I couldn't let you continue creating without the best tools."

"You bought me an oven?" She tried to get her mouth to say something else, but her brain wouldn't cooperate.

"Did I do something wrong?"

"Not at all. This is—" She ran a hand through her hair. "At the risk of sounding trite, this is the nicest thing anyone has ever done for me. No one has ever believed in me this much."

"I think what you do is amazing." He took off his jacket and laid it on the counter. Underneath his jacket he wore a white Henley. The water droplets still twinkled in his hair. He met her eyes, his green ones intense. "I think you are amazing. I know I shouldn't say stuff like that—just friends and everything. But, as your friend, I think you're incredible."

He thought she was incredible? Except, "Wait. I thought you were broke."

He lifted one shoulder, let it drop. "I came into some money and wanted to put it to good use." He gestured at the oven. "Yeah, I'd hoped to be anonymous because I didn't want you to feel like you had to give anything in return or that I was pressuring you somehow. But I also will never lie to you."

All her reasons for avoiding a relationship faded in the light of that level of support. Her mind shuffled through what she knew of Sammy. He was kind, thoughtful, and obviously generous.

She was falling for him. Hard.

She crossed the few steps to him and laid her hand on his arm, his Henley rough under her fingertips. "So, what—you think you're my own personal hero?"

"Maybe. If you let me." His eyes held a question.

Her mouth dried. She tried to swallow and failed.

"Right." Sammy clapped his hands together, the sound sharp in the quiet room. "What are we baking today?"

She blinked. Tried to come back to the moment. "Um, brioche?" Plus she had to start making a plan for the cakes she'd need to make over the weekend. The Adamses' party was Sunday, and the Lindstrom wedding a mere two days after that.

"Don't ask me, I'm just the assistant." Sammy half shrugged. He went to the sink and washed up. "Just point me to a recipe and some ingredients. I'm all yours for the next few hours."

Robin showed him how to mix the dough for the sweet brioche. After it rose she would show him how to braid ropy strands of the dough into a long oval loaf. Some of the dough she would turn into chocolate-filled buns.

Meanwhile, she got to work on starting what she needed for the baguettes. She imagined baking them in the new oven and their crispy crusts when she pulled them out.

An alarm blared.

Robin jumped and looked around in confusion.

"I think your oven is telling you it's preheated." Sammy's slow drawl stopped just short of being a tease. He gestured with his chin toward the digital display.

Ready scrolled in red across the top oven. Robin put a hand to her chest. "I think I'm going to need to check the manual. Surely there's a way we can turn that down."

"Do you want to try it out? Do you have anything you can bake right now?"

"Um, *of course* I want to try it out." She walked to the rack where she had a few simple loaves of white bread proofing. "I've been sticking to simple since you replaced the heating element in Grandma's oven. I didn't know if I would have to take anything back to the house to bake." It seemed a shame for the inaugural bake in this amazing oven to be something so simple as a sandwich loaf.

"I hope today you can pay me in bread instead of cupcakes, because those loaves are works of art."

Yeah, right. "Sammy. These are just normal loaves of bread." She hadn't even carved anything into the top to make a pattern as they baked. "There's nothing special about them." But she had felt a certain kinship with her grandma as she'd shaped each loaf. Maybe bread could be satisfying.

"I guess it's all in how you look at them," Sammy said. "To me they are amazing because I wouldn't even know where to begin. You created them from a little flour, water, and yeast. Amazing."

His words sank deep. To be seen by Sammy sent a tingle down her spine.

I'm all yours... Sure, he'd meant he was available to help her bake. But what if it could turn into something more?

Maybe moving back to Paris wasn't the greatest idea.

Maybe she could find a place to belong in Deep Haven after all.

꽃꽃꽃

SAMMY INHALED THE SWEET, EARTHY SMELL OF THE BAKERY. THESE baking days with Robin were starting to feel more like dates than work.

You think you're my own personal hero? Yeah, he hoped he could be that for her. And more. Too bad she was leaving. Maybe he needed to think harder about smoke jumping with Tucker.

Staying in Deep Haven without Robin seemed like a bad idea. It would feel less like home without her.

If he left, though, he'd give up his dream of building that house on his property and starting a family in the town that he loved. Not to mention letting down the kids who depended on him at the youth center.

The bell on the front door jangled.

"I'll be right back," Robin said. She tugged at the hem of her shirt. Patted her cheeks a few times, pasted on a smile, and pushed through the swinging door. "Hello, Colleen," he heard her call.

The oven chimed. *Timer Ended* scrolled across the LED display. Sammy walked over and opened the oven door. Six loaves nestled inside, their tops browned. He slid them out and onto a waiting cooling rack. Each one was smooth and even. Perfect.

Robin made things beautiful.

He finished the brioche dough and set it aside for Robin's approval. He heard her laughter ring out in the next room. Probably he should check out the sink area, make sure everything was still looking good.

After inspecting the tile, Sammy checked his watch. Oops, he was due to make a delivery for Ella Vassos in five minutes. She needed him to run some of her soaps to Lena's veterinarian clinic. Ella had developed a line that was safe to use for pets, and Lena had promised her some shelf space.

Grabbing his jacket from the counter, he walked out to the dining area. Colleen was on the other side of the counter. She stopped whatever she was saying and looked pointedly at him, then cocked an eyebrow at Robin, who was ringing up her order at the register. Robin appeared to be trying hard to ignore the hints Colleen was sending.

"Sammy Johnson. So good to see you here. With Robin," Colleen said, innocent eyes wide.

Sammy knew he was smiling like an idiot, but those words lit something inside him he hadn't known had gone out. He was with Robin. He wanted to gather those words and tattoo them on his chest.

"I was helping Robin with something in the kitchen."

A knowing smile crossed Colleen lips. "I just bet you were." And then she winked.

Across the bakery display, Robin blushed a bright pink.

What exactly was going on here?

"Sammy, I told Colleen that you have been helping out."

"Oh, so you've been talking about me?" He sure loved to tease Robin. Her face grew even more red.

"Well, I showed her the kitchen earlier." Robin handed Colleen her bag of bread, not meeting Sammy's eye.

Colleen tucked the bag in the crook of her arm and walked toward the door. In a singsong voice, she called over her shoulder, "Enjoy your kitchen work, you two."

Sammy turned to Robin. "What was that?"

"Um…" The contents of the display case must have been super interesting, because Robin kept fiddling with them as she spoke. "I might have kind of told Colleen that I was attracted to you."

Had he really been in the kitchen that long? "Just now?"

"Wellll…" She still wouldn't meet his eyes. "It was last week when she came by."

He couldn't help the belly laugh that sentence created in him. "I'm glad to know the feeling wasn't one-sided all this time." He crossed his arms and leaned against the glass case. "Listen, I don't have long to stay, but I have to know. After the dance you said you don't want a relationship, that you are leaving. Have you changed your mind?"

She pushed an errant hair off her face. He loved that she still looked a little mussed, off-balance. "It was something Colleen said, actually. I couldn't shake her words. She told me that life is always messy, and that there is never a perfect time to fall in love."

God bless Colleen Decker. "Is that what's happening here? Are we falling in love?" He grasped her chin and tipped her face up to his.

"I...I don't know." Her voice wasn't any louder than a breath. "I still want to go back to Paris. I don't think it's fair to you to not be honest about that."

He rubbed her cheek with his thumb. "Thanks for your honesty." He sighed and dropped his hand. "I have to go. Ella is expecting me over at Essentially Ella's in a few minutes. But we need to talk more about that soon." Stepping away felt like he had torn himself into two pieces.

"I'd like that."

He slid into his jacket and stepped toward the door.

"Wait!" Robin came around from the display case and slipped something into his pocket. "A treat for later. I know it's not your regular day to help me out, but will you come and help me with the Adamses' anniversary cake on Sunday?"

Heat flooded him. "You betcha. I definitely will."

Outside, the snow still fell in tiny flakes.

He pedaled toward Essentially Ella's, his thoughts a tangled mess.

He was at a crossroads. Should he sign on with Tucker Newman and become a high-stakes smoke jumper? The alpha male in him stood to attention when he thought about this path. And if Robin really was going back to Paris, he needed something to do where he didn't drive by the bakery every day and think about what might have been.

There was a tug in his spirit toward Deep Haven. He pictured himself staying. Really building a life here, joining in instead of remaining on the sidelines.

Not to mention whatever was developing with Robin. He was reluctant to leave her, to ask her to wait or to leave the business that meant so much to her. And what about his volunteer hours at the youth center? Those kids meant a lot to him.

But what kind of job was there for him here?

All he knew was truck driving and odd jobs. Those things were fine, a great career even, for others. But he was searching for something more. Something meaningful.

What would God call him to?

He steered his bike up to the building housing the Footstep of Heaven and Essentially Ella's. The house used to be a home and now had been converted into two commercial spaces. The bookstore occupied one half and the soap shop the other. Ella Vassos used to live above her shop before she married her husband, former playboy and millionaire Adrian Vassos. The two had built a home nearby and, as far as he knew, the apartment over the store was currently empty.

Walking into Essentially Ella's was a new experience each time. Ella made most of her product in the back room, and whatever scent she was working with permeated the air. Some days it smelled like the ocean, some days like the piney woods of the north. Today, she must have been working on a Valentine's Day product, because a distinct scent of rose-and-chocolate drifted over him.

Ella came out from the back room, wiping her hands on a towel. "Ah! Sammy. Good to see you. I have the delivery boxed up right here." She rested a hand on a large box on the counter. "Is this too big for your bike?"

"Nope. That will fit fine." He thought about the construction supplies he'd strapped on for Robin and bit back a smile. He'd loved the look on her face when she realized he'd carried all of that on his bike. "Straight to Pet Haven Veterinarian Clinic? Or do you want it delivered to Lena's home?"

"The clinic please. Thanks for doing this. I'm so swamped I barely have time to make dinner, let alone deliveries." Ella reached up and secured her blonde hair into a ponytail. "How are you these days?"

"I'm doing fine. Can't complain." He lifted the box off the counter. "Need me to drop anything off at the post office?"

Along with her storefront here in Deep Haven, Ella ran a web store for her product.

"Adrian took that for me yesterday."

"Did I hear my name?" Adrian came out from the workroom at the back of the store, his long hair pulled back, an apron over his dress shirt and chinos. The apron read *Make Soap Not War*.

"I was just saying you went to the post office yesterday." She turned back to Sammy. "Thanks for taking this to Lena. I wasn't going to make it there today, and I know she has clinic hours right now. All those prospective clients." Ella smiled.

Adrian put an arm around Ella. "When I was at the post office I heard that someone donated all the funds to buy costumes for the community theater's spring play."

Sammy stilled. His hands heated.

Ella smiled up at her husband. "I accused him of buying them since I had told Adrian about the need last week when I came back from practice. But he swears it wasn't him."

Adrian threw his hands in the air. "Why would I come home and tell you about it like that?"

She winked at him. "Maybe your ego needed a boost."

"Babe."

"Okay, fine. It's just hard to picture other people here in Deep Haven having the kind of money to just drop on something like that." Ella looked to Sammy as if to have him confirm her thoughts. He was saved from offering an opinion as Adrian offered one of his own.

"Maybe one of the Blue Ox guys was responsible." Adrian took off the apron around his waist and wadded it into a ball. "A lot of those guys have local connections. Maybe they heard about the need and decided to give back to the place that's given to them."

Ella shrugged. "You're probably right."

The tension in Sammy's shoulders loosened. It seemed his secret was still safe. But...something didn't sit right with him. An annoying itch at the thought that no one even considered him a possibility. That they took him for granted. He cleared his throat. "I've got to get going."

"Let me get the door for you." Adrian stepped around him to hold open the door.

The cold air was a slap in the face. A hint of the rose-and-chocolate scent of Ella's store followed him to the sidewalk.

Sammy strapped the box into his delivery basket. Before he could take off, his cell chirped and he dug it out of his jacket pocket. "Vivien. Hi!" He pictured the dark-haired woman on the other end of the line.

"Hey, Sammy. I'm calling because something needs to be done about the youth center."

"Did the furnace go out again? I thought the unit was top of the line."

"The furnace is fine. What I'm talking about is consistency."

"Hold on a sec. I'm transferring to earbuds." He popped his earbuds in and picked up the call again, slipping his phone into his pocket. "Are you still there?"

"Still here. Are you on a job?"

"Yes, but I can talk and ride."

"Good. Here's what I'm thinking," Vivie gushed. "What we need is a full-time director. Someone who is in charge of recruiting volunteers and raising money and stuff like that. They wouldn't need to do all the work, just help keep it all organized."

Sammy smiled at her enthusiasm. If anyone could get it done, it was Vivie. "This all sounds good, but we can't afford to hire a director."

"I've been thinking about that too. There must be grants and things out there that could help. Maybe we should have a bake sale."

"I'm not sure about the bake sale." Though, enlisting a certain baker for help wouldn't be a hardship. "But I like the idea of looking into grants for the position."

"Right? This could really work."

"I'll be excited to see you as director." Maybe this could be a partial answer to his prayers about joining up with Tucker. He'd be leaving the youth center in capable hands.

"What? No. I don't have time for that. I was thinking of you for the director."

He almost drove his bike off the road. "Me? I don't think so."

"Why not? You'd be perfect. You're good with the kids. You're obviously organized. Your work ethic is an inspiration. A side benefit is we all know you can fix whatever breaks in that old building."

He let her words wind through him. He was an inspiration? Maybe he'd been saved for a reason after all.

Except—

"I don't have any qualifications. I didn't even go to college."

"Pfft." He imagined her waving his words away. "College isn't the only way to learn what we need to know in life. What you have to offer is bigger than a college degree."

"We don't even know if we will get the funding." But in the back of his mind, he was already thinking about the money he still had in the bank. Maybe he could set up a trust to support the youth center. Would that be a conflict of interest?

"We'll figure something out. It's too important not to. Just promise me you will think about it."

"I promise."

In fact, he probably wouldn't be able to stop thinking about it. He pictured the log cabin he'd once dreamt of building. If he stayed, he could revisit those plans.

Maybe he and Robin could figure out a way to expand her grandparents' bakery so she could keep creating her cakes.

Maybe she wouldn't have to leave to find a place for herself.

She could find it with him.

twelve

. . .

Robin stood at the worktable in the bakery kitchen, finishing up the Adamses' anniversary cake. After church this morning and grabbing a quick lunch with Sammy at the Trailside Bistro, they came back to the bakery. Everything was going according to her schedule. The cakes were baked on Friday with help from that gorgeous new oven, and she'd mixed the frosting and fondant yesterday. Today they only needed to do the decorating and delivery.

A spike of electricity lit her spine. Her cake needed to be perfect. She tried to absorb some of Sammy's calm as he worked beside her.

She could get used to having a partner. A real partner—one who didn't criticize her every choice or complicate her life.

She marveled at the ease of being with Sammy. He was nothing like Victor. Nothing like any of the guys she'd been around, really. In the food industry, guys were often prima donnas like Victor, and any woman with a little talent threatened them, or they were partyers, hitting the club scene after every shift.

She wanted neither of those things.

Sammy had taught her that men could be kind, generous,

unthreatened by a strong woman, and still look hot in a basic pair of blue jeans and a Henley shirt with the sleeves rolled up.

In fact, she was finding it hard to concentrate when that same man—whose eyes were even more attractive than the corded muscles of his exposed forearms—was standing at the counter next to her.

"Yesterday with the kids was pretty great," he said. "Who knew a bunch of teenagers would be into baking bread?"

They'd spent part of the day teaching a group of kids to bake mini bread loaves at the youth center. It had been fun to watch Sammy interact with the group, alternately joking with them and guiding them as they worked with the dough. During pauses in the baking process, she and Sammy had taken turns helping the teens with their homework and studying for tests.

She paused in the swirl motion she made on the cake and looked up at him. "I know, right? I think they are hungry—pardon the pun—for real things in their life. They're tired of just interacting on screens all the time. You're doing great things up at that youth center." He'd pushed her out of her comfort zone, and she'd loved every minute.

A funny expression passed over Sammy's face.

She put the pastry bag down on the table. "What is it?"

"Vivien asked me if I would consider being the director." Sammy ran a hand across the back of his neck. "They're looking to hire someone full time, to really give their whole attention to running that place."

"What? Sammy, that's awesome. You'd be great at that." Robin's heart twisted.

Sammy braced his hands on the counter behind him. "It would mean a commitment. Staying in Deep Haven."

"So, no smoke jumping, then?" She didn't know if she was happy about that or not. She picked up the pastry bag and started making more swirls. "Are you sure you'd want to give up that opportunity?"

"I'm not sure of anything right now. Not my job, not my future…not you."

She met his eyes. A frisson of electricity spun down her spine.

A blob of frosting oozed out of the tip of the pastry bag. *Focus, girl. This cake means everything right now.* If she didn't get it right, she wouldn't get featured in the magazine. She quite literally couldn't afford to screw this up.

"I know we need to have that conversation, but right now I really need to concentrate on this project." She cleaned up the dripped spot of green frosting. "I'm sorry. I'm not trying to lead you on."

Sammy's face softened. "I get it, Robin. No pressure here. I want this cake to be a success. We'll talk when you're ready."

The tightness in her shoulders eased as she layered on another emerald swirl. The cake was three tiers, starting with a white fondant base with a modern emerald and sapphire pattern swirling around it. The second layer, which she'd just completed, was a solid emerald fondant dotted with gold frosting. And the third layer, which stood on pillars and would be put into place at the venue, featured a marbled agate effect using mainly emerald and sapphire accents with hints of gold throughout.

Sammy took a step closer to her. "Tell me about your favorite culinary school achievement."

"That was, like, ten years ago." She kept her eyes on the cake. If she looked up now, she'd be distracted for sure.

"Come on. I bet you have at least one story you still think about."

"Okay," she said. "Once we had a challenge to make a cake that looked like something real. We had to choose something non-cakey and then shape and paint a cake to look like that thing."

"Sure, I've seen photos and videos of that kind of thing online. It's all cake, right?"

"Right. So, my professor had a favorite metal water bottle he brought to class every day. I figured I would make a cake that matched the water bottle." She swirled on the next two embellishments. "I snuck a bunch of pictures of his water bottle and worked on the project after hours so he wouldn't know. I painted it right down to the long, jagged scratch on the side. Then I'm afraid I did something rather sneaky."

"Straight-A Robin did something sneaky?" Sammy pantomimed being shocked.

She leaned forward, lowered her voice. "I stole his water bottle."

"Okaaay…" He drew the word out. "Doesn't sound like you, but I'll suspend my disbelief."

"I gave it back, I swear." She held her hand up, Scout's honor style. "I finished my cake and put it on the workbench Chef Paul usually used."

"Now I see where this is going."

"Right. The next day, Chef Paul came in and cried out 'My water bottle!' Then he tried to drink my cake." She grinned at him. "Best. Day. Ever."

"I can see it now."

Her phone pinged and she glanced at the screen. Jean Adams had texted her a photo of the table they had set up for her cake.

JEAN

Ready and waiting. See you in a few hours.

She pulled off her gloves and texted back.

ROBIN

Looks great! Do you have your own cake knife and server?

Those pieces of silverware were often overlooked at a party.

Instead of a typed reply, Jean sent back a picture of herself and Palmer dueling with the implements.

She laughed and showed it to Sammy. "These two are a hoot. I hope I'm as happy as they are when I reach fifty-five years of marriage." She looked at Sammy, whose gaze was so intense she had to turn away.

Wowza. Working in the kitchen with Sammy brought a new meaning to the old "if you can't stand the heat" proverb.

She concentrated on putting on a new pair of gloves and breathing deeply. "I'll put the last few swirls on this layer, then the whole thing needs to set for a short time before we move it."

"Roger that."

Yeah, making cakes without those green eyes watching her would be a whole lot easier, but definitely a whole lot less fun.

She finished the cake and carefully stacked the smaller middle portion on top of the bottom one. Using a pastry bag fitted with a star tip, she piped frosting around the edge where the two cakes met, covering up the cracks. From the cooler she retrieved the "Cheers to 55 years!" design she'd piped out of white chocolate the day before. The chocolate was now firm and attached vertically to two toothpicks. Using gold leaf, she covered the chocolate until it gleamed. Holding her breath, she inserted the toothpicks into the bottom layer of the cake so that the words stood up and out just a little from the second layer.

"Wow. That looks amazing. What you do is incredible." Sammy gave her a slow clap of the hands. "Let me snap a photo."

"It's not finished yet." But he didn't listen to her protest as he aimed his smartphone at the cake and took a few pictures. She dusted her hands together. "Okay, now I just need to put together my emergency box while the frosting firms up a little."

Sammy found the tote she'd used for the Snowball Dance and handed it over for her to fill. She packaged up the leftover frosting to use for any damage or other issues that arose during the drive to the Adamses' party. She also put some extra fondant, a palette knife, and extra gold leaf into the tote. Like the Boy Scouts, she wanted to be prepared.

"Let me help you load this in the van, then you can get cleaned up before it's time to go."

Pleasure wrapped Robin's heart as Sammy lifted the bottom two layers of cake in his capable hands. "I'll hold the doors and show you where to put it."

They walked in tandem to the delivery van. Beneath their feet the pavement glistened with a hint of ice, and overhead the sun cast reds and golds into the sky.

By her calculations she would be two hours early, which in her book was right on time. She wondered what time the photographer would arrive. If her cake made it into the magazine, maybe her agate pattern would catch on and be in demand.

She might even have to figure out how to ship cakes.

She reached the van first and pulled open the back doors. The cargo space acted as a perfect place to transport cakes. She laid down a grippy cabinet liner on the floor to help keep the cake from sliding around during the trip on the winding Deep Haven roads.

"Did I tell you there will be a magazine photographer there?"

"Only about a hundred times. I figure I have about a hundred more before I'll need to ask you to stop."

Sammy's teasing chased the chilled February air right out of her.

"It's just a big deal for me, you know? A photo in the magazine could lead to more business. More business puts Fox Bakery on the map. Maybe I can prove to everyone that I can do it on my own. Reclaim some of my old panache." The *La Patisserie* contest flitted through her mind, but she pushed it away. She'd done her best; now it was up to the magazine photographer to decide if she was worthy.

Something black-and-white flashed in the corner of her eye. Must be that pesky cat again. She did a quick check to make sure there was nothing on the shelves in the van that would slide off during the drive. "Okay, you can put it in this space." She moved to the side to give Sammy access to the cargo area.

He stepped forward. "Whoa."

Sammy leaned back as the cat twined itself around his legs.

He stepped forward and the cat moved again.

The cake wobbled.

Oh no! She'd forgotten the center dowel to hold it in place. Oh well, no harm done. She'd fix it in a minute.

Only—

Sammy overcorrected and the cat pushed up against the back of his legs.

In slow motion horror, Robin watched Sammy twist over backward, his foot slipping, his hand shooting out to steady himself.

The cake flew into the air.

In a heartbeat a million years long, he landed on the ground with emerald-green chunks spread over and around him.

And all her hopes and dreams lying in a mess on the pavement.

Sammy was lying in a ruin of cake with the cold parking lot under his back.

Robin's cake.

Robin!

Something soft and warm on his face. He turned to see that cat licking his cheek.

Someone was crying. He wiped a hand over his face and it came away…green.

"Robin." He sat up, his head spinning a little. He pushed to standing and moved toward her. "I'm so sorry. I don't know what happened." He reached out to her.

"It's okay. It's okay."

He didn't know if she was trying to convince him or herself. She held her arms tight to her body, face white.

"We can figure this out." He put his hand on her upper arm. "Let me help you fix it."

She kneaded her hands together. "No, Sammy. There's nothing you can do. I'm on my own in this one."

He gently squeezed her arm. "You don't have to do it alone. I want to be your partner here."

Finally, she nodded once. "Fine. You're right. I could use the help." Her shoulders relaxed a fraction, and she turned and slammed the van doors shut.

He scrubbed a hand over his face, then rubbed at the cake stains on his jacket. Around them lay the debris of the ruined cake.

Under the van, the cat nibbled at a chunk of emerald-coated vanilla cake, a fractured, golden "55" stuck to its fur.

He took a deep breath of the cool, late-afternoon air when Robin turned back around, more color in her face.

"Here's what we're gonna do," she said. "I have ten dozen cupcakes in the cooler we will use. They're for the wedding on Tuesday, but I'm just going to have to remake them later." She pushed past him and to the back door of the bakery. He stepped over the remains of the cake and followed her.

He hoped the cat enjoyed its fancy feast.

"I think I have a design that can work with our time crunch," Robin said over her shoulder. "You know where the cupcakes are. I'll let Jean know we will be there a little late and then start sketching out the design."

Inside the bakery, Sammy shucked off his sticky jacket and washed his hands. *Hooah, let's get this done.*

Grateful for his time at the bakery learning to bake bread and working on the cabinet, he easily found the supplies Robin asked for. He arranged the cupcakes on the worktable in the center of the kitchen while Robin did something complicated with several colored pencils and a notebook.

"Okay. This has got to work." Robin handed him the sketch she tore from the book. "I still have the top layer of the original cake in the cooler. I think I can sculpt fondant into the shape of a peacock head and neck and attach it to that layer. Then we'll fan the cupcakes behind like the tail feathers."

He looked at the sketch, catching the vision. "This looks amazing."

"It'll be even more amazing if we pull it off in—" She looked at the clock on the wall. "One hour."

Robin showed Sammy how to apply a thin layer of white icing to the tops of the cupcakes. Then she got to work on the bird's head.

He watched her out of the corner of his eye. She worked confidently, kneading some blue food coloring into something from a bucket marked Fondant.

Oops. He almost carved the top off that cupcake. He focused back on the task in front of him.

Soon Robin had finished making her bird head. She set the fondant aside, laying it gently on a sheet of wax paper. "I'll teach you to do the easier parts of the piping," she said. She handed him a fabric tube fitted with a silver tip and filled with blue icing. "You're just going to pipe on long teardrops, like this." She demonstrated on one of the cupcakes he had just finished.

"Got it." He took the piping bag and drew on the closest cupcake.

"Not quite."

He startled when her cool, slim hand closed over his as she moved his hand in the proper direction.

"I think you've got it now."

He piped long teardrops until his hand ached. Across from him, Robin filled in the teardrops with an intricate design until the top of each cupcake looked like the eye on a peacock feather.

He glanced at the clock. Ten minutes until they were officially late. "Robin."

"I see it." She brushed a hair out of her eye and finished off the last cupcake. "The cake carriers are stacked next to the cooler."

They loaded the finished cakes into their specialized holders and carried them out to the van. Robin ran back into the bakery to grab some extra frosting and other decorations to refill her emergency tote. If the cupcakes shifted during the drive, she wanted to be able to correct any smudges.

They climbed into the cold van, and Sammy breathed a sigh of relief when it started without protest. Driving as though she had her grandmother, seven antique glass bowls, and a full crock of chili in the back, Robin made her way to the party.

Taking his cue from Robin's silent concentration, Sammy kept quiet during the few minutes' drive through town.

"Sure is dark tonight," he said as she pulled into the driveway. "Cloudy. No moon, no stars."

She turned the engine off and looked at him, a sparkle in her eye. "Yes, but the house is shining bright enough to wish on. I think we made it in one piece, and only a few minutes late."

Opening the van door, Sammy could hear classical music floating out from the home.

They went around to the back of the van and each lifted a few cupcake carriers.

"I'll come back out for the cake topper after we find where these will be sitting," Robin said.

"Lead the way." Sammy gestured toward the house with his chin.

Robin didn't bother knocking on the door but pushed through and into the front hall. On the right the hall opened into a large great room which was strung with what must be a hundred strands of twinkle lights. People filled the room, laughing and chatting with one another. Sammy spotted a buffet table along the wall nearest the kitchen area and an empty table next to it. Robin must have noticed it in the same moment, because she threaded her way around the room until they stopped at the spot.

Sammy began unpacking the cakes. A woman wearing a deep-green dress approached them.

"Robin, dear, I'm so glad you made it."

"Jean!" Robin gave the woman a quick embrace. "I'm so sorry I'm late. And that you won't have the beautiful cake I promised."

"Nonsense, these are lovely. Are those peacock feathers? How clever! Want some help?" Jean met Sammy's eye and put her hand to her chest. "Oh! It seems you've brought your own help."

Under the woman's gaze, Sammy felt his face heating.

"Jean, this is my, uh, friend, Sammy," Robin said. "Sammy, this is Jean Adams. This is her party."

Jean held out her hand to Sammy. "It's so nice to meet you, friend." Then the woman tugged at their clasped hands until he leaned close. "You hold on to this girl," she said sotto voce, "and treat her right. She's one of the good ones."

He couldn't help the smile that spread across his face. "I intend to," he whispered back. "I think she's amazing."

A blond man sporting a full beard and a camera around his neck approached them. Jean released Sammy's hand and reached for the newcomer. "Robin, Sammy, this is my son, Matt, the photographer. Matt, this is Robin Fox, the cake designer I was telling you about. I thought you could help her get set up."

"I'd be happy to help." The man's voice was a deep rumble. "It gives me a chance to ask a few questions and to advise you how to set up your cake for the best lighting."

"Great! I'll go get the rest of it. Be right back," Robin said.

The men waited by the table as Robin went to retrieve the final cake box. Sammy shifted from foot to foot.

"So, are you her assistant?" Matt rumbled.

"I'm just the grunt," Sammy said. "Robin is the talent."

They waited a few minutes more.

Finally, Robin came back in, weaving her way through the party, dodging elbows and furniture. She set the cake box on the reserved table.

Matt and Robin chatted a bit as she set up the peacock. He

asked her about her work at the bakery and her experience in Paris. Sammy noticed that she glossed over her reasons for leaving while speaking well of her colleagues. Good girl. Those quotes would look great in print.

On several of the cupcakes, the colors on the hasty frosting job were bleeding together. Robin handed Sammy a palate knife and showed him how to carefully nudge the color back into place. He prayed no one would notice.

"I love this agate look." Matt gestured to the former cake top doing its current job as the peacock's body. On top of the small cake, the fondant bird's neck sagged a bit, giving the impression it was bowing.

"Thanks. It's the state rock of Minnesota," Robin said.

Matt took a few steps back from the cake and snapped some photos. "It's a great marbling effect." He instructed Robin to stand next to the cake and took her picture from several angles. "Okay, thanks. I think I got everything I need. These are going to turn out great."

Robin turned to Sammy, eyes bright. "Should we head out?"

He nodded, but before they could go anywhere, a tinkling sound filled the air—the party guests tapping their glasses and calling for a speech. People crowded around, facing the center of the room where Palmer and Jean stood, each with a glass in their hand.

Palmer gazed at his wife with soft eyes. "I won't be making a speech. I don't have a way with words." He looked to the crowd. "But I do want to thank you each for coming to celebrate. There was a time when we didn't think we would even make it to ten years, and look at us now." He paused. Cleared his throat. Held up his glass. "To my wife. We may not be perfect, but we are perfect for each other. Thank you for being my bride for fifty-five years. You deserve a medal."

Those gathered cheered and laughed as the couple shared a brief kiss. The clinking sound came again, and Jean raised her glass.

"My turn. To my husband. You stuck with me through thick and thin. A little more thick than thin these days." She ran a hand down her waistline and everyone laughed again. "From the moment you walked into my life, I knew it would be an adventure. Here's to fifty-five more!"

Jean and Palmer linked arms and drank deeply from their cups, the crowd hooting. Then Palmer dipped Jean into a kiss, their empty cups held high.

Sammy watched as Robin made her way through the crowd of well-wishers to speak to Jean and Palmer. Soon she worked her way back to him. "I told them I'd pack my things and that they could just toss the empty containers when they finish the cake."

Together they packed the few items Robin had brought, then carried the totes out to the van, stopping briefly in the hall to reclaim their jackets.

Outside, a breeze had kicked up, chasing away the clouds and turning the stars into frosty diamond lights. Robin shifted her tote to a hip and opened one of the van's back doors. She stowed her load inside, then stepped aside for Sammy to do the same. When he moved back to shut the door, Robin was leaning against the other door, her face tipped to the sky.

"Beautiful night," he said. His mouth dried.

"Beautiful," she echoed. "Almost a shame to go home." She gave him a slow smile.

"Want to take a walk?"

"I'm game."

The road running to Jean and Palmer's house was quiet. They walked in silence for a few moments.

"Thank you again for your help tonight," Robin said. "I'd never have finished without you."

"You never would have needed to scramble if I hadn't dropped that cake."

Robin stopped. She put her hand on his arm. "Don't blame yourself for that. I never should have started feeding that stray cat." Her cheeks were flushed, and the tip of her nose was pink. "I'm glad you were with me."

Sammy could hear the sound of Lake Superior washing onto the shore a few streets away. A scent of pine hinted the air. "This is pretty much a perfect Deep Haven night," he said. "I've always loved winter."

"Mm-hmm," Robin said. "Makes me almost want to reconsider leaving." She glanced up at him under her eyebrows. His heart pounded in his ears. Her gaze dropped to his lips and her own parted.

She shivered and Sammy put an arm around her. "Let me warm you up," he murmured. She leaned against his chest, face still tilted up. "I think maybe I can't be just friends with you, Robin."

"What do you have in mind?"

Did she mean... He searched her eyes. Seeing her gaze flick to his mouth, he dipped his head and pressed his lips to hers. Chilled at first, they soon warmed under his touch. She sighed and leaned into him.

She moved her hand from his arm to the back of his neck. Heat flared and he tightened his grip around her. She smelled like vanilla and buttercream. Before he completely lost himself on this public street, he pulled back.

Smiling into her eyes, he put his forehead on hers. "What do you think? Can we be more than just friends?"

She kept her arm around his neck. "Yes, I think we could try it." She reached up and brushed his lips with hers again before nesting herself at his side and leading them back to the waiting van.

His heart lifted and set sail with the stars.

thirteen

. . .

A girl could be forgiven for basking in her success.

Robin sat in the kitchen of the bakery, reflecting on the past two weeks. First the cake disaster with Sammy and their near miraculous recovery. The photo shoot at the Adamses' anniversary party.

And then the, ahem, celebrating with Sammy afterward. She felt again the warmth of his lips on hers, the grip of his arms around her under the stars.

Then the whirlwind of prepping and delivering the cupcakes for Jacob and Emily's wedding two days later. Sammy had really come through for her at the wedding by bringing a piece he'd built to hold the cupcakes. Small pieces of aspen saplings held up several tiers of round pine shelving. Sprawling out from the main section lay more round platforms. Bisecting the right side of the structure, the extra piece of lace delicately flowed over the pieces, forming a stream-like decoration. Sammy had strung twinkle lights through the edges and over it in an arc. Here and there, greenery popped through. When her flower-topped cupcakes were placed, the overall effect was stunning, like a garden in the middle of an aspen grove. Sammy had taken her vision and run with it.

She stood and paced the few steps from one side of the kitchen to the other. The past weeks since her grandparents had flown to Florida had passed so quickly. They'd called this morning and said their flight home was on time.

She sat down again, drummed her fingers on the counter.

The clock on the wall read ten minutes after eleven. Grandma and Grandpa were due back on the shuttle from the airport in twenty minutes. She got up and moved to the dining area, wanting to see them the minute they pulled in.

She tried to tell herself not to be nervous. They were her loving grandparents for crying out loud.

But, a nagging voice reminded her, in all the excitement she hadn't told them about the changes to the bakery. She chewed on a corner of her fingernail, a habit she'd kicked years ago. But really, had any of those things turned out to be an emergency? She just hoped her grandparents felt the same way.

A white fifteen-passenger van pulled into the lot. Several people got out, including her grandparents. She pushed out the door, suddenly eager for a hug from her grandpa.

Grandpa Jim sported a tan, and Grandma Elaine wore a straw hat decorated with a huge silk hibiscus flower. "You two look amazing." Robin gave each of them a long hug. "Come inside where it's warm."

They all dragged the luggage through the door of the bakery. Inside the door, her grandma paused. "Is everything okay, Robin? You look a little thin around the edges."

"The bakery is fine, Grandma." Deep breath. "But I did have to make a few changes." Robin closed her eyes.

"Changes?" The squeak in Grandma Elaine's voice tightened a vise around Robin's chest.

Her grandma set her luggage next to the door and walked toward the kitchen, Grandpa Jim trailing behind.

Robin hurried to talk to them before they got through the swinging door. "Well, you know that the oven has been acting up. Finally, one day it wouldn't start at all." She told them about the heating element explosion. "It turned out that the oven was fine but the element was faulty. Sammy Johnson and I got it fixed but...well, someone bought us a new one." She'd promised Sammy she wouldn't tell them he'd bought the oven. He didn't want her grandparents to feel obligated to him. And he'd made it clear that he definitely did not want to be paid back. Except maybe in cupcakes.

"Someone bought us an oven." Grandma's voice fell flat. She stopped, blocking the door to the kitchen. "Who would spend that kind of money?"

"The appliance company said it was donated anonymously and that we must have an enthusiastic fan." A slow smile spread across her lips. Sammy was enthusiastic all right.

"An anonymous donor? I'm sorry, I'm just having trouble picturing it."

There was a moment of silence as Robin tried to think of a way to explain it without outright lying to her grandmother. She wanted to keep her promise to Sammy, but she wouldn't lie.

"There seems to be a Good Samaritan going around town providing for people. This must be just another incident." Then her own words struck her.

Sammy.

Sammy must be the Good Samaritan donating to all those needs. It all lined up. A new furnace for the youth center, carpeting for the church after it was listed as a prayer request, even the oven just days after he found out she needed it. She didn't know how he was affording it on a delivery/handyman salary, especially since he kept insisting on being paid in cupcakes, but this had Sammy Johnson written all over it.

How could she have ever thought she wasn't attracted to him? Sammy was generous and kind. He laughed at her jokes. He made up games to help kids pass math. He listened to her, and she loved the way that he made frosting.

No. She just loved him. All of him. She didn't know when it had happened, but right now, yes, she loved Sammy Johnson.

"Still sounds strange to me."

They hadn't heard the half of it. She told them about the Good Samaritan and the other gifts around town. "This oven is top of the line. It's one of those new stackable units. The top is a convection oven, and the bottom is brick-lined. Remember that convention in Paris I told you about? This oven came from one of the European companies I spent time with."

"Sounds pretty fancy—much more than we need for our bread," Grandpa said.

She resisted the urge to roll her eyes at his words. The various functions on the oven would improve anything they baked.

But the moment of reckoning had come.

"Actually, there's something I need to talk to you about." She swallowed against her suddenly dry throat. "I've added cakes to the Fox lineup." She waited a beat, then another. When her grandparents stayed silent, she rushed on. "We had a major water leak, and I had to call the plumber, and then the floor needed to be replaced and there wasn't enough money to pay for the repairs before the health inspector came. I had to come up with the money somehow, so I started baking cakes on the side. Cakes bring in much more return on investment than bread." She stopped the waterfall of words. Held her breath.

"I see." Her grandma's tone wasn't condemning. That was something, anyway. "So you changed the menu without consulting us?"

"I didn't think you would need to know," she admitted. And just like that, she was sixteen again, sneaking in past curfew. That hadn't ended well either. "I'm sorry. I should have told you right away. I just wanted everything to be perfect and non-stressful. I know you don't like the idea of adding cake to the menu."

Her grandma spoke. "It's not that we're opposed to more items than bread on the menu. We never added cakes because we wanted to focus on baking the best bread we could, not get distracted by other things."

"And neither of us could ever get the hang of all that frosting." Her grandpa reached out and put his hand on her shoulder.

She let out her breath in a whoosh. "You aren't mad?"

Her grandpa laughed, a bright sound lifting the weight the room held. "Who can be mad about cake? I remember that photo you sent of some of the things you were creating in Paris. It would be a shame to waste that talent."

"Thank you, Grandpa."

"Is this idea sustainable, though?" Grandma, always pragmatic. "Surely there isn't much call for fancy cakes."

Robin told them about the commissions she'd already received, ending with, "And one of my cakes was already photographed for a magazine." She gave a short description of the Adamses' party.

"Good work, honey." Grandpa Jim was always her cheerleader.

Her grandma cleared her throat. "So, we're not upset that you did this while we were gone. But I don't think we can support it going forward."

A lump rose in Robin's throat. "What are you saying?"

Her grandparents shared a long look. "We're a bread bakery, honey," Grandpa said at last. He reached out and took her hand. "There's not enough room in that kitchen for all of us. I'm not sure what your future plans are, but I don't see how continuing with cakes here would work."

That was okay, though, right? Because she wanted to get back to Paris.

Or did she?

Stiffening her spine, she resolved to reignite the passion she held for France. Besides, she could never live a big life in this small town.

Her grandma headed for the door again.

"Wait!"

Grandma paused at her outburst. Robin closed her eyes briefly, pasted on a smile. Her insides roiled. "You know how I said there was a leak?" They nodded. "I had to change the cabinet and sink because the pipes leaked everywhere and the wood was ruined. And then the floor needed to be replaced because of the warped floorboards. The shelving needed to be moved to make room, but then I discovered it worked better over on the right, so I just left it..." She trailed off, put her hand over her eyes. "I'm sorry. I should've asked before doing all of this. I can move everything back. I can't change the floor or the oven, but I can put the rest where it was before."

Her hands felt like ice.

Her grandma spoke. "We're not mad at you, honey."

Wait. What?

Her grandma opened the swinging door and ushered them through.

A silence fell over them as her grandparents looked around. Robin resisted the urge to bite her fingernails. A wrinkle appeared between her grandma's eyebrows.

"I should show you the best part." She pulled her grandma over to the sink and pointed to the fox floor tile. "Sammy found this tile and thought it belonged here."

"Oh." Grandma put her hand to her mouth. "It's beautiful. Jim, come look."

"I like what you've done to the place," Grandpa chimed in. "The new arrangement makes sense."

"What about not changing anything?" Had they really absolved her?

"Oh, I didn't know what I was saying." Grandma Elaine wrapped an arm around Robin's waist. "I was so worried about your grandpa. Of course you should have made the space your own while you were using it."

"Then why do you still look angry?"

"I'm upset with myself. If you felt you had to keep this a

secret from us, maybe we didn't do enough to show you how much we love you."

"Even when I mess up and don't confess?"

"Of course even when you mess up. Love doesn't quit just because things are hard or people mess up. Do you stop loving someone if they make a mistake?"

"No. Absolutely not."

"Right. And God doesn't feel that way about you either. Love doesn't quit even when you try to push it away. We love you even when you make mistakes because God has taught us how to do it. He loves us even in our most screwup moments. We can only hope to do the same for others."

Like the Grinch, her heart grew three sizes at that moment.

Her grandpa came to their part of the kitchen just as her phone pinged with an incoming email. She glanced at it once, then again. The address line read La Patisserie's Distinctive Bakes. "Give me a second." She moved away from her grandparents, swiped open the message.

"We are delighted to inform you…" She gasped when the meaning of the words became clear.

"What is it? What's happening?" Her grandma put a hand to her chest.

"I got in." Robin took up Grandpa's hands and danced him around the kitchen.

He laughed, then pulled her to a stop. "Got in what? Or where?"

"Distinctive Bakes!" Joy burbled up in Robin. Did the kitchen always have this glow?

"Slow down," her grandma said. "What's Distinctive Bakes?"

"That photographer I told you about entered me into a bake-off competition sponsored by La Patisserie, the magazine. Their annual Distinctive Bakes America competition is in New York City in two weeks. I won a spot." Robin turned her phone around to show her grandparents. "I'm going to New York." She squealed and did jazz hands. "Can you believe it?"

Her grandparents exchanged a look.

Uh-oh.

Her heart dropped at least three feet. "I mean, if you can spare me here." Her grandparents needed her. They'd only just gotten home. Of course she couldn't run off to New York. "Never mind. You just got home. I'll tell them I can't come."

"Don't be silly. Of course you have to do it." Her grandma put a hand out for the phone. "This looks amazing. We're home now. We'll bake the bread. We believe in your talent." She held the phone so Grandpa Jim could see the screen more closely.

"Your grandma is right," he said. "Besides, we've run this bakery for almost fifty years without you. I think we can manage to keep it going while you are in New York."

Robin clasped her hands to her chest. "Thank you! I'm so thrilled!" Maybe if she won some prize money, she could figure out a way to bake cakes right here in Deep Haven. Imagine how Sammy's face would look if she said she would stay. She retrieved her phone from Grandma Elaine and read through the details again. "This says I need to bring an assistant. Grandma, would you want to come?"

"I'm honored that you would ask me, honey. But we just got home." Her grandma glanced at Grandpa Jim, and Robin read her concern for him in the look. "Is there someone else you can call?"

There was only one other person she'd want working alongside her.

She dialed his number. "Sammy, how would you like to go to New York?"

DEEP HAVEN SEEMED VERY FAR AWAY.

Sammy stood in the ballroom at the Marriott in downtown

New York City. The space had been transformed into a baking paradise. Ten workstations, staggered throughout the room, contained an oven, fridge, and stainless steel work countertops. At each station, an apron-clad pair of bakers rummaged through their ingredients, readying their space for the competition. Near the front of the room was the judging area. Several long, empty tables waited for the day's offerings. Three judges would decide the fate of the teams. There was a second round of competitions for junior bakers the next day.

The warmth of the room belied the Saturday morning March chill of the air just out the window.

In their station, he and Robin laid out their own ingredients. Thank goodness their setup was similar to the one at Fox Bakery with the fridge to the left, workbench in the center, oven on the right, and a wash station kitty-corner to that. When his nerves came knocking, muscle memory could take over.

"Do you need me to go over the plan again?" Robin asked. He longed to stroke the auburn curl that had escaped the scarf she'd tied over her hair, but stopped himself.

He held up his laminated 3x5 cards. "I think this detailed agenda is all I need." He'd practically memorized the step-by-step instructions. Pretending it was a football play had gone a long way. "Don't worry. I've got this." He flipped through the cards again, the final card a copy of the rules of the competition. Each team had to present their cakes before a panel of three judges. They would be ranked based on taste and difficulty. Besides fame, the top three teams would be featured in *La Patisserie* and given a cash prize.

He glanced at the clock. T-minus twenty minutes until they officially began. He tucked the 3x5 cards into the back pocket of his jeans, keeping them close by for reference.

He hadn't slept well the night before, this time an unfamiliar bed keeping him awake instead of the customary nightmares. They'd flown in from Minnesota the previous afternoon, him dragging his luggage and a bag filled with Robin's supplies. He shook his head, tried to wrap his mind around the fact that, yes, Robin had asked him to be her baking assistant and, yes, they were in New York, New York.

He'd been in some big cities when was in the Army, but never New York. He hoped they'd get a chance to see some sights after the competition. Maybe even a carriage ride through Central Park.

Robin paced the seven steps their workstation occupied. The tile was going to be permanently dented if she didn't stop. Not that he could blame her—he was about to start pacing too. He put a hand on her shoulder, stopping her progress.

"Robin. Look at me." He waited for her to meet his eyes. "You're gonna do great. Let's breathe." He took a deep breath in and waited for her to mimic him, then blew it out slowly. They repeated the procedure. The panicked look receded from her eyes.

"Thanks. I needed that." Robin tucked her hands into the pocket on the front of her rust-colored apron. "Maybe I'm putting too much pressure on myself for this thing. But winning this contest would be huge for my career. I know winning isn't everything, but I can't help but feel that this is my one chance to do something meaningful."

"I get that." He tugged her hands out of her pocket and held them between his, rubbing them to warm them. "You've practiced so hard, and now it's go time. It's normal to have a few nerves. But this contest doesn't define you. It can't change how amazing you already are."

"Why do I feel like I'm the only one who doesn't belong here?" Robin gripped his hands tight. "I keep thinking someone is going to call me out for being a fraud."

Wow, the crack that Victor had made in her armor ran deeper than he thought. Or maybe Victor had just confirmed all Robin's lies. In that moment, he knew he would do whatever it took to help her believe in herself.

He ran his thumbs over the back of her hands. "You can

never be a fraud. You're just as well trained as these other competitors. You worked in a bakery in Paris, for Pete's sake, not to mention all the schooling and practice you've completed." Her fingers finally warmed in his.

She looked up at him, pale green eyes shining a little hope. "I might need you to keep me calm today."

He dropped one hand and gave her a small salute. "That's what I'm here for."

"I hope you're also here to help bake, because I can't do this on my own." Robin dropped his other hand and his fingers cooled.

"That's *also* what I'm here for, boss." Sammy leaned a hip against the countertop.

A buzzer sounded. Over the loudspeaker, a voice announced, "Five minutes to bake time!"

Robin straightened so fast Sammy thought he heard her spine snap in place. He grinned at her. Now her face held the professional look it always took on when she started baking something.

He took his place beside her at the worktop. "We got this."

Around them their competitors also stood shoulder to shoulder at their stations. Their nearest competition was two women who owned a wedding cake business in Savannah, Georgia. Across from them was a husband-and-wife team from Tennessee. He hadn't met the couple dressed like Mario and Luigi from the video game, but he gave them props for their fun attitude.

Beside him Robin stilled. She stared at the judges' table. "Oh no." Her words breathed out of her.

"'Oh no' what?" He looked in the direction she was staring. A small group of people clustered near the front of the room. A woman in a pantsuit, who he vaguely recognized from a cooking show he'd seen, a man in a navy blue suit and a cowboy hat, and another man dressed in chef's whites with a French flag embroidered on the sleeve all stood chatting with one another.

"The man in the chef coat is Victor." Robin reached up and tucked her hair into her scarf.

"What, like *Victor* Victor? 'The man who stole your work' Victor?" His blood ran hot.

"That's the one." Robin stiffened. "It looks like he's one of the judges."

Sammy didn't know why Victor didn't like Robin, but having him on the judging panel couldn't be good, could it?

"Do we need to report that to someone? Do you think he will be impartial?"

Robin shrugged, a tight movement that moved her shoulders up an inch. "I don't know. I hope so."

The judges moved behind their table as the announcer took up the mic again. "Ladies and gentlemen, start your baking!" An air horn rang out, and the huge digital competition clock began counting down.

She turned to him, the earlier hope in her eyes a distant light. "Nothing we can do about it now. Let's just make this cake shine."

Sammy checked his laminated list one more time before settling in to work. They soon worked as a real team, Sammy measuring ingredients and Robin sifting them into the mixing bowl. The rhythmic thumping of the mixer punctuated their conversation.

"I'll get these pans ready, you watch the batter." Robin lifted the cake pans onto the worktop. They had decided on a castle straight out of a fairy tale. Robin told him it was similar to the cake that had gotten her fired, but with more oomph. The sketches she'd made looked complicated, but he believed in her.

Keeping an eye on the time the batter had been mixing, Sammy also scoped out the competition. The women from Georgia wore flour all over their aprons, and a pile sat on the floor. Some kind of accident, he assumed. In their area, Mario and Luigi sang an Italian song while filling two thin sheet pans. And across from them, the married couple stood in the middle of their station loudly arguing. He caught something about who was in charge of bake times. Scattered throughout the rest of the room were several other teams he didn't have time to check out, bringing the total number of teams to ten.

Uh-oh. The judges seemed to be making their way from baker to baker. He could only hope Victor would leave Robin alone.

Sammy turned off the mixer. "This looks good. Ready with those pans?"

"Bring it on."

He poured the mix into the greased and paper-lined pans. "Don't look now, but we're about to have a visit from your favorite ex-boss."

"Best to just get it over with, I guess. But he'll have to wait until I get these cakes in the oven." She carried the first pan to the oven, bent over and slid it in. As she bent to slide the second one in, Victor approached their workstation.

He gave a low wolf whistle Sammy hoped Robin didn't hear. "A feisty one, that Fox," Victor purred.

"You shouldn't talk about a lady that way." Sammy stood tall, crossed his arms. His gut churned. Who did this guy think he was?

Victor held up both hands in a helpless gesture. "Sorry. Sorry. You'll have to excuse me. I am French. We are a passionate people."

Breathing deeply, Sammy told himself to let it go.

Robin joined them. "Hello, Victor."

"The beautiful Robin." Victor reached for her hand and dropped a kiss on the back of it. Sammy wanted to drop him. Victor motioned to the other two judges, who joined them. "Let me introduce everyone." He made the introductions, ending with, "And this is Robin, who unfortunately had to leave my employ at the end of last year."

If Victor didn't leave the area soon, Sammy's jaw would crack in two. He forced himself to relax. *Had to leave my employ...* As though the man couldn't remember humiliating Robin and taking away her rightful glory. Beside him, Robin chatted with the female judge, describing her vision for the cake they planned.

Sammy concentrated on keeping his fists unclenched.

A sickly-sweet aroma began to permeate the ballroom as the cakes baked. The judges moved to talk to the married couple across the way.

"Could that guy be any more of a jerk?" Sammy's voice came out in a hiss. Across from them, he saw Victor looking down his nose at the silk flowers the wife showed him from their stack of decorations.

"Who?" Robin asked. Her flushed face and wide eyes told him more than her oh-so-casual tone.

"You know who. Mr. Ex-Boss." He nodded at the group of judges as they moved to the next table. "I'd be happy to meet him in the alley to teach him some manners."

Robin braced both hands on the worktop. Her shoulders relaxed a fraction. "Don't bother. He isn't worth it." She spun and looked at the clock. "We've just got a few minutes before the cakes come out, so let's start frosting prep."

Following Robin's detailed instructions, they both moved through the steps needed before beginning the frosting. Sammy began humming the Vivaldi piece from the Snowball Dance. He swayed his hips to the music and did the vine move that Robin had taught him.

Her laughter rang out, and it was worth it.

A timer chimed and Robin checked the cakes. He walked up behind her to see for himself. Perfection.

"I'll put this in the cooler," Robin said.

As the cake cooled in the blast chiller, Sammy worked on making the frosting. He and Robin had practiced the recipe a few times in the Fox Bakery kitchen, but this mixer had different settings. While he messed around getting it just right, Robin piped out the decorations for the cake.

He glanced in her direction. Her errant curl lay across her eye, and she brushed at it. Unclipping the paper clip from his copy of the recipe and instructions, he moved over to her.

"Here, let me." He cupped her chin and raised her face. Catching the auburn curl, he slid the paperclip onto the edge of her scarf, pinning it all in place. He let his hand linger on her chin. Her eyelids drifted shut. His gaze dropped to her lips.

"Thanks." She licked her top lip with a quick flick of the tongue. Heat built between them.

Overhead, the buzzer sounded, then the announcer called out, "One hour remaining."

Robin's eyes flew open. "Oh no! We better hustle." She made the distance to the fridge in two giant, bounding steps.

They finished the rest of the cake in near silence except for a brief word of instruction from Robin here and there.

When the buzzer sounded for the final time, Sammy stepped back to look at the cake. He might not be a professional, but it looked pretty amazing to him.

"Look what you created," he said. He took Robin's hand and twirled her once. "This is incredible."

Her eyes shone. "I know, right? I can't believe I did this—that we did this."

"No, this was all you, babe." No way would he take any credit for any of this.

"You kept me focused." She crossed her arms and leaned back against him. "It is pretty great, isn't it?"

In front of them stood a confection palace. Turrets graced the four corners, gilded in gold leaf. The central structure rose up from the base to a towering height. Tiny people Robin had made dotted the fondant courtyard.

He shook his head in wonder.

They made a great team.

fourteen

. . .

The cake was perfect.

Robin chewed a fingernail as she looked at it from all angles. While slightly shorter than the one she'd made in Paris, this cake boasted more turrets. She'd also taken the time to decorate each turret in its own style.

One of the other contestants wandered over. "You made something awesome!" the gray-haired woman gushed.

And just like that, Robin was thirteen again, hearing her grandma praise her art. *Looks beautiful, sweetie. What a talent.* Her vivacious grandma was everything Robin aspired to be. A compliment from her helped to quiet the voices in her head about not being good enough.

Except, wait. Was that a rip in the fondant covering the east side of the castle wall? The rules stated that she couldn't touch the cake after the buzzer except to move it to the judging area. She glanced around. No one was nearby. Sammy was at the sink washing his hands. She could just—

No.

She would leave the flaw. Cleaning it up would be cheating. Besides, this was her best effort, and if her best wasn't perfect, so be it. Excellence wasn't always found in perfection.

Around the room, other teams were cleaning up and getting ready to move their cakes to the judging area. Voices rang out in a constant, loud murmur, and the scent of cake hung heavy in the air. She looked over at Sammy. He leaned against the worktop, arms crossed, one knee bent. His left cheek was dusted with flour. She walked over and rubbed it off with her hand.

He caught her hand before it could leave his face and held it there.

"We did it." His slow smile ignited an inferno inside.

"We sure did," she said. "Thanks for coming. I couldn't have done it without you."

"You're going to owe me a thousand cupcakes after this." He winked and added fuel to the blaze in her belly.

She pulled away. "Let's get this cake in place."

They had thirty minutes before the first round of judging began. With measured movements, they slid the cake onto a wheeled cart for transfer to the other end of the room.

A movement caught her eye as a man walked up. "Victor?"

In front of them was her old boss. Seeing him earlier had added to her jitters, though she'd tried to ignore his influence. Victor shouldn't have any hold on her life now. She felt rather than saw Sammy move to stand at her side.

"Hello again, Robin." Victor's smooth accent oiled his words. He gave her cake a once-over. A slight sneer appeared on his thin lips. "You finished in time. Congratulations. I see you're still fond of gold leaf. How quaint."

A tingling began in her neck and swept up and over her face. Suddenly unsure that Victor could be impartial, she questioned her earlier words to Sammy. She knew all about judgmental people. They didn't always catch her vision. She'd seen that before in her life.

She clenched and unclenched her sweaty hands.

Beside her, Sammy bristled. A waft of his cologne, spicy with a hint of pine, drifted over her. The familiar scent calmed her.

"What are you doing here?" She crossed her arms.

"Besides judging this contest? I'm scouting new talent. I'm opening a new bakery just outside Paris, in Chantilly, and need a master baker." Victor looked at his hands. Strange, she'd never known him to be shy before. "Until our...disagreement...I'd thought to promote you. A few more years under my tutelage and you could have been something big."

"Seriously, pal? Disagreement?" Sammy's outburst surprised her. "You humiliated her in front of a whole room of people."

"I think she has sold you a lie." Victor curled his lip. "It was she who humiliated me. Questioning my authority in front of the whole staff. Correcting me in front of the judge."

"After you basically stole her cake! Are you calling Robin a liar?" Sammy shot back.

He remembered the story? A warm glow bubbled through her. It would be easy to love someone like Sammy, someone who really saw her. "Sammy, it's fine." She looked at him. Color rose high on his cheeks and his eyes blazed.

"It's not fine. This guy stole your work, fired you, and now has the audacity to say it was all a 'disagreement.'" A chopping hand motion punctuated his words.

She put a hand on Sammy's arm. His bicep tensed. "Let's just get this cake in place."

"Don't worry, ma chérie. We will have all the time in the world to talk after this contest. Maybe I will even help nudge along a good outcome." Victor stood aside and swept an arm in a grand gesture, pointing down the aisle toward the judging area. "I'll walk you up." He moved in front of their cart as though he were a royal escort.

Robin pushed at her side of the wheeled cart.

Sammy moved to help her, leaning close enough to whisper. "I can't believe you would consider any offer from this creep."

Irritation flared. Did he really think she would take Victor seriously? "Just—"

"What did you say?" Victor rounded on them.

Sammy squared up. "I said, you are a creep."

Then just like in a bad movie, Victor shot his cuffs and adjusted his jacket. He cracked his neck once and put up his fists. "Come over here and say that to me."

What was happening right now? "Sammy—"

"Victor, I'm not going to fight you." Sammy shook his head and pushed the cake cart a few inches. "You're not worth it."

"Fine." Victor held up his hands in a surrender and backed up a foot. "But don't think that calling me names will do you any favors. I deserve an apology."

"Come on, man. What's your problem?" Sammy tried to push past Victor. Robin reached out her hand to touch his shoulder, his forearm, or anything just to calm him down. She could see Sammy's back muscles bunching under his shirt. He was just out of reach.

Victor put his hands on Sammy's chest. "You called me a creep, and you are embarrassing me in front of all these people. I demand an apology."

"Not gonna happen," Sammy said.

Everything became sharply etched in Robin's mind as Sammy tried to shrug off Victor's arms.

Victor moved tighter in, his face inches from Sammy's.

Sammy shoved him back. "Get off me."

The move lifted the smaller man up and off his feet. He twisted sideways as he fell, his own arm whacking his face.

"Noooooo!" Robin reached out a hand to catch him, but it was too late.

Victor stumbled, arms wheeling.

Then landed directly on her masterpiece.

Blobs of confection splatted everywhere. She wiped a gob of golden frosting from her cheek. Victor lay there, staring at the ceiling a moment. Around them, a murmur rose from the other contestants.

Half of the cake remained intact, but the other half lay shattered.

She looked at Sammy through blurred vision. Horror filled his eyes.

How could this have happened a second time? First the Adamses' anniversary dessert, and now the one she'd been thinking of as her redemption cake. Maybe God didn't want her baking cakes after all.

On the cake, the torn fondant on the castle's east side winked at her.

"Ladies and gentlemen." The announcer's voice rang loud over the din around them. "Please move your creations to the front of the room."

Victor picked himself up and out of her cake. He brushed off the front of his shirt, then used the back of his hand to wipe the back of his chef's jacket. Frosting streaked up his spine and into his hair. His jaw bore an angry red mark all the way to his left ear from where he'd hit himself.

He tugged at the bottom of his jacket. "I am needed at the judging booth." Raising his chin, he stalked off.

Sammy's gaze turned pleading. "Robin, I—"

She cut Sammy off with a curt wave of her hand. "Don't. I can't do that right now." She wasn't angry. She just couldn't handle his sympathy or apologies right now. She went back to their sink and snagged a rag. Wiping down the cart to get rid of most of the excess frosting became almost hypnotic. Every time Sammy reached to help her, she moved in his way.

She needed to do this on her own.

Because speaking to him would undo her. And if she couldn't shine, at least she could hold on to her last shred of dignity.

She wheeled the cart and the ruined cake up to the judging zone and into place between two of her competitors. She hoped nearly punching out a judge didn't disqualify their team.

The three judges stood in a tight group near their table, whispering furiously. Once in a while Victor threw his arms about in the grand gestures she recognized from working with him. He usually did that when he felt threatened. They were joined by several other people in suits.

The contestants gathered in a small group, waiting it out. Sammy reached for her hand, but she pulled away.

She was on the edge, and one kind word would send her over.

Her heartbeat rang loud in her ears. In front of them, the group of judges broke rank and gathered at the back of their table. Over to the right, the announcer stood at the podium waiting for his cue. The female judge walked over and whispered something in his ear.

"Okay, folks," the announcer said, his voice echoing in the now silent room. "I'm being told that the editors of *La Patisserie* and the judges will need to have a private conference. We will reconvene in thirty minutes. We are asking everyone to vacate the room."

Robin and Sammy followed the other teams into the lobby area.

"Robin." Sammy reached out to her. She let him take her hand. "I'm so sorry. I never should have let him get under my skin."

She blinked hard. Tried for a teasing tone. "My cakes aren't safe around you, are they?"

His face fell. "Maybe I'm not cut out to be a sous chef."

"Then it's a good thing I'm not looking for one." Robin wanted to say more to reassure him, but just then the husband-and-wife team came over to them.

"You sure know how to liven up a baking contest," the husband said and lightly punched Sammy on the shoulder.

Sammy shrugged, a half smile on his face.

"I'm not sure taking out one of the judges will improve your chances," his wife teased.

"I thought it was worth a shot," Sammy said.

"And what a shot!" The man laughed, and he and his wife wandered off.

Sammy's face instantly sobered, and he turned to her again. "Talk to me."

"I feel like my chances for being recognized for my work have been turned into a joke." Robin's stomach sat like a stone inside.

Sammy opened his mouth, but whatever he was about to say was interrupted by the ballroom doors opening. Someone with a clipboard and a headset called, "Come on back in. The judges have made their decisions."

They all filed into the ballroom and stood in a loose semicircle around the front of the room.

"It has come to the attention of the owners of this competition that Victor LaVigne had a previous business relationship with one of the contestants." A murmur swept through the crowd. "They have decided that this means he is unable to be impartial. He has been asked to resign as judge."

People started shouting questions, but the announcer held up his hand for quiet. "Because the rules state that the competition will be judged by a three-person team, we will need to postpone the judging until tomorrow morning when the young bakers are set to arrive. Another approved chef will be arriving then and will take Victor's position."

"What about the Fox team?" someone called. Robin didn't see who it was.

"The Fox team will not be eliminated for their unconventional approach to creating an ancient ruins." The crowd exploded in laughter. Heat burned at Robin's ears. "We will see all of you back here tomorrow at eight a.m. for the announcement of the winners."

The crowd began breaking up. Several contestants came to shake their hands, but the rock still sat in Robin's gut. She saw Victor send a glare at Sammy and then exit through a side door.

Sammy reached for her hand again, but she pulled away.

"I'm sorry, Sam. I just need to be alone."

In the elevator up to her room, she stared at her reflection in the polished walls. A streak of frosting still smudged her cheek, and flour dusted down her apron.

So much for showing the world what she could do.

WHAT WAS HE DOING HERE? SAMMY LOOKED AROUND THE restaurant dining room. Located on the top floor of the hotel, the room was lined with windows. Through the panes, New York showed off, Times Square shining its lights into the room.

When he'd made the reservations last week, he'd anticipated spending a quiet evening with Robin after their grueling day. Maybe even starting a tradition of eating in rooftop restaurants. First Duluth, now New York. He hadn't imagined spending it alone.

Some hero he'd turned out to be.

His body went hot and cold alternately as he reviewed the afternoon. Yeah, Victor deserved what he'd gotten.

But.

The ruin of the cake and the horror on Robin's face turned his blood to ice.

How could he have messed that whole thing up?

The maître d' called his name, and Sammy followed the man to a table next to a window. A romantic table for two complete with candles and a view stared at him. He definitely should have canceled the reservation.

But it turned out that staring at the walls in his hotel room was not an option. He'd tried that for the better part of two hours before his restless energy had chased him out and up to the roof.

The waiter placed a plate of baked trout in front of him. A side of roasted root vegetables lent the dish some color. The smell ignited a growl deep in his stomach.

He picked at the fish, ate a few of the roasted carrots and beets. This plate had nothing on the fish burgers Jack made at the VFW back in Deep Haven.

Pushing aside the remnant of the meal, he dropped some cash on the table to cover the bill. His wallet snagged on something in his pocket. He still had the 3x5 cards. They fell open in front of him and he flipped through. They'd executed Robin's plan perfectly. His face burned as he remembered the teasing they'd received from the other competitors. He didn't mind for himself so much, but he ached for Robin. She'd worked so hard for this only to have her dream crumble at her feet.

The wording on the final sheet caught his eye, the rules for the competition. "Each team must present their cake before a panel of three judges." What if there was a way to redeem this mess? Flicking the card against his finger, he thought it through. Just might work. Now he needed to talk to someone in charge. *Please, Lord.*

He shrugged into his leather jacket and headed for the door. At the hostess stand, a man and woman were checking in. His breath stilled as he recognized the male judge from the competition. Huh. Sometimes God did answer wild prayers.

"Excuse me," he said.

"Don't I know you?" the judge said.

Sammy schooled his face into a look he hoped was contrite. "I'm afraid you probably do. Sammy Johnson. I'm Robin Fox's assistant." He held out his hand.

"Right. The guy who took out Victor LaVigne." The judge chuckled and took Sammy's hand. "I always did think ole Vic needed to come down a notch or two."

"I didn't want to fight..." But never mind, this wasn't about him.

"I'm glad to meet you, Sammy," the woman said. "I don't know about anyone else, but I heard what Victor said to you and your partner. He deserved it."

"I just wish Robin didn't have to suffer for my mistake and Victor's lack of ethics."

The woman threaded her hand through her husband's arm. "Yes, such a shame about that ruined cake. It was so beautiful."

"Tell Robin we wish her the best." The judge started to move toward their table.

"Wait." Now or never. Time to put all the cards—er, cake—on the table. "I actually wanted to ask you something."

"Sure, go ahead." The judge pointed to where the maître d' was waiting for them to take a seat. "But I'm hungry after this long day. Mind if we sit and order?"

Sammy followed them to their place next to a window, noting that his own spot had had a better view. So much for romance.

After the judge had ordered, he gestured for Sammy to continue. "I was looking over the rules," Sammy said. He put the 3x5 card on the table. "See here where it says 'Each team must present their cake before a panel of three judges'? Well, it won't be until tomorrow that we will have a panel of three judges. I wondered if, with our unique situation, we could have a second chance to make our cake."

"Nope. Not a chance." The man drank a long swallow of his water.

"C'mon, honey," the judge's wife said. "There's got to be some way to help."

He shook his head. "I can't do it."

"I'm willing to beg." Sammy leaned forward in his chair. "I don't want any special favors—the rest of the teams could have the same second chance if they want."

"Look at his eyes. It must be true love." Bless this judge's wife and her romantic heart.

The judge sighed. He ran a hand over his brow. "Fine. Let me make some calls. This isn't something that I have full control over." He stepped away from the table.

Sammy drummed his fingers on the tabletop. He willed himself to sit still.

"Have you known the girl long?" the judge's wife asked.

"I've known her since high school." He remembered that girl he'd known and the woman she'd grown into. His chest expanded. She was always on his mind.

"Michael and I were high-school sweethearts too," she said.

Sammy started to correct her, because they weren't really sweethearts, were they? Truth was, he didn't know what they were. He only knew that he loved her. The truth sat in his mind a moment.

"I love her," he blurted.

"Of course you do, dear," she said. "How can you not love those curls and that talent?"

He nodded. But it wasn't just Robin's looks and her flair for cakes that he loved. It went far deeper than that. He loved the way she saw the best in people. He'd seen it in her when she'd worked with Ben and later with the other youth. He loved that she showed resilience in the face of problems. She knew what she wanted, and he admired that.

Wow. He loved Robin Fox.

The judge came back. "It's unanimous. You have your extension. One of our people will contact the other teams. You can repair or replace your cake with what you have on hand, but you only have until six a.m. They need to turn over the baking stations for the junior competition. The judges will be coming in at a quarter past six to be ready for the eight a.m. announcement."

"Thank you! We'll be ready." Sammy shook the judge's hand and turned toward the door.

Behind him, the wife sighed. "Ah, young love."

Too impatient for the elevator, he took the stairs two at a time down to Robin's floor and jogged to her room.

He knocked on the door. No answer. She had to be in there, though, right? He banged on it again. "Robin," he called through the closed door. "I know you're avoiding me right now, but just listen." He heard a shuffle on the other side. "I talked to the judge. They're going to give you another chance."

The door flew open. "What? What are you talking about?" Robin stood there in a T-shirt and—were those fuzzy, polka-dot pj's?

He relayed the information about running into the judge and his wife at the restaurant. "We just have to have something ready by six."

Robin's laugh caught him off guard. "Oh, is that all? Just whip up a cake?" She looked at the ceiling then back at him. "With what kitchen? With what ingredients?"

Oh. Right.

"We can use our old kitchen set-up in the ballroom. As for the rest, we'll figure something out. Come on." He held out his hand to her. "Let me at least try. Listen, Robin, I'm sorry for overreacting earlier. It's just that I care for you. In fact, I realized tonight that I love you, and I want to help you. Ever since my accident I have been looking for something, and I'm realizing that you've changed my life. I want to be with you."

"Okay. Wow. Really, you had me at 'Let me try,' but I'll take the rest too." A spark of excitement lit her eyes. She joined her hand in his. "All right. Let's do this."

He pulled her into the hallway. "Attagirl."

"Um, Sammy?" He turned to her. "I should probably get dressed first."

A few minutes later they rode the elevator down to the first floor. Taking a left when the doors opened, they made the short hike to the ballroom where the contest was. Robin had slipped into a pair of jeans and a sweater, a backpack slung over her shoulder. She tied her hair into a high ponytail on top of her head.

The doors were locked, because of course there wouldn't be anyone there at—he looked at his watch—ten thirty at night. *Think fast, Johnson.* "Wait here. I'll get the front desk to let us in."

"Do you really—" Robin said behind him, but he didn't wait for her to finish that sentence. They hadn't come all the way to New York City just to have a little thing like a locked door stop them.

He ran into the hotel manager coming down the hall. "Ma'am," he called out. "Can you come and open this door for us?"

"I just received word from the competition people to let you in." The manager held up a ring of keys and followed Sammy back to the ballroom.

After unlocking the doors, the manager opened a small panel near the door and flipped the light switches. A faint buzzing filled the air as the room lit up. The cleaners must have already been through, because it looked as pristine as before the competition earlier that day. At the front of the room, the ten cakes stood like soldiers waiting for inspection. Their cake would never pass muster.

"Stop by the front desk when you're done," the manager said. "We'll lock up again." She left.

"Ready, partner?" Sammy grabbed Robin's hand and led her to their station.

Robin took a deep breath. "You know we still have a ton of hurdles, right?"

"I may not have been on the track team, but I definitely can jump." Sammy shot her a grin. Warmth filled him at her return smile.

Robin began poking around the metal shelves of the worktop. "There's nothing here." She slid the backpack from her shoulders and set it on the stainless steel bench. "I still have some of the things I brought from home, a little gold leaf, and some sanding sugar." She began riffling through her bag, setting things out next to her backpack. "But all the cake-making ingredients are gone."

"They probably cleaned all that up and have new stuff for tomorrow."

"Probably."

Aw, shoot. There was that look of defeat again. "Maybe we can order some groceries to be delivered?" He tapped open his phone and searched the internet for a minute. "Looks like we're too late at night for deliveries."

Across from him, Robin held her idea notebook. "If we use parts of our existing cake, we wouldn't need as much stuff."

He straightened. "Of course! The kitchen will have everything we need." He held up a hand at her protest. "You stay here and design something amazing. I'll go get the supplies."

He was halfway to the door when— "Wait. I'll need a list."

Robin jotted some things down in her notebook, tore out the page, and handed it to him. "If they don't have almond extract, get regular vanilla instead."

Ten minutes and all the cash in his wallet later, Sammy pushed a cart loaded with baking supplies into the ballroom. A few other bakers filtered in. He paused a moment to look at Robin before she noticed him. She had found a chair and sat hunched over the bench, scribbling fiercely in her notebook. Her hair had been retied into a high messy bun, a few wisps around her face. She'd pushed up the sleeves of her sweater.

She took his breath away.

She glanced up. Her face glowed. "You found flour."

And yeah, he couldn't help the way his chest puffed out. Knights fighting dragons had nothing on him. Of course, he was the cause of all this mess in the first place. His chest deflated. "They had everything on your list. And"—he picked up two cups from the cart—"coffee."

"You're a lifesaver."

"What's the plan, boss?"

She took the cup he offered and spun her notebook around to face him. "Remember the peacock cake for the Adamses' anniversary?"

Remember the last time he'd ruined one of her cakes? Um,

yes. He rubbed at the back of his neck. "You want to do that again?" He looked at the drawing she'd made. "Oh, wait. I see."

She'd taken the original plan of the castle cake and adjusted it so the crushed half would have the agate-style finish of her peacock cake. It appeared as though the castle was tumbling out of the gemstone.

"The cake wouldn't be structurally sound if I just tried to rebuild the other half again. If we follow this plan, we should be okay." Robin demonstrated which parts of the old cake would be stripped away to make room for the new. "We can even leave a few of the destroyed parts and just layer them with some colored sugar. It will look like a geode." She looked up at him, eyes bright. Her full lips...

Nope. Too close. Much too close. They had too much to do for any other shenanigans. Sammy took a step back. "Okay. Put me to work."

fifteen

· · ·

This was...totally wild.

Robin tugged out the hair tie from her messy bun and then flipped her hair back up into the hair tie and secured it back on top of her head.

She checked the clock on the wall. Twenty minutes until go time. Not long enough to run back to the room to change. She glanced down. Her sweater and jeans showed signs of the night's activities—a smear of frosting on her right arm, a dusting of flour across her thigh. She brushed at both.

Oh well.

Sammy, on the other hand, looked amazing. He'd shed the blue button-up shirt he'd worn last night and now wore an apron over his T-shirt and dark jeans. By all rights he should be swinging an axe, chopping down trees—not helping her in a baking contest, for crying out loud. Atlas himself would be jealous of those burly shoulders. She blinked. She didn't have the time to be noticing Sammy's shoulders. Or the faint hint of golden stubble on his chin.

Get it together, Robin. She wiped her hands on her jeans. "Thank you again for helping."

She had been crying into her room-service chicken strips and

French fries when she heard Sammy's knock on the door last night. Wallowing. Yes, she'd been wallowing.

And then Sammy had walked in. Saving her. Again.

Their all-night baking session had been exhausting and exhilarating by turns. She'd grabbed a quick nap while the cakes cooled for two hours, but then had been decorating, drawing agate swirls and creating geodes until her eyes crossed.

Sammy stopped wiping down the counter. "Don't even say that. We never would have had to pull an all-nighter if it wasn't for my macho stunt."

"I liked you being macho." She could admit it now.

"Still, I shouldn't have done it."

"Just be careful around these cakes, eh?" She winked at him.

He smiled back at her, holding up three fingers. "I'll be extra cautious. Scout's honor."

The cake had turned out exactly how she'd pictured it. She'd adjusted the decorations on the castle side to pick up some of the emerald and cobalt tones of the agate side. They moved it into place next to the other cakes.

People began trickling into the room, including the two judges from the night before. Robin and Sammy helped the competition crew clean their baking station to get it ready for the young chef team scheduled to start at eight.

A few of the other contestants came by to compliment them on their cake rescue. Sammy flexed his muscles once. "That's me. The superhero of cake rescues." He'd smiled at her, and heat pooled in her belly.

They watched as the judging team made their way around the cakes, pausing often to consult each other and to jot notes on their clipboards. The clock ticked over to eight o'clock, and everyone in the room streamed to the front.

"Ladies and gentlemen, the judges have made their decisions. All winning teams are requested to come to the front to receive your prize, and for photos." The announcer's voice boomed over the general hubbub. Everyone quieted. "The runner-up is Team Higgins, with their Titanic cake. They win a premium kitchen suite of appliances." The husband and wife hugged each other and then danced up the aisle.

"And in third place, we have Team Sweet Peaches with their Alice-in-Wonderland cake. They'll be taking home a ten-thousand-dollar prize." Everyone cheered for the team of chefs from Georgia as they went forward for their prize. Robin clapped along. Team Sweet Peaches' cake, a towering structure resembling a topsy-turvy stack of teacups straight out of *Alice in Wonderland*, deserved the prize.

"Next, in second place with a twenty-thousand-dollar prize, we have Team Fox with their Gemstone Castle."

Sammy looked at her, a crazy grin on his face. "I think they just called your name."

"Yours too. Our team." She grabbed his hand and dragged him to the front of the room. People clapped and cheered. Onstage, the judge made some joke about this cake being still intact, but she barely heard him. She didn't care what people thought. She didn't even pay attention to the final team called. The verdict rang in her ears.

Second place.

Someone needed to pinch her, because her dreams were coming true.

Twenty thousand dollars could be a brand-new start. Maybe even in Deep Haven.

The contest winners stood in a group to have their photo taken, then individually with their trophies and oversized presentation checks. Robin's face began to ache from all the smiling.

When they were released from photoshoot duties, Sammy moved with her out of the throng. "Congratulations, superstar. I'm proud of you." He gave her a hug. Too soon he broke contact. She spun away from him as someone tapped her on the shoulder, offering their congratulations. When she turned back, he was gone. She stood on her tiptoes, trying to see his broad shoulders through the crowd.

Her heart sank as, instead of Sam, she saw Victor making his way directly toward her. With him was a tall, lanky woman dressed head to toe in black—a turtleneck and slim dress pants, stiletto heels.

"What do you want, Victor?" She refused to shake the hand he held out to her. "More drama?"

"Au contraire! I've come to apologize."

She speared him with a look, raised one eyebrow. Apologize? Yeah, right. Although, he *did* look pretty rough with his red face, his hair slightly disheveled. She wondered if it had been a difficult day for him with the others involved in this contest. He lowered his voice and spoke again. "I'm sorry about yesterday. I behaved very poorly. I will even apologize to your lumberjack, if that would help."

"He's not my—Whatever. Never mind. It's over now."

"Can you forgive me?"

Forgive him? Probably. Eventually.

Trust him? Never again. "Fine. Victor, I forgive you." She held out her hand to belatedly shake his. Her stomach roiled at his clammy hand. She concentrated on her heartbeat for a moment, then two, until she'd calmed. Yes. She could forgive Victor. She believed in forgiveness.

He gave her fingers one last squeeze, then let go. "The other reason I came over here is to offer you a job."

"Victor. Come on. You can't believe I would work for you again." She put her hands on her hips. Was this guy for real?

"No, no, you are right. Let me introduce Valerie." He gestured to the woman standing beside him.

The tall woman stepped forward and offered her hand to Robin. Robin gripped the cool, slim hand and pumped it once. "Nice to meet you, Valerie."

"Likewise."

Robin looked at Victor for more explanation.

"Valerie is opening my new patisserie, Bakery LaVigne, in Chantilly. She has full control of hiring and firing. I am too busy in Paris to oversee anything. She is completely in charge."

"I want you to consider coming to work for me," Valerie said. "Chantilly is an up-and-coming market for new bakeries. You would have full creative control while I take care of the business end of things. I think we could be a great success."

Robin blinked at her. "I don't know what to say." She'd been to Chantilly many times during her years in Paris. Located to the north of the bustling city, Chantilly held all the charm of France and more. Village shops lined cobblestone streets, and the city even had an honest-to-goodness castle just outside of town.

"Say you'll come and check it out at least." Victor smoothed down his hair as he spoke.

"Yes, we'd love to have you come and take a look. Victor speaks so highly of you." While not exactly warm, the woman did seem sincere.

Robin shot a glare at Victor, who had the nerve to give a little shrug.

"I do think highly of you. I'm just not a very expressive person."

Whatever. She refocused on Valerie. "Why me?"

"Victor showed me some of your sketches. I think your innovative ideas are perfect for the new market. If you don't want to come, that's your decision, of course, but this would be a great opportunity for you to make a name for yourself."

Robin just bet Victor had shown her some ideas. Probably the ones from the book she'd left behind. But still, she had a point about this being a good opportunity. "What's your timeline for opening?"

"We already had a soft open. I have temporary staff for now, but I am hoping to fill the permanent positions as soon as possible. Would it be possible for you to fly to Paris right away?"

"You can use your prize money to relocate," Victor put in.

Valerie put a hand on his arm, and he closed his mouth. "The bakery will of course reimburse you for any expenses you incur as you relocate."

"Relocate to where?" Sammy joined them as Valerie finished speaking. In his hands he held something made from wood.

"Robin is moving back to Paris where she belongs." Victor crossed his arms, a smirk on his lips.

"What?" Sammy wheeled to her. "What is he talking about?"

"I'm giving her a job," Victor said.

It hadn't struck her until this moment. A job. In France. To make a name for herself. The thought caught her, and for a blinding moment, dazzled her.

Then Sammy rounded on him, clenching and unclenching his fists. "I'd like to hear all of this from Robin, if you don't mind."

Victor held up his hands in surrender. "As you wish. Remember what I said, Robin. Full control of the bakery menu, as well as recognition for your efforts." Victor took Valerie by the elbow and they left.

But all she saw was the confusion in Sammy's expression.

"Robin," Sammy said. "What is going on?"

She swallowed, cast her gaze to the departing chef. "I...I'm going to France." She was just trying out the words to see if they fit, really, but as soon as they were out, the thought congealed, clung.

A beat, and then Sammy thrust the wooden object into her hands. "Congratulations on your win."

She turned it over. Two spoons joined by a wooden chain lay in her hands. "What is this?"

"It's Norwegian love spoons," Sammy said. He buried his hands in his pockets. "I carved it out of some of the leftover wood from the cabinet I took out of your grandparents' kitchen."

Oh. My. So sweet. So beautiful.

Intricately carved designs ran along the bowls of each spoon. She identified Lake Superior, a peacock, a bicycle, and even a tiny representation of the Fox Bakery. Two foxes chased each other through a grove of pine.

And in that moment, the room grew hot. Tight.

She looked at the spoons and the chain joining them, and a possible future spooled out in front of her. Life in Deep Haven, baking bread and an occasional cake...the never-ending winters...a quiet life. A safe, boring life.

No more espressos on the Seine. No more international travel on the weekends. No more art and creativity and—

"I can't believe you're really thinking of going to Paris. You— I mean, I know you lived there, but I thought that was done. You're not—you belong in Deep Haven, Robin—"

Heat flared in her belly. "You know going back to France is my dream. It's always been my dream—"

"I thought—" His jaw clenched. "I thought what we had was a pretty good dream."

His voice had fallen. And now her throat filled, her eyes burning.

It had been. A nice dream.

But this was her *life*. "Sammy, I—"

"Do you want me or not, Robin?"

She stared at him, and something white-hot burned inside her. "I don't know, okay? I mean—don't pressure me!"

But his mouth tightened. "No pressure. Because I think it's pretty clear that you don't want to come back home with me."

She stared at him, her jaw tight. Fine. "Maybe not."

Sammy stilled. His gaze searched her face, so much hurt in his own.

Her throat clogged, her words a knife between them. She swallowed several times. *Please understand.* "I'm going to take my prize money and move back to France, to Chantilly. I want to try again."

"Try again with Victor?" he said, almost in a whisper.

And yeah, he had a point. But Victor had promised it would be her and Valerie. "Not really. I'll be in Chantilly with Valerie. She and I will work together. I won't have anything to do with Victor."

He looked away, as if in disbelief.

"We'll split the money." She knit her fingers together in front of her. "You can use yours to buy a new truck, or to move to Montana or Wyoming or whatever. Join Tucker's crew. Have an adventure."

Her words seemed to ignite him, and he grabbed her arm and pulled her to the relative privacy of a corner of the room. "That's not what I meant, and I think you know it."

She did know it, and seeing the pain in his eyes made it worse. Her voice softened. "Sammy, we can figure it out. We can video chat all the time."

He winced. "Why bother? You never wanted a long-distance relationship. Besides, it's becoming clear that we want very different things out of life."

Maybe they did. "I need to do this. Can you understand?"

"No, don't think I can. Why can't you be happy in Deep Haven?" Sammy leaned closer to her. "You won't find what you're looking for chasing a mountaintop experience all the time."

"Is that what you think I'm doing?"

He lifted a shoulder.

"At least I'm not hiding away in Deep Haven too scared to try anything new."

Sammy pressed his lips together. The silence between them stretched thin like a rubber band pulled too taut.

"I hoped I would be enough for you. That we could have adventures together. I hoped you would be happy with a life in Deep Haven." Sammy looked down at the floor, then raised his gaze to meet hers again. He stood up straight and reached out a hand toward her. "I love you, Robin, and I want a life with you."

Oh. She closed her eyes. "I guess I want more."

She shouldn't have opened her eyes again, because he was struggling to form words, the hurt cascading over his face.

But he couldn't seriously think that she'd give up Paris for...

Oh. He did. And if Victor hadn't offered her the job, she would have gone back to Deep Haven, ready to build a life.

With him.

"Please, Sammy—"

"You're choosing to go to France—*with Victor*"—he threw a thumb over his shoulder in the direction Victor had walked off—"instead of figuring out if we have a future."

"I'm not going with Victor…" But she couldn't complete the sentence, because that's *exactly* what she was doing.

"There's not much more to say, then, is there?"

"Sammy—"

"No. I'm not enough for you, and I never will be. Not when your head is in the clouds. Not when you can't even imagine having enough right here. It's not like this thing would have worked out anyway. You're right. You'd never fit into Deep Haven." Sammy turned and walked out of the ballroom.

Robin's feet were rooted to the floor as she watched him go.

"Excuse me, miss?" Standing there was the announcer. "I have your real check." He held out an envelope to her, *Team Fox* scrawled across the front in a flowery font.

She took the envelope. It shook in her hands. Everything she had ever wanted. Recognition for her talent. A job in a bakery in France with full control. Money for a new start.

Yep. This should be the happiest day of her life.

If she could bring herself to open the envelope.

THE LOSS OF ROBIN PHYSICALLY ACHED.

Two weeks after their blowup in New York, and Sammy still caught himself rubbing at the middle of his chest. It never helped.

I guess I want more. Her words echoed through his mind, fueling the pain.

Translation: You're not enough.

He sat on his bed in his mom's house, back to the wall, legs stretched out in front of him. Beside him on the bedside table, his phone buzzed, Seth's name on the caller ID.

"Hey. What's up?" Sammy crossed his ankles.

"It's been a while. Thought I'd check in."

"I thought maybe you had a job for me."

"Not at the moment. I'm at your front door. Want to let me in?"

Sammy hung up and jogged downstairs to the door. He and Seth did a half hug, half backslap.

"How was New York?" Seth took off his jacket and Sammy hung it up.

"Fine, I guess. It's big."

"Okaaay..." Seth raised his eyebrows, but didn't pursue the statement. "I stopped in at the bakery. Elaine and Jim have a picture of you and Robin with your winning trophy displayed on the counter."

Sammy rubbed his temple. "Second place."

"What's that?"

"We placed second, not a winning trophy." He led Seth into the living room. They sat on opposite ends of the couch.

"The looks on your faces could have fooled me."

"Mind if I put the TV on? There's a rerun of Monday night's game." He flipped the channels until he found ESPN. Onscreen, the Minnesota Timberwolves battled it out against the Dallas Mavericks.

"Look, Seth, why did you really come by?"

"I haven't seen you around. I'm wondering what happened in New York. I'm concerned for my friend."

"We took second place. Robin moved back to France. I came home. What's to tell?" He rubbed at the spot on his chest again.

"Not fooling me, man." The fans roared as the Mavs scored a point.

"Fine. I thought we had something going, you know? Robin is really, really special. I thought maybe she felt the same way about me."

"But she doesn't? Too bad. She asks you to come all the way to New York and then drops you?"

Yeah, that sounded bad. Except... "It wasn't exactly like that." Sammy found himself telling Seth the details of his trip. Clearing his throat, he added, "She chose France over me."

"Sounds to me that she needed to try again over there. Maybe redeem some of the bad memories from when she had to leave."

"I suppose."

"If you love her, let her go and all that."

"You're such a good guru." Hopefully Seth could hear that it wasn't all sarcasm.

"Anytime, buddy. Anytime."

They both watched as the Wolves' point guard drove hard to the basket. He went up for a layup and was fouled hard by the Mavs' power forward.

Sammy turned the game down. This would be hard enough to admit without having to say it loudly. "She called me a coward."

"What?" Seth broke his gaze from the TV to look at him.

"She said I am hiding and that I'm too much of a coward to move forward."

"I see."

Sammy rubbed his hand over his hair. "The thing is, she's right."

Seth returned his attention to the television. "I don't know if it's cowardice preventing you from acting."

"Maybe not in all things, but in some things." Sammy watched as the point guard's second free throw tickled the bottom of the net. "I mean, yeah, I still have the hang-up about driving, and that's not cowardice, I don't think. But not making a decision about what I'm doing with myself...I think she's right. I'm just scared." He turned the game back up.

Seth reached out for the remote, then muted the game. "You know that heroes act even when scared, right? Might be cliché, but it's true. Maybe try doing one thing scared." He clicked the mute button again. Onscreen, the Timberwolves' small forward stepped in to take a charge, hitting the court with a thud. The whistle blew, putting the Mavs in foul territory.

They sat in silence and watched the Timberwolves pull out a 101 to 98 buzzer beater over the Mavericks. Seth slapped his knees. "Welp. Time for me to head out."

Sammy walked him to the door. "Thanks for the pep talk. I'll think about what you said." He shut the door behind Seth, then returned to his room and sat on the edge of his bed.

He pulled open the drawer to his nightstand and picked up the envelope on the top of the stack of envelopes with *Williams* on every return address. The paper felt rough under his fingertips. One corner of the envelope was bent and dirty. He tapped the envelope against his palm.

Maybe try doing one thing scared.

With a swift movement, he tore the envelope open. Inside was a folded piece of lined notebook paper. He pulled it out.

Dear Mr. Johnson,

This will be the last time I write to you. I certainly don't want to bother you. You've already done so much for our family, just by pulling my son to safety.

I don't know if you have read any of the other letters I wrote to you, but let me say again how

*incredibly grateful I am. My son would not be
alive if it wasn't for your heroic action.*

Sammy almost threw the letter in the trash. He closed his
eyes, then forced them open again.

He scanned the document for where he'd left off.

*Teddy's surgery is scheduled for tomorrow.
He's feeling pretty low. I keep telling him to be
brave, but I think he's losing hope. If you are a
praying man, please pray for Teddy.*

You remain in our prayers,

Melissa Williams

Surgery? What was this about? Sammy searched the drawer,
noting the dates on the postmarks of the letters. He put them in
order and began to read from the beginning.

The letters told a story of a prolonged medical battle. Teddy
had never fully recovered from a broken leg he'd gotten in the
accident. He'd gone through multiple therapies, but nothing had
worked. In the second-to-last letter, Sammy read that the team at
Children's Minnesota, a hospital in Minneapolis, decided to
remove Teddy's badly damaged leg. He would be transferred to
an inpatient program at Sister Kenny, a rehab specialty clinic
located in Golden Valley, a Minneapolis suburb.

He'd had the surgery over two months ago.

Melissa had slipped in a photo with that second-to-last letter.
A boy of about ten lay in a hospital bed, a smile on his face. Even
from a photo, Sammy could see that the boy was faking.

Melissa ended with the words:

We've taken the following verse as our theme verse for this time in Teddy's life: "Wait for the Lord; be strong, and let your heart take courage; wait for the Lord!"

Her words sank deep inside him, filling in the cracks in his heart. Maybe he wasn't truly a coward, but he was acting like one. Hiding behind his accident and recovery instead of moving forward with his life. Instead of pursuing God's best, he'd just been coasting.

That ended today.

Heroes acted even when scared.

He went back downstairs and found his jacket as the sound of the garage door opening echoed through the house.

His mom came into the hall and hung her jacket in the closet. "Hi, honey."

"Hi, Ma."

"Everything okay?" She reached out and touched his arm.

"I'm gonna take the truck to Minneapolis."

"Um, okay." She blinked several times, and her eyes searched his face.

He forced a smile. "I've done a lot of thinking about it, and I think I need to go see Teddy Williams. I read the letters." Okay, maybe he'd only thought about it for five minutes before making a decision, but any longer and he would have talked himself out of it.

His mom put her hand to her mouth for a moment before taking his hand. "I'm proud of you. Want me to drive you to Minneapolis?"

"That's super tempting, but I think this is something I need to do on my own."

"Okay. Text me when you get there. And if you stop on the way." His mom squeezed his hand. "I'll be praying."

Moments later he stood in the driveway, facing down his truck like it was an angry bull and he the bullfighter. The green Ford Ranger had been like a friend to him. Over the past year and a half or so since his accident, he'd sat in the front seat a few times, starting the engine and checking that everything still ran.

Every time he'd broken out into a cold sweat.

He tugged his gloves on tighter. Took a long breath. His exhale wisped into a cloud in the frigid air.

The truck door opened with a protesting screech, and the leather front seats crackled as he sat. True to form, the engine revved up with just a turn of the key.

His heart raced in tune with the motor.

His hands dampened in his gloves. He flexed them on the steering wheel. Breathed a prayer. *Let my heart take courage, Lord.*

Resisting the urge to close his eyes against the memories, he eased the truck into reverse and backed out of the short driveway and onto the road.

Choosing against the radio, he sat ramrod straight in the seat. He held the steering wheel so tight his knuckles began to ache.

All the way through town he practiced deep breathing. He had to make it the four hours to Minneapolis.

This was too important for failure.

An hour into his drive, his grip loosened on the wheel. The roads ran dry and clear. He flipped on the cruise control and eased his foot off the gas.

His shoulders came down from around his ears.

The sun began to sink lower in the sky, lighting the few clouds with reds and golds.

A motion caught his eye as a deer leapt in front of his truck. It was caught in the headlights for a moment as he stood on the brake.

He blinked away the darkness descending over his sight. The truck tires squealed. The front fender caught the tail end of the deer, and Sammy came to an abrupt halt. He glanced in the rearview mirror. No cars.

Hands shaking, he pulled off to the side of the road. No sign of the deer. He got out of the truck and fell to his knees.

Vomited in the snowy grass.

But as he stood and checked the front bumper, a sense of peace ran through him. The bumper was fine. The deer, apparently, also fine.

God had saved him again, but this time he wouldn't question why. God had given him a good life. It was time to fully live it.

He climbed back into the cab of the truck, hands steady. The dashboard clock told him he would be arriving at Sister Kenny just before dinner time.

A few boring hours later, he made it to the Twin Cities. After a quick stop at McDonald's, he pulled into the rehab's parking lot. The sun cast a golden glow over the rehab center as it set in the west.

He walked under the portico and into the brick building. The sharp smell of disinfectant raised his heart rate. A ghost pain flickered through his legs, but he pushed through it. He followed the nurse's directions, stopping outside a room with a hand-lettered sign: Teddy Williams.

He knocked on the door with one knuckle.

"Come in." A woman's voice.

"I brought contraband," he said. He held up the McDonald's sack as he came into the room. A small boy, towheaded and thin, lay in the bed, his lower half covered by a sheet. The sheet flattened to the bed much earlier than it should have. In the chair next him sat a woman with the same nose as the boy.

"Sammy?" she said and rose to her feet. "Sammy Johnson?"

"That's me. You must be Melissa and Teddy." He shook the take-out bag. "I hope I haven't missed dinner."

"Honey," she said to the boy. "This is Sammy. He's the one who rescued us. Sammy, this is Teddy." She crossed the room and shook Sammy's hand. "Thank you so much for coming. I'll just leave the two of you alone."

Sammy pulled another chair next to the bed. He unpacked

the hamburgers and fries onto a wheeled table at his elbow. Teddy sat in bed, arms crossed, chin tucked to his chest.

"I suppose you're here to cheer me up."

Sammy smiled at the kid's attitude. He recognized a bit of himself from his first days of therapy. "Nope."

Teddy's head snapped up. "What are you here for?"

"To eat a hamburger." Sammy took a big bite of his Big Mac. "Want some ketchup for your fries?" he asked around the bite. He unearthed some ketchup packets from under the napkins in the take-out bag and squirted them onto a napkin. Keeping his eyes on his food, he kept eating.

A few bites later he saw Teddy's fingers reach for a fry. Then another. Sammy had nearly finished his burger when he heard the crinkle of the other Big Mac being unwrapped. He popped a fry into his mouth and met Teddy's eye.

"You have no idea what it's like." Teddy's tough exterior was melting in front of Sammy's eyes.

He shrugged. "You're right. I don't."

The kid choked on his bite. Sammy handed him a cup of water. "Everyone is always trying to convince me that they know what I'm going through. They don't."

"But I do know what it's like to do hard things. Look, I'm not here to tell you that things won't be hard. But remember, when things get hard, you've got people to lean on. Your mom and dad, your medical team. And now you've got me."

"What do you mean?"

Sammy found a pen and tore a scrap of paper off the McDonald's bag. He scrawled on it. "There. That's my cell number. You can call me anytime." He handed the paper to Teddy. "I'll give it to your mom too, and she can call if you don't feel up to it."

Teddy stared at the slip of paper. "Why are you giving this to me?"

"So you can call me when you need to rant, or a burger. So you've got someone in your corner. Because that's how I made it through my therapy. That's how I'm doing anything at all—the support I receive every day."

"Thanks."

Sammy stood. "I'm gonna head out. But you be sure to use that phone number." Teddy nodded, his face bright.

Out in the hall, Sammy leaned against the wall for a breath.

Melissa came toward him. "Thanks again for coming. It means a lot to me." She stood next to him. Her face had relaxed since Sammy walked in earlier. "I hope you don't mind, but I eavesdropped a little." She shrugged. "Overprotective, I guess."

Sammy waved away her concern. "I get it. You don't really know me." *Tell her. She deserves to know.* The words moved through his mind, settled in his heart. He pushed off the wall. "Melissa, I need to tell you something."

They walked the hallway as he explained about his head injury in the Army and the subsequent seizures. Then finally, he told her about what happened on the day of their accident. "If I'd taken my meds, I probably wouldn't have had that blackout right before coming around the corner. I would have seen you sooner, braked quicker. I could've gotten you and Teddy to a safe place instead of nearly running you over." He straightened his spine. Time to rip this Band-Aid all the way off. "It's my fault that Teddy is lying in that hospital bed. I'm so sorry."

Melissa folded her arms and looked steadily at him. A nurse brushed past them. Overhead, the PA called for Dr. Klein to report to the rehab room. Sammy forced himself to continue meeting Melissa's gaze. She deserved that much.

"Sam. How could it have been your fault? I'm the one who hit that deer." He started to break in, but she held up her hand to silence him. "No. I understand how you feel. I've blamed myself for this for so long too. But the truth is that the accident was just that—an *accident*." She leaned closer to him. "I'm sorry this has tormented you for so long. You were never to blame. In fact, you saved us that day. My son wouldn't even be here if you hadn't acted so quickly to get him out of the car."

He rubbed his thumbs over his eyes. "I should have—"

"No. No more blaming yourself. You are forgiven by me, though I never blamed you, and by God, who knows your heart." She began walking again, and he followed after her, ten thousand pounds lighter.

Their walk took them back to Teddy's door. "I guess it's time for me to head back home," he said.

Melissa laid her hand on his arm, halting him. "I appreciated what you said to Teddy in there. You're really good with kids."

Her words penetrated through to his heart.

Yes. Yes, he was.

And just like that, his life seemed to snap into place.

sixteen

· · ·

CHANTILLY, EARLY APRIL

The culmination of all her dreams stared her in the face.

Robin stood in the paltry glow of morning. Sunlight struggled through the windows at Bakery LaVigne in Chantilly, France. She wrapped her arms around herself as she surveyed the store.

In the month she'd lived here, she'd streamlined the kitchen, added a small seating area indoors, and changed the menu to better suit her strengths. The public area of the bakery was black trim and white walls, with black-and-white checked floors. The dining space had two white tables with three black, bistro-style chairs each.

In an act of whimsy, she'd hung a small painting of a fox near the cash register. She'd found the painting in an outdoor market on the Seine in Paris. Her grandparents had encouraged her to grab on to this opportunity to move back to France, and she was grateful to them. Though she had a small apartment over the bakery here in Chantilly, she spent most of her free time on her days off wandering the streets of Paris. From her apartment, she could catch a train and be at the Eiffel Tower in an hour.

Damien, the clerk, handed her a small espresso cup. "We have a brief lull. Perhaps you want to take your coffee on the patio." His French accent turned "the" into "zee."

The door to the kitchen opened, and a hint of cinnamon swirled out on the heels of Jackie, the pastry chef. Robin closed her eyes and imagined being in Grandma Elaine's kitchen, watching Grandpa Jim roll out his famous cinnamon raisin walnut loaf.

She threw back the espresso in one long gulp. "I'd rather get back in the kitchen. The Gerards will be in for their order soon."

Keeping her hands busy kept her mind from wandering. At least that was the theory. In practice she found herself daydreaming about a pair of green eyes and the man behind them. Some of Sammy's last words haunted her. *I hoped you would be happy with a life in Deep Haven.*

Except what was wrong with wanting big things? Wanting to shine bright?

You won't find what you're looking for chasing a mountaintop experience all the time. Sammy again. His comment prodded an ache in her heart. Was that really what this was? An attempt to live a life that wasn't sustainable?

She mixed up a final batch of fondant to finish the Gerards' cake. After rolling it out, she cut the remaining shapes and added them to the top of the cake.

She took a step back to look it over. Perfection. The modest two-tier cake resembled an English garden. Tiny shrubs ringed even tinier flowers. She'd even planted a miniature fountain in the middle. Flowers and greenery tumbled down the sides. Moving as quickly as a sloth, Robin and Damien boxed up the order. Through the plastic window on the top of the box, Robin saw that the cake remained unharmed. She carried it through to the display in the front of the bakery.

The bell jingled. "Bonjour," the customer said. "I am here for my cake."

"Welcome, Ms. Gerard." Robin went around the counter to greet her customer. "I have it right here."

"Please, call me Zoe. We're practically the same age." Zoe peered inside the plastic window. "Magnificent! You have created exactly what I asked for." She spun to Robin, took both hands into her own, and then pressed a kiss on each of Robin's cheeks. "You are a rock star. I will tell all my friends about you. This is going straight to social media." And that wasn't nothing. Zoe's social media following numbered in the hundred thousands.

Robin's cheeks warmed. She gave a little shrug. "It's what I do."

"And you do it so well," Zoe said. "I wish I had this much talent." Zoe left the bakery, cradling her cake like a stack of fine china.

Praise, recognition of her talent, a life abroad. It was all she'd ever dreamed about.

Why did it feel so hollow?

"Damien, I will go sit on the patio after all." She pushed out the door and sat in one of the wrought iron bistro chairs to the right of the entrance. The cool, damp metal gave her a shiver. Overhead, the weak sun sailed through a pale blue sky, its rays doing nothing to warm her heart.

A clattering on the cobbles caught her attention. She shielded her eyes from the sunlight. She caught a glimpse of white-blonde hair. "Elise?" Her friend came into view.

"Robin! I am so glad to see you!"

She jumped up and gave her friend a squeeze. "What are you doing here?" The two friends had been in contact multiple times since Robin's move, but they'd never had the opportunity to meet up.

"I had to come and see you and your bakery," Elise said. "So when I had an unexpected morning off, I couldn't wait another minute." Elise twirled her around. "Look at you! You are very French today."

Robin glanced down at her clothes. Her slim black jeans, dark turtleneck, and canvas shoes did look very petit bourgeois. The apron on top cemented the outfit as bakery chic.

She put her hands on her hips and struck a pose. "I'm trying to look the part. Let me show you around." Robin looped her arm through Elise's and took her into the bakery.

She introduced her to Damien and Jackie, the chef. Then she pointed out all the little improvements she'd made to the space and had her taste a fig jam tart piping hot from the oven. Elise oohed and aahed in all the right places. Pausing in front of the little fox painting, she asked, "And this?"

"I found that in Paris." Robin's voice broke. She brushed a tear from her eye.

"Ah, I understand." Elise laid a hand on Robin's shoulder. "Show me your apartment and we can talk all about it."

Robin led her friend up the back stairs and into her studio apartment. The small garret tucked under the eaves held a daybed, which pulled double duty as a bed for Robin and a couch for visitors. Not that Robin had any visitors. Or much space in the room. A dresser only big enough for five T-shirts, four sweaters, a couple pairs of pants, and her threadbare jammies stood to one side. Her shower and toilet were tucked under the eaves on the other side of the hall. She took her meals in the kitchen of the bakery.

They sat on the daybed, knee to knee. A cloud passed by her round window, throwing the room into shadow.

"Now, tell me why you are unhappy."

Robin tried for a laugh. It came out with a croak. "Who said I'm unhappy?"

Elise put a hand on her knee. "We lived together for four years. I know when you're faking it."

"Fine." Robin looked toward the window. "I thought coming here and being part of this bakery would be the greatest thing. When I was in Deep Haven, I kept dreaming of moving back here. This was all I wanted."

"Except you sacrificed love."

"He doesn't want me." The thought twisted in her heart, a sudden sharp pain.

"Did he tell you that?"

"He said, 'It's becoming clear that we want very different things out of life.'" She tried to add an edge of sarcasm but failed. "He wanted me to settle."

"I think maybe he just wants you to choose him." Elise patted her knee again.

The words rang inside Robin. They had a sliver of truth.

Elise stood, warming to her subject. "Also, he's not wrong. You can't always be chasing the high. We have to live in the normal, the everyday. You have to love your life for the regular times too."

"You're the second person who has said that to me." She winced at the memory of the hurt on Sam's face as he said it.

"Why can't you see it? You want to bake amazing cakes, and that's fine, but sometimes life is about making bread too. It can't be all sugar all the time. Bread is deeply satisfying, a foundation of life—like love." Elise paced in front of her. "You think you don't fit in anywhere, but it's just not true. You fit in here, and you fit in your small town back home. You just don't want to believe it because you want to be a superstar with cakes on magazines and all the adoration of Paris. Also, fitting in and belonging aren't the same thing."

"I guess you're right." She kneaded her hands in her lap.

"Oh, I know I am. Life is a journey lived out one step at a time. We need to walk out our faith and our life with a long faithfulness, not living on mountaintop experiences."

"But how do I do that?"

"Only you can answer that, my friend." Elise put a hand on her hip. "Ask yourself, is my dream to bake here in France, far from my family and other 'loved ones'?" She winked broadly as she put air quotes around the last words. "Or is it okay for my dream to change?"

"I'll think about it."

"Good. Now, I need another one of those tarts before I head back to the train station."

Robin swatted her friend on the arm, and they headed downstairs.

"Damien, I'm going to walk Elise to the train station." Robin served each of them another jam tart, and then they walked out into the sunshine.

Buildings rose tall along the cobbled streets on the way to the train station, a brisk ten-minute walk.

"Thank you for coming," Robin said. "I needed to see a friendly face. I needed the truth-telling even more."

"Anytime. I'm glad it worked out." Elise linked her arm through Robin's. "I expect to see you in Paris some afternoon."

Soon the station appeared. After a quick hug, the friends said goodbye, and Robin headed back to the bakery.

A block away, she spotted a man standing just outside the open bakery door. As she drew closer, fragments of his American accent drifted toward her. His back was broad and his blond hair cut close to his head.

Could it be? She quickened her steps, and the bell on the door jingled as he went inside.

A sprout of hope began pushing its way up through her heart.

She pushed the door open. The man stood near the counter, his back to her. She stepped toward him, heart pounding.

She reached out for the man as he turned around.

The stranger gave her a quizzical look. "Do I know you?"

Robin's throat swelled. "Oh. I'm sorry. I guess not."

Up close, this man was several inches shorter than Sammy, and his hair was all wrong. It was just her wishful thinking painting Sammy back into her life.

A woman came from near the cash register with a paper bag in her hand, grease from the pastries inside dotting the paper. "C'mon, Steven. Let's get to the castle before the line starts."

The man wrapped his arm around the woman's waist, and they walked off in the direction of one of Chantilly's famous sites.

Robin watched them for a minute before walking up the stairs to her little apartment. She opened the top drawer of her dresser. Nesting in one of her T-shirts lay the love spoons Sammy had carved for her. She picked them up, studying the pictures again. A small bicycle. A tiny peacock. A fox chasing another along one edge.

She tucked the spoons into a pocket of her apron. The apron with the Bakery LaVigne logo scrolled across the top.

It was all wrong.

She reached back and untied the strings and lifted the apron over her head. She didn't need the adoration of all of Paris or Chantilly. She only needed the adoration of one man.

It was time to make some new dreams.

SAMMY SAT IN THE STANDS IN THE HIGH-SCHOOL GYM, WATCHING the baseball team work out on the floor. Despite being early April, Deep Haven had had seven inches of snow dumped on it last week, so practice was being held inside.

Ben had texted earlier in the day.

BEN

Got my history grade. I passed! Am eligible to try out for the team. Come cheer me on?

How could he say no to that? So Sammy was sandwiched between Seb Brewster on his right and Dan Matthews on his left. Other parents and fans sat scattered across the rest of the bleachers.

There was more to life than baseball, but on days like today it was hard to remember what they might be.

So many things had happened over the past few weeks since visiting Teddy in the hospital. He now called Teddy or his family regularly to talk through the difficulties the boy was experiencing in his recovery. Teddy would be fitted with his prosthesis soon.

He'd made two calls the day after visiting Teddy. One to Tucker to turn down the smoke jumping offer. And the other to Vivien to accept the full-time director's position at the youth center. They had applied for a few grants while he'd quietly deposited some of his insurance money into the youth center account.

On the gym floor, Ben trotted toward the coach, who pointed him toward the pitching area. Ben hustled into position and threw a few fastballs to a kid in catcher's gear. Then he changed his stance and pitched a knuckleball, then a changeup.

The whole group of teens ran through some infield and outfield throwing drills, and then the coach had them circle up center court.

"Looks like we'll have a pretty good team this year," Dan said.

"We'd better. We're due a playoff run," Seb shot back. On the court, the group of new baseball hopefuls broke rank.

"I'm going to go talk to Ben," Sammy said. "See you guys at headquarters later?"

"You betcha," Dan said. "See you there."

Sammy made his way through the teens and parents littering the court until he found Ben. He clapped him on the shoulder. "You looked good out there."

"Thanks, Mr. J." The kid's grin stretched wide. "Coach says I did well. The roster won't be official until next week, but as long as I keep my grades up, I'm golden."

"That's great, Ben! Let me know if you need more study sessions." He gave Ben a salute and walked out of the gym to his

Ford Ranger. He'd promised his mom a loaf of walnut raisin bread on his way home.

Sam passed by a few people braving the not-quite-cleared sidewalks. He gave each of them a Minnesota hi sign, flicking his index finger up from the steering wheel. As he made the turn into the Fox Bakery parking lot, he narrowly avoided Casper Christiansen behind the wheel of the municipal snowplow. The volunteers had been working all week on clearing snow, him included. If Casper didn't finish up tonight, Sammy would take another shift tomorrow.

He pushed through the bakery door. The familiar sweet, yeasty scent assaulted him. Why had he promised his mom he would come? Elaine Fox stood behind the cash register. A picture frame perched on the counter—a print of him and Robin with their prize at Distinctive Bakes.

Looked like he would be getting a side of heartache with his daily bread.

"Sammy! Good to see you." Elaine came around the counter and gave him a hug. "Are you here for a baguette or a raisin loaf?"

"You know me well," he said, a smile creeping up on him. "Raisin loaf today."

"Coming right up." Elaine moved back behind the counter and began bagging up his order.

Don't ask about Robin. "How is Robin doing?" *Shoot!* His mouth had a mind of its own.

Elaine paused. Her lips tipped up briefly. "I don't think Chantilly is everything she hoped for. But she's a smart girl. She'll figure it all out."

"I believe in her. She was made for big things. I'm glad her dream is coming true."

"You helped her realize that dream." Elaine touched the edge of the photo frame. "By the way, we have people coming in all the time asking for her caramel mocha cupcakes. I haven't the faintest idea how to make them. I don't suppose you know?"

"Actually, I do." An image of Robin, hair tied on top of her head, laughing as she mixed the cake mix, flashed through his mind and speared itself somewhere in the vicinity of his heart. A ghost of chocolate mocha hovered in his nose. "The secret is in the fresh espresso. Or so Robin always said."

"Are you looking for a job? I need someone to make those cakes." Elaine clasped her hands together.

A lumberjack turned baker? Why not? Robin had already introduced him to how fun the kitchen could be. "If you're serious, I could probably come by once a week."

"Works for me," Elaine said. "We'll need to work out a payment schedule."

"Didn't Robin tell you? I work for cupcakes." He grinned at Elaine and took his raisin loaf.

Sure, being back in the bakery would be bittersweet, but maybe with time, the sweet would be all that remained.

seventeen

. . .

He ought to feel proud of himself.

A few days after talking to Elaine at the bakery, Sammy surveyed the youth center around him.

When their grant had come through, Vivien had immediately begun planning this night. The other volunteers, parents, and youth who used the center had gathered for a party to celebrate having their first full-time, paid staff member. Him.

Standing in the center of the chaos of tonight's party, Sammy knew he'd made the right choice in turning down the smoke jumping job. He had a calling to Deep Haven, to help the town in any way he could. And to follow through on building a house out on his land. Something made with big logs to stand the test of time.

He already had big plans mapped out for how they could benefit more kids. Thinking about the tutors he wanted to line up made his heart quicken. He couldn't wipe the smile from his face. He could be a hero to kids every day, in small ways. Being a firefighter or smoke jumper wasn't the only way to protect and serve.

Crepe paper streamers and crooked signs proclaiming "Congratulations" papered the walls. Near the door a table groaned under a huge spread of food. Over in the corner a "Welcome home, Sammy" card hung over a freshly painted desk and a brand new chair with a huge bow pinned to the back.

And yeah. This place did feel a little like home.

He'd also come to grips with the idea that he and Robin were on different paths. He loved her, but he needed to let her live her life the way she thought best. He was ashamed that he'd ever implied that he wanted her to change. He'd sent her a text just that morning.

SAMMY

> We should talk. I'm sorry for the things I said in New York.

She hadn't replied, but that was okay too. Tomorrow, after the party stuff had settled down, he would try to call her. Apologies should be delivered in person if possible, but a cell phone would work in a pinch.

"Hey, Mr. J. Want to lose?" Ben Zimmerman held up a pair of Ping-Pong paddles, his eyebrow raised.

"Bring it on."

One game of Ping-Pong turned into two when Ben beat Sammy and Sammy immediately challenged him to a rematch. When Ben got up on him by five points, Sammy laughed and surrendered. He handed his paddle over to Tiago, who was waiting for a turn.

Vivien walked over to him, her arm around Boone. Boone kissed the top of her head. "I'm going to go grab us a Coke," he said. "Sam, do you want one?" Sammy shook his head.

"Everyone's having a great time," Sammy said after Boone left. "This was unnecessary, but thank you for doing it."

"You deserve it," she said. "Everyone wants to celebrate you. I think you underestimate how much this town relies on you."

"You've got that backward. I rely on them." Sammy stood taller.

"Boone tells me you helped out on the snowplow after last week's storm."

"He told you right." Sammy's white-knuckled driving had soon turned to a loose-gripped enjoyment as he remembered why he loved being in the cab of a snowplow so much. High above the street, white snow draped over all the winter grime, helping his neighbors—it just felt right.

"I'm glad to hear you're claiming your life back."

"Just trying to move forward in courage and not in fear."

Vivien gestured to the groups of young people all around the room. "The kids obviously love you."

"The feeling is mutual." Sammy smiled at Tiago, who was jumping up and down and cheering. The kid must have beaten Ben at Ping-Pong.

"That other grant came in for paying your position for the next few years. There won't be much left over for extras though." Vivien tossed her sable ponytail over her shoulder. "I'm sorry that we're starting you on such a shoestring budget."

"About that. I have some ideas to bring to the next board meeting." He had to restrain himself from word-vomiting all his ideas at her right now. "Some fundraisers I think could bring in enough money to buy matching furniture. The kind that can take a licking and not disintegrate."

"Sounds good. I'll set it up." Sammy had agreed to be the youth center director on the condition that Vivien continue to be chairman of the board.

Boone came back carrying two cans of Coke and handed one to Vivien. When their fingers brushed, Vivien smiled up into Boone's eyes. The love between them almost sizzled. They walked away, Boone's arm wrapped around Vivien's waist.

Sammy felt a pull in his gut. Envy, or something close to it. If he closed his eyes, he could almost smell the shampoo Robin used. Just because he'd decided to step aside and let her pursue her own path didn't mean it would be easy to let her go.

Near the front of the room, Peter Dahlquist rapped on the food table, getting everyone's attention.

"I'd like to propose a toast," he said. "Sammy, for as long as I've known you, you've been selfless. From your time as a linebacker on the football field to your recent days serving this town. I'm glad we can all be here tonight to celebrate you and to wish you well in your new endeavor. To Sammy!" Peter raised his can of soda and took a long swallow.

"To Sammy!" rang out from around the room.

He felt his face warm. A tingling, electric sensation started in his chest and spread to his whole torso.

"Speech!" Seth called out. Soon the whole room called for a speech.

Sammy made his way to the food table. He hadn't eaten yet, but he would have to check out his options once this speech was over. "You all know me," he said. "And you know I'm a guy of few words."

"Since when?" someone near the back of the room called out. A ripple of laughter ran through the crowd.

"Okay, so I'm a guy of lots of words, but not profound ones." His eye caught on an item displayed at the end of the table. Was that a cake or just another pan of bars? He edged nearer to it. "Some of you know that at the beginning of this year, I was at a crossroads." His attention split between what he was saying and the cake, he almost missed the flash of an auburn head ducking through the gathered crowd. Was that—Could Robin really be here? His heart rate picked up as he attempted to focus on his speech. "My legs are fully healed, and I started itching for more than being a courier and handyman."

"You'll still come and help me paint my front room, though, won't you?" Edith Draper hollered from her place in the front of the group.

"Anything for you, Edith. You're my number one customer." The party chuckled in appreciation. He must have imagined the familiar curly hair. Rats. He was probably just willing it into life.

"After talking to some of you, and hearing some hard truths, I came to realize that I could never leave Deep Haven. This place means too much to me. Anyway, thank you for this party, and thank you for your support now and always."

The crowd erupted in cheers. Sammy's face heated, and he quickly turned and reached for a plate. After piling it high with a ham sandwich, chips, pickles, and Jell-O salad, he made his way toward the cake.

The two-tier confection was ringed with red, orange, and blue-green illustrations. A fox chased a peacock, an agate swirled near a tiny bakery, a pair of bicycles rested together alongside a lake. He took a slice and then swiped a piece of frosting. A hint of almond lingered on his tongue.

His breath caught. There was only one person who would have baked this. He set down his plate and scanned the room. There! Another flash of auburn hair almost to the door.

"Robin!"

She stopped, her hand on the doorknob, then turned and looked at him. He started toward her, but a hand on his shoulder stopped him. Peter.

"Great speech," the big man said. "For what it's worth, I'm glad you're sticking around."

"Thanks." How quickly could he end this conversation?

"Seth told me you considered joining a smoke jumping outfit." At Sammy's nod, Peter continued. "We can always use good men on the fire department here in town. Let me know if you get a hankering to fight a fire." And then, blessed relief, he clapped Sammy on the shoulder and walked away.

Sammy took two steps toward Robin. Was she really going to leave before saying anything? "Wait!" he mouthed at her. Her eyes crinkled in a smile. Edith Draper stepped into his path.

"I'm glad we aren't losing you to parts unknown," she said. The older woman had a knack for making him smile.

"I won't be going anywhere for a very long time." He gave her a quick wink. "I couldn't leave my favorite customer."

"Oh, you." She gave him a little swat, and he leaned down and kissed her on the cheek. Just then his mom came up, opening her arms wide. He stepped into them, hugging her tight. Over her shoulder, he checked on Robin.

Still there.

"I'm proud of you, Sam," his mom said. She released him, then held on to his upper arms. "Of course, I'd be proud of you no matter what." She let go of his left arm and dug in her pocket. "The Williamses sent you a note for tonight." She handed him an envelope. He tore it open and a photo slid out. Teddy stood on a new prosthetic limb, holding two thumbs high into the air.

Congratulations on your new adventure,

the card read.

Teddy says two thumbs up to the man who helped him do hard things. The youth of Deep Haven are lucky to have you.

Sammy wiped at a stinging in his eyes.

At the door, Robin shrugged and put her hand on the knob again.

"I'm sorry, Mom. We'll talk more later." He bent down and kissed his mother like he'd done for Edith. "Right now I need to catch a girl."

His mom turned, and he saw her react as her eyes landed on Robin. "Go," she said and gave him a little push.

He felt like a linebacker again as he dodged his way through the room. No one else was getting in his way.

Until...

Finally.

"Robin."

HOW HAD SHE EVER FELT THIS WAS "LESS THAN"?

Robin stood at the door of the youth center. Around her, friends and neighbors laughed and teased each other.

She'd arrived late to the party, purposely trying to keep her arrival quiet. She'd wanted to be in, deliver the cake, and be out again without anyone spotting her. This was not the time or the place to reunite with Sam. But the warmth of the party had drawn her in, kept her from escaping into the cold April air.

She'd hidden behind Seth during Peter's toast and Sammy's speech. She'd caught a glimpse of his smile, the glint of humor in his green eyes. She'd watched Sammy checking out the cake. Would he recognize the work she'd done? Okay, the cake probably wouldn't tell him all the things she wanted it to say, but he couldn't blame a girl for trying.

She'd thought she heard him call her name, but then he hadn't come to her. Just as well. She'd resolved to not stay long. She'd watched as he greeted first one person and then another. Over his mom's shoulder, he mouthed something to her, but she couldn't make it out.

Enough.

It was time to leave.

She closed her hand on the cool doorknob.

"Robin."

Sammy.

She couldn't stop the smile that bloomed on her face as she met his eyes. "I got your text message."

A light lit his eyes, turning them the color of a spring morning. "I can't believe you're here." Sammy reached out a hand but stopped short of touching her.

She let go of the doorknob. "I just got back last night."

"Is everything okay with your grandpa?"

"What—oh, yes. He's fine. I didn't come back because of that."

His eyes held hers now. "Why did you come back?"

She felt rather than saw a few curious gazes cast their way. "Come by the bakery tomorrow. We can have that talk."

"There's no way I am waiting that long." Sammy shoved his hands in his pockets.

She glanced at the people milling around. "I don't want to have this conversation in front of fifty of Deep Haven's finest." She wanted to be seen and known, but this might be a bit much.

Vivien walked up and patted Robin on the arm. "Love the cake, Robin. Well done. Thanks for bringing it. But you must have been working on it all day."

Robin shrugged, held Sammy's gaze. "It's not the first time I've made a cake under pressure."

Colleen chose that moment to walk through the door. A cold blast of wind hit them. Colleen held hands with a tall, dark-blond-haired man. "Robin!" she squealed and threw her arms around her friend. "It's so good to see you. I thought you were in Paris."

Colleen held Robin out at arm's length. "Oh! This is Jack." She pulled the man forward. "My fiancé." Colleen dangled a hand in front of Robin, the glint of a diamond on her third finger.

"Colleen! Congratulations." She gave her friend another swift hug. Out of the corner of her eye, she saw Sammy shaking Jack's hand.

Robin gave Sammy a small shrug. There was no way she was having this conversation in the middle of a party.

Sammy turned his head left and right. "Congrats, Jack and Colleen. We'll have to catch up later. Right now I need to talk to Robin."

He reached for her hand. The warmth of his palm ran all the way along her arm and into her heart. "C'mere." He led her to a small room smelling faintly of dampness and lemon and tugged the door shut behind them.

"Did you just pull me into the janitor's closet?" Rags and cleaning supplies filled one shelf while another held footballs and baseball equipment.

The floor space was only large enough for them to stand still in the middle of the room, practically touching.

It was her new favorite room on the planet.

"It was the closest quiet space I could think of." Sammy looked down at their joined hands and dropped hers like it had burned him. He smiled sheepishly. "Maybe I should have waited for tomorrow." He put his hand on the doorknob behind him.

"No! Wait." Robin placed her hand on his chest. His heart thrummed against her palm. "You're right. I can't wait until tomorrow either."

His breath hitched. "So, you got my text? That can't be why you came home. I only sent it this morning."

"I didn't come home because Grandpa Jim was sick or because I lost my job again. I chose to come home. I decided late last week, actually."

Sammy inched a hand up until it covered hers on his chest. "How long are you in town for?"

She let a slow smile cross her lips as she looked up at him. "I'm here to stay."

His eyes widened. "What are you saying?"

She flipped her hand over so she was holding his. "Sammy, I'm so sorry for the things I said. You're the bravest man I know. I never should have said otherwise."

"No. You were right. I was hiding. Your words shook me out of the coasting course I'd been on. I'm the one who is sorry. You were only chasing your dreams, and I should have supported that." He squeezed her hand, his touch sending a jolt of electricity through her. "I was only angry because I was hurt that I wasn't being chosen again. All my life I've been second fiddle, the lineman and not the quarterback. Your choice needled that spot in my heart."

"I am so sorry. I realized my choices must have felt that way to you. I never wanted to hurt you."

"I know that now. I forgive you. Can you forgive me for not understanding that you needed to go back to France? I should have stood by you. You are amazing, and you deserve the opportunity to show your talent to the world."

"I've already forgiven you." She put her other hand over their clasped ones.

"You don't have to give up your dreams. I'm pretty committed to Deep Haven right now, but once I get the youth center on firmer footing, I'll follow you to France. We can figure something out."

"Turns out a bakery in France isn't my dream."

"Well, what is?"

"You."

His Adam's apple bobbed, and her mouth dried.

"I choose you, Sam. Here in Deep Haven. I feel seen when I am with you. All the praises and accolades in the world are empty without you. I love you, Sammy Johnson." Her heart soared as she spoke the truth. She wanted Sammy—and Deep Haven—now and always.

His eyes filled with passion, and he bent to her. "I love you, Robin Fox."

She slid her hand around his neck as their lips met, and his arms moved to wrap around her waist.

He kissed her with a hungry passion, his lips tasting of almond frosting.

How could she have ever thought Paris was better than this? Coming home to Sammy was the best decision she'd ever made.

He moved her toward a shelf and pressed her against it, knocking a football over. It bounced twice, the sound loud in the small room. She broke away from him, a nervous giggle in her throat.

"Probably not the most romantic place for this," Sammy said. He ran his hand through her hair.

She bent, picked up the ball, and handed it to him. "You will always be the quarterback to me."

He took the ball and, without looking, put it back in its place on the shelf.

"So, what happened to smoke jumping?"

Sammy shrugged and put his arms around her waist again. "I realized that all I wanted to do was to help Deep Haven stay the amazing place that it is. I couldn't imagine a better place to settle down and raise a family. Smoke jumping would have been a job, but staying in Deep Haven is a calling."

"I get that now." She saw that a life here could be an even bigger adventure than the one she had planned for herself.

She thought briefly about her brothers, Grayson and Oliver. Hoped they were out there finding big dreams too. Maybe someday they would even find their way back to Deep Haven. "Hey. I didn't see your bike out front. You must have ridden in with your mom. I don't suppose I can talk you into me giving you a ride home in the oh-so-sexy bakery van?"

One side of his mouth quirked up. "I did come here with my mom, but I drove my truck. I can see if she's okay with driving it home."

"Wait. You drove? Like, you were the driver?" She wrapped her arms around his neck, crossing her wrists. He nodded. "That's amazing."

"I'm actually driving a lot now. Even got back on the snowplow team. And I drove to Minneapolis."

She couldn't help the giggle that bubbled up. "Boy, when you do things, you don't do them by halves."

He tightened his arms around her. "Yep. That's something you should know about me. When I'm in, I'm all in."

"What was in Minneapolis?"

"I went to visit Teddy, the boy who was in that car in my accident. He's so brave. His leg never fully healed, so they had to amputate it. We've been video chatting once a week while he goes through rehab." He dropped one arm and dug in his pocket. "Here's a picture of him."

Robin took the photo. A smiling boy with two thumbs up grinned back at her. "He looks so healthy."

"He's come a long way."

She handed the photo to him, and he tucked it back into his pocket.

"Everyone will be wondering where the guest of honor is." She moved her other arm from around his neck and took a step back. "We should get out of here before they come looking."

"Maybe one more minute." Sammy caught her by the waist and pulled her close again. He bent and kissed her. Slower this time, like they were just getting started. A promise for more. When they broke apart, Sammy took her hand in his. She smoothed down her hair, and he smiled at her. "Don't worry. No one will notice."

They walked out of the small room hand in hand.

And ran straight into Seth.

"There you are," Seth said. He looked between the two of them, then gave Sammy a mischievous grin. "Hi, Robin. So good to see you."

She gave him a small wave. "Hi, Seth." So much for sneaking back into the party.

Seth turned to Sammy. "I brought the plans you requested for your cabin. The architect finished them up this week. He modified them from your old plans just how you specified. Want to take a look?"

Sammy shot a glance her way. "Absolutely."

They carried the plans to a nearby table. Sammy pointed out the various parts of the plan he liked the best. "Here's the kitchen. I want it to be big enough to entertain. Everyone's favorite room is the kitchen."

She saw a square marked Oven. "That appears to be a very large oven."

"It's a double oven." He hesitated. "I ordered one of them brick-lined."

A tingle raced along her spine. "Did you buy me another oven?" Yep. She loved this man.

His voice dropped an octave. "I figured I should put all those baking skills you taught me to good use."

"Sure you did." She put her hand on his back and bent to the plans again.

He pointed at another spot. "This will be the center of the home—a living room with a fireplace anchoring it. The room will be big enough for parties and having groups over to watch games on the big screen."

She could listen to him talk about this house all night. She didn't worry about the way it was laid out or the number of bedrooms he had planned. She knew whatever it looked like, it would be perfect.

Because any place with Sammy was home.

THANK YOU FOR READING *HOW SWEET IT IS*! DON'T MISS OUR NEXT Fox Family novel, *It's Your Love* by Rachel D. Russell, bringing Grayson Fox back to Deep Haven in a sweet story of second chances.

"A charming story about love least expected!"
—Susan May Warren, *USA Today* Bestselling Author

IT'S YOUR
Love

A DEEP HAVEN NOVEL

THE FOX FAMILY SERIES

RACHEL D. RUSSELL

When Grayson Fox is asked to return home to Deep Haven and run the wrangler activities for the local camp, the last thing he expects is to run into the one woman he never wanted to see again. Worse...she's his boss. But Grayson has big hopes for a life back in Oregon, and he must keep the promise to the camp in order to keep his dreams alive.

Just because Beth Strauss has stuck around Deep Haven doesn't mean she doesn't want a bigger life. And becoming the camp assistant director is the first step to that bigger life. Of course, standing in her way happens to be the one man who has always managed to derail her dreams, the way too arrogant Grayson Fox.

But if they want to keep the camp afloat and their dreams live, these two must learn to work together. But will these enemies become sweethearts, and if they do, will they find something better than the dreams they're striving for?

The next delightful installment of the Fox Family series!

LOOKING FOR MORE SWEET ROMANCE IN DEEP HAVEN? START YOUR JOURNEY WITH STILL THE ONE.

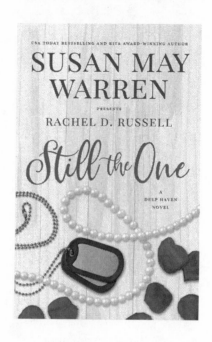

It's never too late to finish a love story...

Former Army Ranger Cole Barrett has a new mission objective—sell his grandfather's house in Deep Haven, and leave the town that contains his childhood hurts for good. Unfortunately, the tenant in the garage apartment refuses to move. Even worse? It's his childhood crush, Megan Carter, and her son.

Wedding planner and single mom Megan Carter loves Deep Haven. To her, it's the place where she makes dreams come true —at least, everyone else's. Hoping to purchase a local B & B and turn it into a premier event venue, she's oh, so close to her down payment...until Cole Barrett returns to Deep Haven. Even if he's not back to fulfill a silly childhood promise to marry her, she never expected him to evict her!

When a blizzard strikes Deep Haven, and Megan is overrun with wedding catastrophes, it takes a former Ranger to step in and help. Besides, the more he comes to her rescue, the sooner she'll be able to move out...and he can move on. And that's what they both want, right?

Return to Deep Haven with this magical tale about the one who got away...and came back.

CONTINUE YOUR DEEP HAVEN JOURNEY WITH MORE STORIES BY
ANDREA CHRISTENSON

He can't buy his way out of trouble this time...

Housekeeper-slash-entrepreneur Ella Bradley prides herself on being ready for anything. After all, with a father who died—and lied to her—and a stepmom and stepsister who despise her, she has no one else to depend on. But on the biggest night of her life, she's unprepared to be trapped in an elevator with the man of her dreams.

Wealthy prince-to-a-fortune Adrian Vassos wants nothing more than to shed his reputation as a party boy and prove that he is a savvy businessman. Even, a gentleman. But when he's trapped with a woman who knows his reputation but not his face, he gives into the temptation to be someone else, and lies.

When serendipity brings them together again—this time to work off community service—can their combined sentences spark a new ending? Maybe...if Adrian's lies don't find him out. Again.

The magic of Deep Haven enchants in this modern-day Cinderella story.

He just wants to erase his past. She can't seem to escape hers. But facing it might put their future in jeopardy.

The day Jack Stewart walked out of jail, he vowed to keep his conviction a secret. The whole thing was just a terrible mistake, and he did his time. Now he wants a new life in a sleepy town where no one knows his name. Deep Haven is the perfect place to start over as a chef. The last thing the former pararescue jumper wants is to get involved. But when Boone Buckam—the guy he owes for getting him out of the slammer—asks for help, how can he refuse?

Colleen Decker has already escaped evil once—as a teenager, she was kidnapped by a murderer. But she's put all that behind her as a trauma nurse in Minneapolis. Or maybe not, because a freak mistake in the ER sends her past crashing down on her. She needs a timeout in her hometown of Deep Haven. She doesn't plan to stay—even when she's roped into the job of flight nurse for the town's Crisis Response Team chopper. Colleen's not sure why she's drawn to danger, but she'll be safe enough—after all, she'll need training, and her teacher is a handsome former pararescue jumper. What could go wrong?

When Jack said he didn't want to get involved, he especially meant his heart—but being with Colleen feels like a fresh start. He'll even climb aboard a chopper again, despite his vows. They're headed for a happy ending...

But secrets never stay buried in a small town. And when disaster strikes one snowy night, they'll both have to decide if the past will destroy them...or if it just might lead them home.

Escape with this perfect Deep Haven drama about discovering a season of second chances.

connect with sunrise

Thank you so much for reading *How Sweet It Is*. We hope you enjoyed the story. If you did, would you be willing to do us a favor and leave a review? It doesn't have to be long—just a few words to help other readers know what they're getting. (But no spoilers! We don't want to wreck the fun!) Thank you again for reading!

We'd love to hear from you—not only about this story, but about any characters or stories you'd like to read in the future. Contact us at www.sunrisepublishing.com/contact.

We also have regular updates that contain sneak peeks, reviews, upcoming releases, and fun stuff for our reader friends.

As a treat for signing up, we'll send you a free novella written by Susan May Warren that kicks off Sunrise Publishing's Deep Haven Collection! Sign up at https://sunrisepublishing. com/free-sampler/.

acknowledgments

When Team Deep Haven began to plan out another installment of stories for the Deep Haven Collection, I quickly raised my hand and asked to write a bakery story. I love all things about baking bread and I knew Deep Haven needed a quality place for quality bakes! I identify much more with Grandma Elaine and Grandpa Jim in this story in that way. I don't have the same creative flair with frosting and cakes that Robin exhibits.

A project like this takes good leadership and great insights. I'm grateful to the Sunrise Team—Susie, Lindsay, Barbara, and all the rest—who spent time working with this novel until we were all satisfied.

Writing about a bakery in Deep Haven took me to a new favorite location: Brick Oven Bakery in Northfield, MN. Many thanks to owner, Dean Christensen, for patiently answering my questions and allowing me to take a million photos. Your hospitality was as wonderful as your bread. And, yes, I realize this introduces yet another spelling of the iconic Deep Haven last name. We all know which spelling is the correct one.

A huge hug and thank you times one thousand to my writing besties, Rachel and Michelle. This book wouldn't exist without you! Wherever our next projects take us, know this: you're stuck with me forever.

To my amazing family: we've been through a ton of upheaval and uncertainty during this past season of life, over the course of writing this book. You've each done a remarkable job navigating the route. Thanks for taking the journey with me. You're all my favorite.

    All glory to God

    Andrea C.

about the author

 **Andrea Christenson** lives in Western Wisconsin with her husband and two daughters. When she is not busy homeschooling her girls, she loves to read anything she can get her hands on, bake bread, eat cheese, and watch Netflix—though not usually all at the same time. Andrea's prayer is to write stories revealing God's love. Visit her at www.andreachristenson.com.

facebook.com/andrea.christenson.author

instagram.com/andrea_christenson_author

twitter.com/AndreaC_Author

bookbub.com/authors/andrea-christenson

amazon.com/stores/Andrea-Christenson/author/B08M9FQVMZ

other deep haven novels

Fox Family Collection

How Sweet It Is

It's Your Love

The Way You Love Me

Deep Haven Collection

Only You

Still the One

Can't Buy Me Love

Crazy for You

Then Came You

Hangin' by a Moment

Right Here Waiting

Once Upon a Winter Wonderland

Deep Haven Series

Happily Ever After

Tying the Knot

The Perfect Match

My Foolish Heart

Hook, Line, & Sinker

The Shadow of Your Smile

You Don't Know Me

How Sweet It Is: A Deep Haven Novel
Fox Family Series, Book 1
Published by Sunrise Media Group LLC
Copyright © 2023 by Sunrise Media Group LLC

This book is a work of fiction. Names, characters, places, and incidents are either products of the author's imagination or used fictitiously. Any similarity to actual people, organizations, and/or events is purely coincidental.

Scripture quotations are taken from the Holy Bible, New International Version®, NIV®. Copyright © 1973, 1978, 1984, 2011 by Biblica, Inc®. Used by permission of Zondervan. All rights reserved worldwide.

Scripture quotations are also from The ESV® Bible (The Holy Bible, English Standard Version®), copyright © 2001 by Crossway, a publishing ministry of Good News Publishers. Used by permission. All rights reserved.

For more information about Andrea Christenson, please access the author's website at the following address: www.andreachristenson.com.

Published in the United States of America.
Cover Design: Jenny Zemanek, jennyzemanek.com
Editing: Susan May Warren and Barbara Curtis

Made in the USA
Columbia, SC
30 January 2024

31178192R00169